Robert B. Parker's
Wonderland

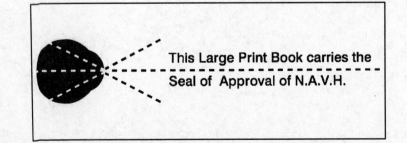

This Large Print Book carries the
Seal of Approval of N.A.V.H.

ROBERT B. PARKER'S
WONDERLAND

ACE ATKINS

THORNDIKE PRESS
A part of Gale, Cengage Learning

GALE
CENGAGE Learning·

Detroit • New York • San Francisco • New Haven, Conn • Waterville, Maine • London

GALE
CENGAGE Learning®

LIBRARY OF CONGRESS CATALOGING-IN-PUBLICATION DATA

Atkins, Ace.
  Robert B. Parker's wonderland / by Ace Atkins. — Large Print edition.
    pages cm. — (A Spenser Novel Series) (Thorndike Press Large Print Core)
    ISBN 978-1-4104-5773-8 (hardcover) — ISBN 1-4104-5773-7 (hardcover) 1.
Spenser (Fictitious character)—Fiction. 2. Private investigators—Massachusetts—Boston—Fiction. 3. Boston (Mass.)—Fiction. 4. Large type books. I. Title.
PS3601.T487R638 2013
813'.6—dc23   2013008097

Published in 2013 by arrangement with G. P. Putnam's Sons, a member of Penguin Group (USA) Inc.

Printed in the United States of America
1 2 3 4 5 6 7 17 16 15 14 13

For Joan.
Nobody tougher.

1

Henry Cimoli didn't mince words.

"Have I ever asked you for a favor?"

"Nope."

"In all the years I've been knowin' you and Hawk," Henry said, "I haven't asked for jack squat."

"Jack or squat has never been stated."

We sat at an outdoor table at Kelly's Roast Beef, facing the ocean at Revere Beach. It was early spring, and people had rediscovered shorts and T-shirts. I was particularly interested in the return of the skirt, bare legs, and high heels with thin straps. Not that Revere was a fashion mecca. Revere was a working-class town and Revere Beach was a working-class beach. But you could live well on the beach, and the seafood and Italian restaurants along the boulevard were very good. I had ordered a bucket of clams from the take-out window.

"I take calls for you guys, keep Pearl when

you and Susan want to leave town and moon over each other."

"Pearl loves you, Henry."

"Do I complain?"

"She says you withhold affection."

The wind was sharp and cold, but the sunshine warmed you during the lulls.

I sampled a few fried clams from the bucket. Sadly, I learned Kelly's did not serve Blue Moon ale, or any beer, for that matter. One cannot enjoy fried clams with a Coke Zero. I dipped a few more in tartar sauce, and studied a leggy brunette in a flowy skirt standing outside the beach pavilion. She kept the skirt from blowing away with the flat of her hand while she walked. Maybe Revere was on the verge of becoming fashionable.

A couple paunchy guys in coveralls stained with grease got up from a table and patted their stomachs. One belched. Perhaps not.

"Do I detect a request for a favor?" I said.

"Why?" Henry said. "Because I'm saying I never asked for one?"

"Did I tell anyone about the time you wore lifts to that Hall of Fame banquet?" I said.

Henry stood about five-four and weighed about 134 pounds. But 133 of it was muscle, and in his youth, he'd gone toe to toe with

Willie Pep. Some of that still showed in his face. He had a lot of scar tissue around the eyes; his knuckles looked like thick pebbles. He was a hard and tough man despite my claim that he had once been a member of the Lollipop Guild.

"So you owe me?" he said.

"I'd do it anyway."

"What?"

"Whatever you're going to ask."

"I don't like asking for stuff," Henry said. "I wasn't brought up that way. Say no if you want. Don't worry about what I said. I'm just ticked off about all this crap."

"Fried clam?"

"You could lose a little weight, Spenser," Henry said. "Z told me you've been into the donuts again. You know how many calories are in one donut?"

"Next you'll want me to give up sex."

"Women make you stupid."

"Not all," I said, eating more clams. A blonde had taken the brunette's place, wearing wedge heels, tastefully frayed chino shorts, and a light blue button-down shirt with several buttons open. She wore designer sunglasses on top of her head and shifted her hips as she strolled.

"She could." Henry motioned.

"Talk slower," I said. "I can't understand you."

"So you want to hear it or did you drive up to Revere on a Sunday to eat a bucket of clams?"

"I'm motivated equally."

Henry craned his wrinkled neck over his shoulder, watching for anyone within ear-shot. Satisfied that a young couple with a toddler posed zero threat, he turned back. "We got some problems at my condo," Henry said. "I tried to handle it myself, but the cowards sent three guys the other night. They told me if I didn't shut up, that they were gonna toss me out my window."

"What floor is your unit?"

"Fourth floor."

"You're so light, you could blow away."

"This ain't funny."

"Okay. Tell me about these guys."

Henry shrugged. Several seagulls landed on a table next to us, and started to scrap over half an onion roll.

"The guy talkin' was a thick-necked steroid freak. He had a tattoo on his neck and crazy eyes."

"Lovely."

"Other guy was black, not as juiced-up, but just as thick. Third guy was older, with long hair and a goatee. Didn't look that

10

tough. Maybe he's the shooter. He had that look, trying to show he was a hard guy."

"Names?"

Henry shrugged.

"I didn't ask for references."

The gulls yammered a bit until the victor took his spoils and flew across Beach Boulevard.

"What's it about?"

"Some asshole wants to buy up the condo and buy us all out," Henry said. "It's a decent price. But I like the place and don't want to move. I mean, look at the fuckin' view."

"It's fucking grand."

"And there are memories and all."

Ten years ago, Henry had met a woman. She was ten years younger and she had given him eight good years. Lots of dinners and trips to the Cape. Two years ago she'd died of cancer. He never spoke of it, but in his office I'd seen a prayer candle next to an old photograph. They'd bought the place together, Henry moving out of the gym and fifteen minutes away to the condo.

"So I won't sign the paper," Henry said. "A few more of us feel the same way. There's a nice Jewish couple up on eight who don't want to leave, either. One of these dumb shits made an anti-Semitic

11

remark to the woman when she was bringing in her groceries. Used some bad language about her in front of her fucking husband."

"Who's the guy wants to buy the building?" I asked. "I could pay him a visit and reason with his more enlightened side."

"If I just needed head busting, I would have called Hawk."

"Where is Hawk?"

"Miami," Henry said. "Guarding some rich broad in South Beach."

"You know the company who wants to buy your building?"

"Nope," Henry said. "They sent some lawyer to come speak to the board."

"When was this?"

"Last week."

"And you publicly objected?"

"I ain't alone," Henry said. "Half of us want to stay, others just want a fast buck. They're old and tired and looking for the easy way out."

"Why not just take their money," I said, "if it's a fair deal? Move back into your apartment at the gym. Maybe it's time for Z to find his own place."

"The money is okay but not great," Henry said. "I was considering it until they started to press. I don't like people pressing. Pisses

12

me off. Being told what to do."

"I can relate."

"Figured you would."

"When's the next board meeting?"

"Tuesday night at seven," Henry said.

"Do they serve refreshments?"

"All the bullshit you can eat."

"Wonderful."

"I sure like to know what kind of piece of crap sends some hoods around to harass a bunch of old people."

"I can most certainly find that out."

2

"You told Henry that I was putting on weight?"

"I told him that you ate too many donuts," Zebulon Sixkill said. "He decided you had put on weight."

"Is there no loyalty from my Native American apprentice?"

"Pale Face shouldn't take more than his fair share."

We were running along the Charles River that Tuesday morning. The promise of an early spring had turned to gray skies and spitting rain. But it was warm enough to wear athletic shorts and a blue sweatshirt with the sleeves cut off. Z was pushing me a bit, keeping a faster pace than I preferred. My pace was slow and even, knowing I could outlast him on the five-mile route along both sides of the river. Maybe if I'd been a D-1 running back like Z, I'd have been swifter of foot.

"How long have you known Henry?" Z asked.

"Since I was eighteen."

"You and Hawk?"

"Hawk and I."

"So there isn't much you wouldn't do for the man?" he asked.

"Nope."

"Me either," Z said. "He didn't have to give me a place to stay when you started to train me. I was a mess. All that booze and sloppiness. On the juice. I still don't know why he did it."

"Because he saw some promise," I said. "Henry has always had an eye for talent."

"He's a good man."

"Yep," I said. "How are you with everything?"

"I drink sometimes," he said. "I don't drink because I'm an alcoholic. I drink because I like the taste."

"You can stop?"

"Sure," he said. "Just like you."

"In the past, I struggled with the stopping."

"I can stop."

We jogged for a bit, working to control our breathing, rounding the bend of the river by Harvard Stadium. I had just invested in a new pair of New Balance 1260s, feeling patriotic hitting the ground in American-made running shoes.

"Must have been something to trust me," he said. "When we met."

"I needed someone to pass along my knowledge to," I said. "And also could use a little help from time to time."

"And you will put in a good word with the state," Z said. "As a reputable citizen of the Commonwealth, noting my fine and upstanding character."

"Three years," I said. "The law says you're under my watch for three years."

"And then?"

"You have a private investigator license and trade."

"Not much of a future as a head breaker."

"Unless you're Hawk," I said. "But Hawk is equal parts ass-kicker and philosopher."

"The Thoreau of Thuggery?"

"Susan is right."

"About what?"

"You've been hanging around with me too long."

"So where do we start with Henry?"

"I'll make some calls," I said. "And we observe."

"Wait for those guys to show up?"

"Yep."

"And Henry will push the point?"

16

"Henry is not a subtle man."

We turned north onto the Harvard Bridge, making our way toward MIT, where we'd follow the bike path below Mass Ave, past the Longfellow Bridge and over to the dam, where we'd cross back over into the city. Z had yet to let up on the faster pace, seemingly still annoyed I'd taken an extra donut last week.

"Would be good to know who hired them," Z said.

"We can ask nicely," I said.

"Does that ever work?"

"Almost never."

3

The Harbor Health Club had been upscale longer than it had been low-rent. I knew it when it had been low-rent, before the waterfront was rebuilt with luxury hotels, slick office buildings, and million-dollar condos. Henry had changed with the times, adding the latest Cybex machines, treadmills, and stationary bikes. There were a lot of mirrors, a juice bar, and cubicles to meet with personal trainers. Henry had even recently added a glass-walled workout room, where women participated in something called Zumba. Z and I had little interest in Zumba but appreciated the taut young women in sweat-stained spandex who filed out of the room. Some of them even smiled at us as we took turns on the bench press. We decided to add more weight in appreciation.

"Maybe we should take a Zumba class," I said.

"Might hurt our reputation."

"Or maybe we could recruit some of the young ladies to the boxing room?"

"Susan might not like that."

"Who would know?" I said. "She's lecturing at the University of North Carolina this month on the psychology of adolescents."

"Years of research?" Z said, sliding onto the bench and slowly repping out 275 as if the bar were empty. He took his time, pausing the bar on his chest as I'd taught him, not pushing the weight but working on breathing and controlling the weight.

Henry walked up to study us, watching as Z clanged the weights down on the rack and stood up. He wore a white satin tracksuit, right hand in his pocket and a grin on his face. "You turkeys gonna pump some iron or just ogle my clientele?"

"I'm teaching Z the proper way to accomplish both."

"You ever think about investing in some workout clothes?" Henry said. "They've improved in the last century."

"Not everyone benefited as much from Jack LaLanne's death," I said.

Henry snorted. Z smiled as I slid onto the bench and started into a slow rep.

"I'll have you know this workout suit is custom-fitted," Henry said. "Probably cost more than your whole freakin' wardrobe."

I paused the weight on my chest, pushing out a couple more reps. I wanted to say something about shopping in the kids' section but kept it to myself, concentrating on the weight, the pause of the bar on my chest, exhaling as I pushed the weight upward. I finished the twelfth rep and re-racked the weight.

"Any more trouble?" I said.

"Nope."

"Thought we might follow you home tonight."

"I don't need babysitters," Henry said. "I need you to do that detective thing. Find out who these crapheads are."

"Crapheads have muddied the water," I said. "The prospective buyer is a corporation with an address listed as a P.O. box. The corporate contact registered with the state seems to be a phony."

"What about their lawyer?"

"I called him," I said. "He was less than forthcoming."

"Hung up on you?"

"Twice."

"I told you he was a prick."

"He's a lawyer," I said, shrugging.

Z had moved on to triceps presses with a fifty-pound dumbbell. He made it look easy.

And for me, it wasn't as easy as it used to be. Of course, I wasn't in my twenties and just a few years away from college football. I had lasted only two years at Holy Cross before joining the Army, never being a fan of the rah-rah coaches or taking orders.

I switched places with Z. He'd pulled his long black hair into a ponytail, his wide face covered in sweat. The front of his gray T-shirt read *Rocky Boy Rez, Box Elder, Montana.*

"Is there a lot to do in Box Elder?" I asked.

"Why do you think I stayed in Boston?"

"Numerous liberal coeds wanting to right their ancestors' wrongs?"

"Nope."

"Or because you worked for a bloated, self-absorbed, immoral creep and sought spiritual guidance from a Zen master?"

"There was that," Z said.

We met Henry in the parking garage thirty minutes later. I was driving a dark blue Ford Explorer that year, decent legroom for men of a certain size. Henry pulled out in a white Camry, and we followed him up Atlantic and down into the Callahan Tunnel and intermittent flashes of fluorescent light, taking 1A up past Logan, through Chelsea, and on into Revere Beach. I had the radio tuned low to a jazz program on WICE, Art Pepper

21

on horn. The tired triple-deckers and sagging brick storefronts whizzed past.

"A good friend of mine used to vacation in Chelsea," I said.

"You're kidding," Z said.

"Have to know the guy," I said. "Grew up in Lowell."

Henry lived in a 1960s condo with the architectural inspiration of a Ritz cracker tin. The condo building was ten stories, with small jutting balconies hanging from each unit and a wide portico facing the water. A sign over the entrance read *Ocean View* in a fine, detailed script. I parked just across the street in an empty slot by the beach. I had cracked the windows and the wind had kicked up a bit, slicing in the sound of the ocean and smell of salt.

"And what's the plan if they approach Henry?" Z said.

"Persuade them to stop."

"How far do we go with the persuasion?"

"Fists," I said. "No guns. Unless they want to up the ante. But we carry to make sure. This is not one of those situations where you make that play first. Other times call for it."

Z pulled a .44 revolver from a shoulder rig. He popped out the cylinder, checked the load, and clicked it back into place. It was a big gun. But Z was a big man.

I watched for Henry locking his car and carrying his gym bag up a concrete walkway to the condo's front entrance. I offered Z a piece of bubble gum, but he declined. I chewed and admired my reflection in the rearview mirror, looking rakish in my Brooklyn Dodgers cap and leather bomber jacket. I fiddled with the radio a bit. I smelled the salted breeze coming from the sound.

I glanced up to spot three men surrounding Henry's slight figure under the portico. One of them knocked the gym bag from his hand. Henry responded with a left hook to the guy's nose. The guy went down. His buddies rushed Henry and started pushing him. Henry set into a fighter's stance.

"Saddle up," Z said. "Here we go."

4

One of the men pressed his hand to his nose, lots of blood oozing through his fingers. Henry had done well. "You come at me again and you'll get it in the bazoo, too," Henry said.

The men weren't listening. They had switched their attention to Z and me after we drove up and slammed the Explorer's doors. We all stood in a happy grouping under the portico. No one moved or spoke. Henry stepped back and lowered his dukes a bit. "Nice night," I said.

One of the men was olive-skinned, with the build of a fire hydrant, and a tattooed neck bigger than his head. He was walleyed, with a skinny mustache and goatee and black hair cut short and combed forward to disguise a receding hairline. His pal was black, with a long face, patchy beard, and that thousand-yard jailhouse stare. He'd gotten pretty good at it, flicking his eyes

from me to Z, watching our hands and waiting for one of us to make the play. The
bleeder was taller than the other two, and
older, maybe my age, with a thick head of
brown hair and a lean, weaselly face. He
also had a goatee with some gray in it.

He leered at me. It was hard to be scary
while stemming a bloody nose with one
hand.

"Henry, you want to introduce us?" I said.

"Yeah, this is Moe, Larry, and Fuckface."

"Nice to meet you guys," I said. "Especially you, Fuckface. I've heard a lot about
you."

"Go fuck yourself," Walleye said. His thick
neck melted into his leather jacket.

"How much are you guys getting paid for
the shakeup?" I asked. "Because it's really
not worth it."

"Fuck off."

"Bad language is scary," Z said. "You
scared?"

There were guns there. There were always
guns. But no one made a play for the guns,
because once they made that move, there
was no going back. So we stood around at
awkward angles under the portico, three
against three, no one wanting to move. A
lot of noise of crashing surf and buffeting
ocean wind. I shifted my weight from one

leg to another. I'd recently purchased a pair of steel-toed Red Wings for such an occasion and my feet felt solid and confident in them. Beside me, Z loosened his shoulders and rolled his neck from side to side. Henry stood beside him and spit on the ground between us and the jolly trio.

"Walk away," I said. "And don't come back."

The black man was nearly as tall as me and had spent a lot of time in the weight room. His biceps tightened and flexed in a black denim jacket. His mouth curled into a smile, showing off a couple gold teeth as he rubbed his patchy beard. "How about we just fuck all y'all up? Don't make no difference to me."

"Doesn't make *any,*" I said. "You should be more careful about letting double negatives slip into everyday conversation."

"Fuck your momma," he said.

"Much better," I said.

"Oh, yeah?" Henry said, sliding into a fighter's stance. "How'd you like me to turn your ass into a hat?"

Z looked to me from the corner of his eye. He was relaxed and ready.

Walleye made the first move, tackling me around the chest and driving me back into a thick column, knocking the wind from me.

He pounded sloppy, short punches into my ribs until I finally head-butted him and drove him backward. Z was into a scuffle with the black gentleman, landing a solid, bone-shaking right into the man's temple. Walleye took another run at me as my hands instinctively lifted up to protect my face and I jabbed him twice, landing the second one. A third jab set up a perfect right, and the right rolled into a hook, with all that space under the portico giving me a nice pivot on the back foot to knock Walleye sideways. I turned to Z, who was holding the man's collar with his right hand as he punched him with his left. Walleye gathered his feet and made another attempt. My feet ached to try out the boots, and within a few feet, I kicked his legs out from him, an audible crack coming from his shin as he lost his balance and fell to the concrete. There was a lot of blood. My right hand was swelling but my breathing was cool and controlled as I pulled a .45 auto from Walleye's belt. Z's black hair had loosened and fallen in his face as he turned to me and grinned, the black man at his feet, Z's foot on his neck, and the man's face scraped and bloody from the rough concrete.

Z searched the man and pulled a Glock from his jacket pocket.

Somewhere in the fight, the man Henry had hit had run away.

There was blood all over Henry's white satin workout jacket. But he was smiling until he noticed the blood and said, "Holy Christ. Someone is paying for my damn dry cleaning."

"I have a terrific deal for you guys," I said.

"Fuck you," Walleye said.

Z looked at me with disgust.

"He can't fight," Z said. "Lacks verbal skills."

"Here it is," I said. "Tell me who hired you and I won't call the police."

"You fucking assaulted us," Walleye said, curled in a ball and holding his busted shin. The black man looked up from the ground and closed his eyes. He wasn't buying it, either.

"Okay," I said, reaching for my cell phone, dialing 911. I rattled off the address to the condo.

"Okay," Walleye said. "Screw it. Okay."

"Does this mean you wish to cooperate?"

"Don't call the cops," he said. "I'm on parole."

"Maybe you should seek other job opportunities," Z said.

"And not fight like such a goddamn pussy," Henry said.

"That, too."

"Go to hell," Walleye said.

"Careful, you're bleeding on my new boots," I said.

Walleye got to his feet slowly. His eyes flicked from Z to me. Z would not relinquish his foot from his pal's neck.

"Let him go," Walleye said. "And give our fucking guns back."

"Name?"

"Jesus Christ."

"I doubt it," I said.

"I want my fucking guns back."

"Nope," I said. "You got two seconds to give me a name or I'll see you at your arraignment."

"I don't know her name."

"Her?" I said.

"Yeah, a woman. Nice body. Big tits."

"Oh, her," Z said.

"She should've come herself," Henry said. "She could've done better."

"I just got word about a job," Walleye said. "My cousin told me to meet this broad at the HoJo at Fenway. At that Chinese restaurant. You know the Hong Kong Café?"

"Name?"

"I don't remember," Walleye said. "I was too busy staring at her bazooms and counting the money."

"How'd you keep in touch?"

"She wrote her cell number on a napkin. Told me not to use it unless it was an emergency."

Z smiled and shook his head. He helped the bleeding man to his feet, smoothing down the man's denim jacket and brushing his shoulders as if he were a tailor. I reached into Walleye's back pocket and lifted his wallet. I handed it to him, and after a few seconds, he extracted a folded napkin and handed it to me. I read it and neatly placed it into my jacket.

"A pleasure doing business with you guys," I said.

They limped unhappily back to a beaten Chevy sedan, Rust-Oleum polka-dotting the doors and hood. The windshield was cracked and the muffler sagged from the rear end, catching the condo's drive and sparking for a moment before the car turned south on Beach Boulevard and into the night.

"Now you pissed 'em off," Henry said. "Whoever this is won't waste the effort on amateur hour next time."

I shrugged. Z grinned in expectation.

5

"So you just called her?" Z said.

"Yep."

"And she's coming?"

"Yep."

We shut the doors to my Explorer and walked toward the Hong Kong Café attached to the HoJo. The cracked asphalt glowed dully under the streetlamps. "I guess this couldn't have waited or she'd be onto us?"

"The contact point was a Chinese restaurant," I said. "I happened to be hungry and like Chinese food."

"And it didn't hurt that the woman was described as having a nice body and large breasts."

"I only have eyes for a cold Tsingtao."

"I'll sit at the bar," Z said, and made his way through the restaurant.

I decided on the moo shu pork along with an order of spareribs and an egg roll. No need to be gluttonous. The waiter quickly brought me a cold Tsingtao. Z lifted his identical bottle from the bar and gave a slight nod.

As I drank, I was ever vigilant for a gorgeous woman blessed with ample bosom. Although no woman compared to Susan Silverman, it was important to remain vigilant. I had years of experience at detail work. A keen, appraising eye. Of course, I wasn't sure if the woman would come or not. For all I knew, Walleye might have dialed her up right after our chat and told her what happened. But guys like Walleye are seldom proficient at explaining why their asses were just handed to them, and, more often than not, pretend it never happened. It wasn't great for business.

I watched the door from the lobby and dug into the spareribs. From where I sat, I could see through a large bank of windows over a pool still covered, waiting for summer. Behind the pool and a large concrete wall, the lights of Fenway blazed, although the Sox were on the road. Rain had started to fall in the bright electric lights, giving a halo effect around the stadium.

A cold beer in one hand and a warm pancake in the other; life was good. Z looked bored.

An hour and a half after I called, a striking woman walked into the Hong Kong Café.

I summoned my detective abilities to study her body to see if the description matched. Z watched her subtly from the bar. He raised his eyebrows. She was the kind of woman who expected men to stare.

The woman was tall, maybe five-ten in heels, with stylish, layered brown hair. Her eyes were large and dark. She had a pert nose, prominent cheekbones, and very large, sensuous lips painted bright red. She had the figure of someone who worked out and used weights. Perhaps she had even attempted Zumba.

The dress hit just above the knee, a black wraparound number with a deep neckline. Studying her legs, I guessed the boots cost about as much as my rent.

I stood and walked over to her.

"Do I know you?" she said, with the slightest trace of a British accent. I hadn't noticed it on the phone.

I gave Walleye's name and said he couldn't make it.

"Why?"

"Tonight's his night for the Big Brothers program."

She gave me an appraising glance. "You

33

look tougher," she said.

"What you see is nothing," I said. "I got a Balinese dancing girl tattooed across my chest."

Even though she failed to smile, I motioned her to my table. The waiter had already cleared the plates and left me the check and two fortune cookies. He soon reappeared and asked if the lady would like to see a menu. She did not. Nor did she wish to have a cocktail.

Up close, she appeared older than I had first guessed. Which wasn't a bad thing. A very fit woman in her forties with crinkles at the corners of her eyes and subtle laugh lines around her mouth. She wore large diamond earrings. Her makeup was impeccable, and she smelled of expensive perfume.

She smiled at me. I smiled back.

"And?" she said.

"Yes?"

"What's the emergency?"

"Those people at the condo are giving us trouble."

"That's not our problem," she said. "That's your problem."

"They ain't backin' down."

I said it just like that, with the "ain't" and the dropped *g*. I figured I'd go for the thick-necked Southie type. It went well with my broken nose and Irish heritage.

"You take care of it," she said, studying the inside of her wrist, where she wore a gold watch twisted backward.

"You guys sure want this property," I said. "Why not just go for somewhere easier?"

"I don't pay you and your friends to think," she said, chin dropping, eyes intent.

"These people got friends," I said. "It could get messy."

"How messy?"

I shrugged. "Some people might get hurt. You know?"

She stared at me and crossed her legs. I followed the legs. Her eyes caught me staring. She widened them and bit her lip. "You have until the end of the week," she said.

"The boss is some fuckin' ball buster, huh?"

The rain fell in a neat slant in the stadium lights behind her.

"I am the fucking boss," she said, standing. "If you attempt to follow me or make any trouble . . ."

"So we're not friends?"

"Not likely," she said.

I smiled and shrugged.

She shook her head and walked away, sliding into a stylish little raincoat she'd kept slung over her arm. It matched her boots. She lifted the hair off her neck as she settled into the coat and knotted it tightly at her waist, heels clicking hard on the tile floor. Without a word, Z laid some cash down on the bar and followed her out to the parking lot.

I paid, pocketed both fortune cookies, and walked out into the rain. I turned up the collar on my jacket and headed up Boylston, cutting over to Commonwealth, where pink and purple magnolia blooms fell in the bright glow of streetlamps.

Let the kid do the work, I thought.

6

Even though I was my own boss, I liked to arrive at the office early. I enjoyed the banter with the women at the designer showroom across the hall. I appreciated the routine of making fresh coffee, listening to it brew atop my file cabinet as I sorted through bills and searched for the occasional check that slipped through my door. Pearl had come to work with me that morning, and she curled herself up on the couch, sighing deeply, and returned to sleep as I turned to study more spring rain. Rivulets zigzagged across the windows facing Berkeley Street. Ella sang softly on my computer while I made a list of phone calls on a yellow legal pad.

I had just picked up the phone when Z opened my door and sank into my client chair with a thud. Pearl lifted her head with great attention but, recognizing Z, took another long sigh and returned to her morning snooze.

I put down the phone. I crossed off the first name on my list.

"You worried?" Z said.

"I got your message," I said. "I had started to think that woman had taken you prisoner."

"I wouldn't fight it," Z said, standing up from the chair and removing his black leather jacket. He hung it on my hat tree by mine and reached for a coffee mug. He poured us both a cup and slid one in front of me.

"Hawk usually brings donuts."

"I promised Henry you'd cut down."

"Have we not covered confidentiality in the snoop business?"

Z shrugged. With some more practice, he might shrug as artfully as I.

"So," I said.

"Four Seasons."

"You worked a tail job to the Four Seasons?" I said. "My God, how did you survive?"

"I left the car with the valet," Z said. "Just like you said. Twenty bucks, by the way."

"Expense it."

"I found a place to sit in the lobby," Z said. He folded his arms across his chest and sat up straight in the chair. "I watched her talk to the man at the desk and then take the elevator. I followed her and walked the opposite way on the same floor."

"Did she come back down?" I said.

"Nope."

"You get a room number?"

"Hmm," Z said. "Would that help?"

"Maybe you could have relied on your heritage and tracked her boot prints in the carpet."

Z just stared at me over the rim of his mug. He took a sip and sat it back down on the desk.

"Do we have a name?" I said.

"I had a beer at the bar."

"Bristol Lounge."

"Yeah, at the Bristol Lounge."

"Good place to have a beer."

Pearl jumped from the couch and trotted over to me, setting her head in my lap and looking up at me with baleful yellow eyes. I did not need to be Cesar Millan to know she wanted to take a stroll in the Public Garden. There were fresh flowers to sniff and squirrels to chase. I patted her head and waited for Z to finish.

"I pretended like I was going to charge it to my room," Z said. "I gave the woman's room number. I dropped a twenty-dollar tip on him before I signed."

39

I nodded. "Boston ain't cheap for a gum-shoe."

"Just as he snatched it up, I asked if the room was under my name or my boss's."

"And what did he say?"

"He told me the name of the hotel guest."

"Smart."

"How do you think the Cree won the Battle of Cut Knife?"

"That exact thought had just crossed my mind."

"J. Fraser."

"J. Fraser." I placed my Red Wings up on the edge of my desk and noted a few new scuff marks on the edge. My A-2 bomber jacket and Dodgers cap hung neatly on a hook beside Z's jacket. I scratched Pearl's ears. She shook herself, and her collar jingled on her neck. I looked down at my yellow legal pad and tapped my pen in contemplation.

"Okay," I said. "So we're one step up the food chain."

"Nice to know who J. Fraser is."

"You write down her license plate?" I said.

"Looked like a rental," Z said. "Didn't figure it would matter."

I reached an open palm across the desk as he handed over a scrawled paper from his pocket.

"Detective work," I said. "Watch and learn."

I picked up the phone.

7

I don't care for computers besides using them to type reports, calculate a sometimes depressing income, or as a makeshift juke-box. I do not e-mail, surf the Web, or use Facebook. An electronic message was an instant record, and in my business, it was best to discuss private matters in person or on the telephone. There were also times when a phone call was faster and more thorough than a computer. So by the time I finished my first cup of coffee, I had con-nected J. Fraser's BMW to a Massachusetts corporation called Envolve Development. It took two calls.

"Aha," I said.

"A clue?" Z said, sitting with Pearl on my office couch.

"Better than a clue," I said. "A lead."

"We know who is trying to force out Henry?"

"Sort of."

"And what do we do now?" Z said.

"This requires additional contemplation." I stood up, reached for my jacket and baseball cap. I tossed Z his leather coat and grabbed Pearl's leash. "When stalled, walk a dog."

"What number crimestopper tip is this?" he asked.

"Let's call it thirty-seven."

We took Boylston up to Arlington and followed the sidewalk to the wrought-iron gates of the Public Garden. A lazy drizzle watered the bright orange and bloodred tulips. The wind swayed the loose branches on the willows while ducks floated aimlessly across the lagoon and under the bridge. I placed one hand in my jacket and pulled down the bill of my ball cap. Pearl strained at the leash, pawing hard toward a squirrel. The squirrel worked on a stray bit of popcorn, unconcerned.

"You ever let her off the leash?" Z said.

"Chaos might ensue."

We walked the pathways, heading east, the Financial District looming far over the Common and Tremont Street. We passed over Charles and into the Common, the State House's gold dome gleaming from atop Beacon Hill. City lights shone wetly across Boylston.

"Okay, J. Fraser works for a company called Envolve," I said. "Now we need to learn more about Envolve and why they want that condo."

"I am willing to conduct as much research as needed on Ms. Fraser."

"Have we forgotten she sent three thugs to put a beat-down on sweet Henry Cimoli?"

"Nope," Z said. "And since when is Henry sweet?"

"He was sweet one time in 1974," I said. "Someone should have written a poem."

"Do you want me to go look up some records?"

"Stick to Ms. Fraser; I'll stay on the paper trail," I said. "Divide and conquer."

"What if she notices me following her?"

"You're an Indian," I said. "Be both silent and stealthy."

Z nodded. "I will remind myself."

"It would be good to know the company she keeps," I said. "Don't worry about Henry. The men they sent have been properly discouraged."

"Until they send for better men."

"Nobody is as good as us," I said.

"What about Hawk and Vinnie?"

"Sure," I said. "But we're on the same team."

"That's comforting," Z said. "I would hate to go against Hawk."

"I did a long time ago," I said. "It wasn't much fun."

"Once we find out why this company wants Henry's building, what's next?"

"We ask Henry," I said. "The next move is up to him. But I don't think he wants to sell. Just be left alone."

"We can create a buffer."

"Yep."

"You think him not selling has to do with the woman he lived with?"

"I do."

"He never mentioned her to me," Z said.

I nodded. Pearl panted heavily, nails scratching at the pavement, crouching and moving toward a group of pigeons. I gave her some extra lead, and after a few steps, she broke into a perfect point. I smiled with pride at Z.

"Some dog," I said, and made a gun with my thumb and forefinger. I carefully aimed for Pearl's benefit. "Pow."

8

Two more cups of coffee and one tuna sub later, I had pretty much learned all the Internet knew about Envolve Development. They owned a lot of commercial real estate in the city, a shopping mall in Worcester, a hotel in Lexington, and a couple of condos in Revere. They were mentioned in passing in stories about corporate philanthropy, a brief item here and there about new construction or the purchase of a new property. A recent story in the *Globe* blamed them for the massive gaping hole by the now-defunct Filene's Basement in the Financial District. No names were given, but there were some stern words from the Boston City Council and stiff fines levied.

I called Envolve's corporate office and asked for a J. Fraser. The peppy woman who answered told me there was no such employee. I asked if she was sure. Still peppy, she assured me there was not. Being an ace investigator, I ran the name of J. Fraser with that of Envolve Development through Google. Nothing. I read back through the news stories for something that might help.

On the second read, I recognized the byline of a pal I had not seen in some time. I dialed up Wayne Cosgrove and invited him for a drink. Wayne seldom turned down a drink.

"You still hanging out in the Ritz?" he said, a slight hint of Virginia in his voice.

"I can drive down to Dorchester."

"Nope," Wayne said. "I'd rather come to you. The Ritz sounds nice after a rainy day."

An hour later, Wayne walked into the old Ritz bar and joined me at a small table facing the Public Garden. I liked the bar because it offered the best nut sampler in the city. And it was just around the corner from my apartment. I stood and shook Wayne's hand. Since the last time I'd seen him, he had grown a beard and let his hair get long. Both had some touches of gray that went well with his threadbare brown corduroy coat and plaid button-down. His shoes were wingtips, well worn and careless without socks. He looked like he should be teaching a sociology class at Harvard.

"Glad you haven't been laid off."

"Back on the beat," Wayne said. "After a

47

lot of time on the desk."

"What did you like better?"

"I can't say I miss afternoon meetings."

"Which allow you to file stories and meet old pals for cocktails."

"So where have you been, Spenser?" Wayne said. "I take it you want something, because you always call when you want something."

"I am deeply offended."

"Cut the shit," Wayne said. "I'm cheap. Get me a bourbon."

"You and William Faulkner," I said.

" 'A man shouldn't fool with booze until he's fifty, and then he's a damn fool if he doesn't.' "

"Bill say that?"

"He just might have."

An old Asian man in thick glasses wearing the formal dress of a waiter came by and asked for our order. I ordered a couple glasses of Blanton's, neat, with ice water on the side.

"Where water should reside," Wayne said, settling into the chair and watching cars pass along Arlington, spewing water from the gutters. The businessmen and women getting off work made their way to the downtown bars and restaurants, carrying umbrellas and wearing slick coats.

The bourbon arrived. We sipped for a while. The old Ritz was a truly good place for a late-afternoon drink. There were comfortable leather chairs, English hunt paintings, and on cold days, of which there were many, a crackling fireplace. Even though it had chain ownership, it would always be the Ritz, feeling more like the salon of an old estate than a hotel bar. I toasted Wayne with my glass. He had already finished his.

"How is Susan?" he asked.

"Teaching at Chapel Hill for the semester."

"How's that going?"

"It makes sex tough."

"Unless it's phone sex," Wayne said. He grinned.

"Yeah, but I always get tangled in the cord."

I motioned to the waiter for another drink for Wayne.

"So what do you need to know?"

"Besides just unveiling the great mystery of the common man's everyday world?"

"Yes, besides that."

"You wrote a story about a real-estate development company called Envolve."

"Since the paper has shrunk, I cover a little bit of everything."

"So you know Envolve?"

"Maybe," Wayne said. "They all have silly names like that."

"They ran into some trouble with that big hole next to Filene's Basement."

"Oh, yes," Wayne said.

"Any reason they might be particularly hot for a run-down old condo in Revere?"

Wayne shrugged. He leaned forward, thinking more of the question. "It might be unrelated. But . . ."

"Go on."

"You ever read the paper, Spenser?"

"Mainly just *Arlo and Janis.* Sometimes *Doonesbury.*"

"Well, if you cared to read more than the funny papers, you may have heard that Massachusetts just passed a law to bring casinos to our great Commonwealth."

"Gee, that rings some bells."

"There are three licenses up for grabs," Wayne said. He sipped a bit of whiskey. "One in western Mass, one down south that is pretty much a shoo-in for the Wampanoag tribe, and then one close to the city. That's the big one, and lots of big players are making their bids."

"You think that's what's happening?"

"How hot for the property are they?" Wayne said.

50

"Enough to send some thugs out to facilitate the purchase."

"Smells like casino land to me."

"Who are these guys?"

"Envolve is probably just the purchasing company," Wayne said. "If it's one of the biggie gaming companies, they would never use their own names. If they did, the owners' price would soar."

"Who are the players?"

"Well, the front-runner is Rick Weinberg's outfit."

"Why do I know that name?"

"Ever been to Las Vegas?"

I nodded.

"Well, he owns half of that," Wayne said. "His old man was a bookie who ran bingo parlors in Philadelphia. He's been working to bring casinos into Mass for years. That's what these casino companies do. They try to push the legislation, laying out millions of dollars to lobby, and then hope they get a license if the law passes. And securing land in Revere would be a major step."

"So how does one secure a license?"

"There is a four-person board, consisting of the governor, the secretary of state, and the speaker of the house. When they convene —"

"Which they have not."

51

"Once the board convenes, they will select that fourth member and begin the licensing process."

I nodded.

"Where is it?" he said.

I told him.

"Sounds like a puzzle piece that fits nicely with the old Wonderland dog track." He ran a finger around the edge of his bourbon glass. He nodded. "It's a rumor. But a good one."

"And who owns the track?"

"I'm not sure," Wayne said. "I can make some calls."

"And I can check on Weinberg."

"Well, he's not the only one trying for this license," Wayne said. "He has some real competition with this guy named Harvey Rose, who is the hometown favorite. Rose's buying into the Suffolk Downs parcel."

"Tell me about him."

"Ex–Harvard professor," Wayne said. "Got a Ph.D. from MIT. Hell, he's not Joe Broz, if that's what you're asking."

"God rest his soul."

"But when it comes to money and power, throw out the rules." Wayne tossed back more of the bourbon. "Weinberg and Rose and a few other long shots are fighting like hell now that the gaming law has passed. I would be very interested if Weinberg was trying to turn the old dog track into part of his casino proposal. We just assumed everything would happen at Suffolk Downs. It's already got the land and it's on the county line. Much closer to the airport and downtown. And you throw in horse racing to the layout and it makes sense."

"What do you think about all this?"

Wayne shrugged. "Some say it could be a massive influx of cash, more jobs, more tourists. A true boost to the sagging economy."

"Do I detect a note of pessimism for your fellow man?"

"You detect realism," Wayne said. "I don't want to know how you got pulled into this, but watch your back."

"For a Harvard prof named Rose?"

"What about 'Las Vegas outfit' did you not understand?" Wayne said. He took a long pull of bourbon. "I don't write obits. Even for old friends."

"Mobbed up?"

"Weinberg has a reputation," he said. "Rose, not so much. He's a number-cruncher. I mean, if he wasn't CEO of a gaming corp, he'd be working for Gillette or Capitol One. Or go back to teaching at Harvard Business School."

"So why work for a casino?"

"Because it's a machine for printing money," Wayne said. He smiled and finished the bourbon, then stood up.

"It's nice knowing an ink-stained wretch like yourself. I couldn't make those connections with a keyboard."

"There aren't many guys like us left," Wayne said. "You can't trade technology for shoe leather."

"Keeps me bucks up and you in high-end hooch."

The waiter asked if we would like another round. We declined and he laid down the check in a handsome leather cover.

"That's why I always liked you, Spenser," Wayne said. "You are the most sophisticated thug I ever met."

9

Before meeting Wayne, I had started braising a nice slab of brisket by placing it in a Dutch oven and adding some chopped carrot, parsnip, and onion. I sprinkled in a bit of kosher salt, pepper, coriander, Worcestershire, and a can of tomato paste and chicken stock and left the whole thing to cook at 350. When I returned, my apartment smelled heavenly. I put on a Duke Ellington album and started work on a tomato jam. I felt a jam would go nicely with some biscuits and a hunk of white cheddar.

A pleasant darkness had settled over Marlborough Street. I popped the top from a Sam Adams Alpine Spring, cracked a window, and watched the streetlamps glow on the wet sidewalks. I made the biscuits, cut them on a butcher block, and placed them on a greased cookie sheet to bake.

I felt so overworked, I opened another Sam Adams and called Susan. After four rings, she picked up.

"I was in the shower," she said.

"Does your phone have a camera?"

"Can't you think of anything else?"

"Well," I said. "Despite your absence, my apartment smells like Shangri-La."

"I would have thought you would have been at my place, gazing lustily at my photograph."

"May I serenade you with 'Moon River'?" I said.

"Let Andy Williams rest in peace," she said. "I've just finished with a very lengthy lecture."

I hummed the first few bars and drank some more beer and looked out at the streetlamps. A couple walked hand in hand along Marlborough. They were not talking, only smiling. Content. "And what was today's lecture?"

" 'Functional Subgrouping and Other Innovative Methods for Resolving Conflict.' "

"I can fly down immediately to speak as an expert."

"Kicking the crap out of someone has not been proven an innovative approach."

"Someone needs to do more research," I said. "What about threatening?"

"Is that what you've been up to?"

"Henry Cimoli asked for a favor."

56

"And Henry Cimoli never asks for anything."

I took another sip of beer. I checked the timer on my biscuits. Pearl sniffed at the oven. She looked disappointed that I was not paying closer attention to the impending meal.

"He in fact noted that very point."

"I take it the favor did not require you and Hawk greasing gym equipment."

"Nope," I said. "He asked for me to use my own time-tested method for resolving conflict."

"And the conflict?"

Susan sounded a million miles away. Her voice was never a substitute for the smell and touch and presence of the whole package. I sighed and told her about the conflict.

"Not a smart negotiation," Susan said.

"Nope."

"And what if these people offer more money?"

"That's up to Henry," I said.

"And who are these people?"

"I'm pretty sure they need Henry's apartment as a block in a big-time casino development."

"I thought that hadn't been decided."

"Ducks are being placed in a row."

"Ah, the infamous ducks," Susan said. "So

what do you do now?"

"Make sure no one harasses Henry."

"You can't do that forever," she said. "And besides, he'd hate that."

"True," I said. "It would slight his honor."

"Why don't you just call Quirk or have Rita's firm file a civil suit?"

"That might slight my honor."

"To report a crime?"

"I'd rather handle this myself," I said. "I think the players here have been adequately discouraged. Now we want to discuss the issue with the source."

"And if they return to harm Henry?"

"I will discourage them even more."

"By yourself?" Susan said.

Pearl stopped sniffing and looked up at me with pleading yellow eyes. She had developed a sixth sense for when biscuits were ready.

"Nope," I said. "I'm using the opportunity to train my Native American apprentice."

"That is something."

"It is."

"And how is he doing?"

"Tough and resourceful," I said. "He's getting better about making his own decisions. He isn't just waiting for me to tell him."

"Always a good thing."

"He continues to train with Henry," I said. "Besides a sloppy left hook, he could probably put half of Boston in the hospital."

"Can you note that in a job referral?"

"Yep."

"And his drinking?"

"He drinks," I said. "But he continues to control it."

"Like you."

"Like me."

"Does training Z have something to do with your Lone Ranger complex?"

"Is that a thing?" I said.

"You mean a psychiatric condition?"

"Yep."

"Most definitely."

"Returning to those thrilling days of yesteryear," I said. "How about you call me later for an adult conversation?"

"Perhaps."

"I think my biscuits are burning."

"Has it gotten that bad?"

"You have no idea."

10

The next morning, I drove twenty minutes to Revere and parked in an empty space along the beachfront to wait for Henry's white Toyota. The waves tumbled along the sand while I listened to player interviews after a heartbreaker with the Yankees. Even with the addition of Adrian Gonzalez, I did not feel optimistic about the season. I thought about calling Mattie Sullivan. But she would probably just offer that they were sucking big-time.

I ate two corn muffins and drank a large coffee. I searched around the dial for some palatable music. When that failed, I turned off the radio just as Henry's car appeared from a parking garage. I squashed the sack from Dunkin' Donuts and followed.

Susan was right. Henry would hate to have a babysitter. As far as he was concerned, the matter was over. There was a conflict and then a fight. The fight was won and it was finished. But in my experience, greedy people seldom consult rulebooks or play by honorable standards. Case in point, sending a trio of goons to bust the kneecaps of a formidable but old man. I kept on Henry as he took the tunnel into the city and hung back as we approached Atlantic. I parked outside the aquarium for a good ten minutes before grabbing my gym bag and heading into the Harbor Health Club.

"What took you so long?" Henry said. He was watching a pudgy middle-aged woman in a headband perform an assisted pull-up.

"Sorting my underwear to color," I said.

"Bullshit," he said. "I spotted you at the curb. You were eating a fucking donut."

"It was a corn muffin."

"How many?"

"One."

"Since when do you eat one of anything?"

I shrugged. The woman completed her reps with significant assistance from Henry. She got up from the machine and wiped her brow with a hand towel. She called Henry a brute. I grinned and mouthed the word "brute."

Over her shoulder, Henry shook his head and mouthed the words "Up yours."

I changed into shorts and an old gray sweatshirt and walked back to the boxing room. I wrapped my hands and faced the mirror, working on a quick round of shadow-boxing. After the first round, I picked up a leather jump rope and amazed and delighted myself with a few tricks. I had a good sweat going. Then I pulled on a pair of sixteen-ounce gloves for some heavy bag work. Henry strolled into the room, arms crossed over his chest, and watched. He listened as I worked out some frustrations in a barrage of combos. I tried out a few different ones Henry had never seen, just to show off a little. The three-minute round finished with an electronic buzz. I placed my gloves on top of my head and walked to the water fountain.

Because of the gloves, Henry thumbed the button for me.

"I just got a call," Henry said. "Condo board can sell with majority of votes. It's in the original deed or something."

"Not good."

"I tried to round up some support," he said. "I've lived there for ten years. Doesn't that mean anything?"

"You'd have a good case to sue."

"For crissakes," he said. "How long would that take? I'll be dead by the time they write the check."

I leaned in for more water. Henry pressed

the button again.

"Unless we had something on them," Henry said.

"You got a good case for harassment."

"That's chickenshit stuff," he said. "They'd lie their way out of it. I want to know who these people are. Stick it to them. You know, hit 'em where they live."

"What would you say if the proposed buyer wanted to knock down your building for a casino?"

"Now, that's something," Henry said. "Jesus, how long were you gonna keep that from me?"

"I don't know for sure," I said. "I'm still connecting the dots."

"These people gave us a lot of grief. If we could make them pay through the nose . . ."

"But is that enough?" I said.

"You mean that they get what they want?" Henry shrugged. "I've been thinking of expanding the gym. With that much cash, I could afford to build a second apartment. Maybe it's time for a change anyway. When I'm up there sometimes I kind of think on things."

I nodded. I knew who he was talking about.

"How good is the source on this casino business?"

"Solid," I said. "But not definite."

"The board would need more for leverage."

"Still working on it," I said. "But you need to know, the more I push, the more they might push back."

"Good thing I got some first-class sluggers who owe me," he said.

" 'Tis."

"So until we settle, it's gonna get a little dicey?"

"Yep."

"Where's Sitting Bull?"

"Sleeping."

"What the hell?"

"He watched your place all night last night," I said. "This morning we traded."

"You fucking guys."

"Don't cry, Henry," I said. "You might break something."

"You fucking guys."

11

Tired yet dogged, I returned to my offi
learn all I could about Rick Weinberg
his gambling empire. I found many inte
views with *The Wall Street Journal, The Nev
York Times,* and *Forbes.* But what held my
attention most was a profile on a site called
vegasinc.com on a new hire for Weinberg. A
woman named Jemma Fraser.

"Aha," I said.

She was indeed a British citizen, a heavy-
weight in the gaming industry, and the VP
of Weinberg Entertainment. According to
the interview, Jemma Fraser looked forward
to opening up new markets in states where
gaming has been illegal. She also talked a
bit about her own experience in Hong Kong
related to casinos in Macao. I added an "oh-
hoh" to the "aha." They worked well together.

I printed off a few of the stories and a
corporate bio and added them to the Ocean

file. By noon, I had pushed my body
 mind to their limits and decided to
ke a pilgrimage to Eastern Lamejun Bak-
 for some flatbread and hummus. I also
rew in some Armenian pickles, Kalamata
ives, and fresh feta, to keep up my
trength.

I stopped off a second time at a grocery
in Harvard Square for a six-pack before
heading to Susan's place. There was much
to be done.

All seemed well at Susan's. I emptied her
mailbox, checked all the locks, and ate
standing up at her kitchen counter. I enjoyed
a beer and caught a bit of Susan's perfume
lingering. I closed my eyes and smiled and
entertained the idea of a ticket to Raleigh-
Durham for the night.

But Pearl needed to be fed and walked.
Sixkill needed to be instructed in the ways
of the gumshoe. And Henry's interests
needed to be protected. Perhaps more
protected than ever, once it was known by
the players that he wanted more money.

I cut off a wedge of feta and slid it onto a
piece of flatbread I'd heated in the toaster
oven. The morning classes at Harvard had
let out and the streets were filling with cars
and students. You could hear them as they
passed Linnaean Street, debating the aca-

demic issues of the day. I ate a couple olives and opened up the hummus. The Avery White Rascal ale tied it all together nicely.

I dialed up Rita Fiore. A secretary said she wasn't available, but Rita called back twenty seconds later.

"I hear Susan is out of town." There was a huskiness in her voice.

"But her kitchen holds such sweet memories."

"You're sniffing around her kitchen?" Rita said. "That's pretty whipped, Spenser."

"I'm standing up eating a Mediterranean feast with some cold brew from Boulder, Colorado."

"Shall I chill the martinis?"

"Would you do me a favor?"

"Why, of course."

"Speak lawyer to me."

"Are you in jail again?"

"Nope," I said. "I have a client. Actually, it's Henry Cimoli. You remember Henry?"

"The old boxer."

"Yep."

"And?"

"And a casino developer from Vegas is trying to push Henry from his home."

"Do tell."

"I believe a billionaire casino developer is rubbing his greedy hands together for

Henry's condo," I said.

"What do you mean, you believe."

"The buyer has remained hidden," I said. "And I need some hard proof."

"And you're calling for one of my young and energetic paralegals to go and pull some property records for you?"

"Ownership will be buried pretty deep."

"What's in it for me?"

"If this is what I think it is," I said, "your firm could be negotiating for a substantial amount of money."

"Not my area of expertise," Rita said. "I'm strictly criminal. But Cone, Oakes, and Baldwin does employ several lawyers that would salivate at the proposal."

"Of course they do."

"And lawyers do love money," Rita said. "How come you're not going to lecture me on principles or your moral code?"

"Henry will need more backup than I can provide."

"I'm sure the firm can file a nasty civil lawsuit that could tie up their people for some time."

"Until they make an offer."

"That's generally the way it works."

"The company belongs to Rick Weinberg."

"Wow," she said. "I heard Donald Trump spit-shines his shoes."

"The company he's using in Boston is called Envolve Development."

I gave her addresses and needed information both on the Ocean View and Wonderland. She was quiet for a moment, and I heard the scratching of pen on paper. "I'll send one of the kids to wade through the property records," she said. "If the ownership is intentionally hidden, this could take some time."

"And how can I reimburse the firm for their precious time?" I said.

"I think you know."

"That property belongs to Susan."

"I prefer to think of it as a rental."

"How about a two-martini lunch instead?"

"Sold," Rita said.

I hung up, placed what remained of my feast into the grocery bag, and drove to my apartment. Pearl was very happy to see me. The early-afternoon sunlight was golden and filled the Public Garden. Willow branches fingered and trailed the edge of the lagoon, leaving soft dimples. A mallard hen and drake paddled around the pond, winding their way to the bridge. The hen was molting, getting ready to make her nest and lay her eggs.

I had always respected ducks. They understood monogamy.

12

Rita called the next day. Three of her best paralegals could not tie Rick Weinberg to Envolve, the company that owned Wonderland, the offer on the Ocean View, or the assassination of Abraham Lincoln. I offered to pay for her time anyway. We settled on the martini lunch at Locke-Ober before it closed for good, and more scintillating conversation.

After I hung up the phone, I nodded at Z, who sat in my client chair.

"Anything?" Z said.

"Nada."

"So we know, but we don't know."

"When the legal trail fails, follow the illegal," I said. "Write that down somewhere. It's a good tip."

Z nodded. He went back to reading the *Phoenix.*

"Get some rest," I said. "You'll watch Henry when he locks up. We'll switch in the morning."

"Where are you headed?"

"A den of iniquity," I said.

"Send me a postcard," Z said. He never looked up from the newspaper.

Twenty minutes later, I sat in a red vinyl booth in the back corner of the Tennessee Tavern, which was perched at the precipice of the Mass Pike at the corner of Newbury and Mass Ave. The place was appropriately smoky and dark. As usual, the bartender brought me a draft beer and a shot of Wild Turkey that I never ordered.

Lennie Seltzer grinned. "Cheers," he said.

"Salut'," I said, and drank the shot. The whiskey had been finely aged a good six months, which developed qualities of a heady diesel fuel. I quickly cleansed my palate with a cold Budweiser.

"So what have you heard about Rick Weinberg in Revere?"

"He's one of a lot of players," Lennie said. "But Weinberg's got a freakin' hard-on for a Boston casino."

"Nicely said."

"Thanks," Lennie said, popping a cigarette into the corner of his mouth and lighting up with a pink Zippo. "Want another round?"

"I have a pint of cough syrup in the car."

"So yeah," Lennie said. "These guys are fucking serious. All of 'em. The carnival is coming whether we like it or not."

"What about the Wonderland dog track?" I said.

"What's the property record say?"

"Corporate names buried a mile deep," I said. "I can't make the connection. Officially it's in bankruptcy."

"I miss that place," Lennie said. "I liked watching the dogs run and chase that rabbit. Lost a lot of business when those fucking PETA weirdos got riled up."

"Maybe they had a point."

"Dogs were bred to run," he said.

"Some are bred to fight," I said. "That doesn't mean it's a good thing."

Lennie shrugged. He squinted his eyes at me and smoked some more. "I know Weinberg is here and looking," he said. "But I hadn't heard anything about him and Wonderland."

I drank some more beer. I didn't want to be rude.

"Everything is changing," Lennie said. He blew a stream of smoke upward and crushed the cigarette. "Don't matter what we want. Bookies like me are in short supply. First the fucking Internet and now legal gambling in Boston. Christ."

"What's the old guard have to say about it?"

"You're talking about Gino Fish?" Lennie said.

I nodded.

"Why not ask your friend Vinnie?"

"I'd rather ask you."

Lennie shrugged. "Gino tried to keep it out," he said. "Greased some palms. They greased more. Hell, we lost."

"What about now?"

"Don't know."

"Is Weinberg connected?"

"He's a fucking casino mogul from Las Vegas," Lennie said. "What do you think? He ain't Walt Disney. I'd really watch my ass if I were you."

"I'm proceeding with caution."

"So let me get this straight," Lennie said. He spread his arms on the back of the booth. "You want me to find out who owns Wonderland because you can't."

"Yep."

"Okay," Lennie said. "I just wanted to hear you say it. Remember your old pal sometime when you don't need nothing."

A working girl in a very short black leather miniskirt and black mesh top with a red bra underneath stumbled into the bar. She gave Lennie a sloppy wink. Lennie acted as if he didn't know her. "You been busy, Spenser," Lennie said. "Jesus H. You blew away Jumpin' Jack Flynn."

"That wasn't me."

"Hawk?"

"Flynn broke the rules."

"What's that?"

"You don't mess with kids."

"Hoods got rules?" Lennie settled back, amused.

"You have rules."

"Yeah," he said. "The fucking golden rule. Whoever has the most gold makes the fucking rule."

"Speaking of."

"Hold on, hold on," Lennie said. He shook his head and scooted out from the booth to find a stool at the end of the bar. I stayed in the booth and finished my beer. The working girl nuzzled Lennie's ear as he dialed his telephone. He lit another cigarette and pushed the girl away, the bartender bringing him another beer. Ten minutes and three cigarettes later, Lennie returned to the booth.

"And?"

Lennie spread his hands wide, cigarette dangling from the corner of his mouth.

"What's in this for me?"

"A favor to be named later?"

74

"Good enough," Lennie said. "Yep, Weinberg has the Wonderland track sewn up. He bought it right after it closed. He may have even funded the crazies wanting to protect the puppies to make sure it went tits up."

"May I ask where this information was obtained?"

Lennie tucked another cigarette into the corner of his mouth and stared at me with great pity.

"Solid?" I said.

"Ain't it always?"

It was dark when I started back to my apartment. A mile down Commonwealth, I spotted a tail. To make sure, I jockeyed down into the South End for a few blocks. As I lifted my phone to call Z, the car took a sharp turn and disappeared.

That night in the Public Garden, I held Pearl's leash with my left hand. My right rested on the butt of my .38.

13

The next morning in Revere, I spotted Z's car. But no Z.

He had parked at a meter across from the Ocean View, a couple spaces from a beach pavilion. I tried calling him, but there was no answer. I left my Explorer on Beach Boulevard and walked up to the front entrance of Henry's building. I called Henry. There was a lot of wind off the water and it made the cell signal reverberate like a seashell. He buzzed me in and met me in the lobby. Henry looked like he hadn't slept. His white hair was disheveled. I had never seen Henry disheveled.

"They came back," Henry said. "Those rotten bastards."

I nodded.

"They hurt Z," he said. "Rotten bastards."

"How bad?"

"Bad."

I followed Henry to a small sitting area

76

off the lobby. Z sat nearby on a metal folding chair, his head tilted back, a bag of ice on his nose. He had scratches and welts across his forearms and biceps. His blue jeans were torn, boots scuffed. In his other hand, he gripped a bloody towel.

"What happened?" I said.

Z removed the ice and looked at me. He had a busted blood vessel in one eye, and his nose looked broken. One of his legs was stretched out, knee locked. The other leg rested comfortably on a boot heel.

"Two of them," Z said. As he spoke, I noted a cracked tooth. "I got one of them down and the other pulled a gun. They got my gun and both took turns."

"How's the leg?"

"I think my knee is screwed," he said. "Again."

"On the plus side, your nose will look more like mine."

Z did not answer. He leaned over and spit blood into his cup. He looked up at me. A bloody towel hung loose in Henry's hand.

"We'll find them."

"Shouldn't have waited for the gun."

"Maybe," I said. "Or maybe you'd be explaining two stiffs to Quirk right now. He may be less lenient on you."

"I stopped fighting back."

"Didn't sound like much of a fight."

"I quit," he said. "I didn't fight back after a while. I think they thought they'd killed me."

"Takes more than two men."

"You never get beat like that." He leaned forward, head in his hands, not looking me in the eye.

"I have."

"When?"

"So many times I try and forget."

"Being shot isn't the same as two men coming down on you," he said. "I want to kill them."

"You follow that path, and you'll work sloppy. Just like in a fight."

"How much more sloppy can you get?"

"Two against one," I said. "They took turns holding a gun."

"Never happened to me," Z said. "Last man to beat me was you. But you didn't try to kill me."

I shook my head.

"You need a doc to check you out," Henry said, pressing the bloody towel to Z's face. "Then me and Spenser will come back here and talk to the folks who seen it."

"I don't need a doctor," he said. "This is bullshit."

I nodded to Henry. We both helped Z up

78

from the folding chair. Z slipped his arm around my neck and limped along, with Henry opening the door for us. Z spit out blood onto the ground while we walked together. He was silent the whole ride to the hospital.

14

"How's it going?" Susan asked.

"Swimmingly."

"As in the freestyle or as in treading water?"

"The latter," I said. "How could you tell?"

"I hear it in your voice."

" 'If it was only the dark voice of the sea.' "

With the phone cradled between my ear and shoulder, I pulled a cold Amstel from the refrigerator. I popped the top. "Z was hurt today in a fight," I said. "I just left him at Henry's. He broke his nose, chipped a tooth, and reinjured his bad knee."

"My God," Susan said.

"He took it as well as could be expected," I said. "Z is not the type to complain. More than anything, he seemed disappointed with himself."

"Did he do anything wrong?"

"Nope," I said. "But he hasn't been doing this as long as I have. Yet he expects to achieve similar results."

"And one does not become you in a few months."

"It takes a lot more donuts and beer."

"And experience."

"That, too."

Pearl was resting on the couch and gnawing on a rubber bone. I had tuned the television to the Sox against the Devil Rays. After, there was a Lee Marvin festival on TCM. *Point Blank* was up first. I had asked Z to join me. Z said he wanted to be alone for a while.

"Does he know he is a work in progress?" Susan said.

"I thought he did," I said. "But now I'm not so sure. I think he believed I was the only man who could best him. Maybe Hawk or Vinnie, too. But not just a couple thugs in Revere."

"Can he still help you?"

"He's pretty badly hurt, Suze," I said. "More his ego than his body."

"You recall he refused therapy with me or anyone I recommended."

"Yes."

"And AA."

"He believed he had the situation licked with a new outlook and new profession."

"You need to get him working as soon as

possible," Susan said. "It doesn't have to be hard work, but he needs to prove that he can be helpful. If not, he may fall into a funk and start thinking of himself as a complete failure. That feeds upon itself."

"Maybe a professional shrink is paid to worry?"

"Z has a troubled history," she said. "He has not been in recovery long enough to mend all his broken places."

"Does anyone ever?"

"The longer the period from the last fall, the better," she said. "Self-pity from failure can sometimes be very comfortable."

"Henry will check on him."

"And who will check on Henry?" she said.

"I know a sergeant at Revere PD," I said. "He's got a guy watching the place. I'll provide escort to and from the health club."

I looked out on Marlborough Street. The window was open and everything smelled and sounded like spring. Only the slightest chill off the harbor shooting through downtown and the Common.

"Get him working."

"And what if he fails again?" I said.

"It's not the failure," she said. "It's the time it takes to bounce back."

"Years of being a shrink?"

"Years with a professional thug."

15

The next morning I found myself sitting in a semicircle of folding chairs, listening to a bunch of old people gripe. Z joined me at the Ocean View for the group encounter. His massive arms were crossed over his chest, hand-tooled cowboy boots crossed at the ankles. His face looked like bruised fruit and he had walked in with a noticeable limp. Besides the obvious injuries, I did not care for the blurred and unfocused look in his blood-shot eyes.

"If they come back, I'm gonna blow their schnitzel off," said an old man. He was tan and wrinkled, with a very prominent nose. His hair was an inky black. "You blame me?"

"Nope," I said.

Z was quiet.

Schnitzel Shooter was joined by a fat woman in a leopard-print muumuu, a skinny and wrinkled woman with bright red hair, and a man in a blue polo shirt and chinos that hit him mid-stomach. The high-waisted man was introduced to me as Lou Coffone, board president. He looked like a condo board president. In fact, his polo had been monogrammed with the word *President* in case of confusion.

Coffone shook my hand and introduced the others, also members of the Ocean View board. I was disappointed to learn Schnitzel Shooter's name was actually Buddy.

"They ruined his Cadillac," said Muumuu. "Slashed the tires. Cut the roof. Keyed the paint job. He loves that car. We've had it how long?"

"Thirty goddamn years," Buddy said.

"My friend was hurt, too," I said. "Perhaps you noticed."

"Sorry, Big Chief," said the red-haired woman. "I saw what happened."

Z did not respond.

"So now these guys decided to mess with the Ocean View big-wigs?" I said to Henry.

Henry nodded. The board members looked to one another, nodding. Coffone hiked up his pants even higher and stood next to the red-haired woman. Her hair was artfully tamed by a couple of gold pins and what I assumed was a massive amount of Aqua Net. Buddy was apparently with the woman with the leopard muumuu. Lovely couples.

"Now they've screwed themselves," Henry said. "The board wanted to settle with the holdouts."

"Even with the possibility of more money," I said.

"I don't like these people," Buddy said. "Never would trust them."

Z just listened. He recrossed his arms.

"Our residents are more scared than ever," Coffone said. "We filed reports with the police in Revere, and they're going to post some cops here. But some of us are still afraid to go to the corner store. That's no way to live."

"I had that Cadillac forever," Buddy said. "I was going to give it to my grandson so he could cruise for chicks. Original paint was the color of vanilla ice cream."

"Mr. Sixkill here may have to have knee surgery," I said.

"We will not be liable for what happens to you," Coffone said. "That's between you and Mr. Cimoli."

"No one is liable for anything," Henry said. "But some of you may want to get your heads out of your asses and develop a little appreciation for what's going on here."

"And what's being done?" Buddy said.

"Other than people fighting on our door-step?"

"To protect you and your damn car," Henry said.

Coffone held up his hand. Stoic and in charge. "What about this casino we're hearing about," he said. "Is this just gossip and rumor?"

"It's more," I said. "I'm sorting out the details."

"We are open to options," Coffone said. "But I also must do what's best for all our residents."

"I would expect no less," I said.

"So what do we do?" Coffone said.

"Stay tuned," I said.

Buddy snorted. Muumuu rolled her eyes, looking as if she had had years of practice. Coffone walked over to a coffee urn and filled a foam cup. He returned, rocked back on his heels, and stared at the linoleum floor. "Nobody is happy how things are going," he said. "Nobody likes being harassed or hosing off blood from our sidewalks."

"If the buyer is who I believe it is," I said, "you should be able to name your price."

"I can name a pretty freakin' big price," Buddy said.

I never doubted Buddy for a moment. But I kept my mouth shut.

"We can't hold off forever while you snoop around and people are getting beaten up," Coffone said. "Their attorney says if we wait any longer, the offer won't be good."

"Of course they will say that," I said.

"They say they have no knowledge of the harassment," Buddy said.

"They would say that, too."

"I told Spenser we want to be compensated for this aggravation," Henry said. He walked over to the coffee urn and poured two cups. "If these people came to us like real human beings and told us what they wanted, we'd be done. But you don't come in with threats and intimidation trying to rush the process. Now I want to bleed them for some more cash."

"What if one of us is really hurt?" Buddy said. "That Indian kid can take it. But Jesus, we're old."

Henry handed me a cup of coffee. "Spenser will nail 'em," Henry said. "What the hell do you people have to lose? He's a high-end investigator and is doing this for me as a favor. His associate had the shit kicked out of him trying to help. You should be kissing his ass."

I smiled modestly to the elders. "Not necessary. My ass is fine."

Z did not even crack a smile.

As the meeting broke up, Henry and Z followed me out to the parking lot. I tried to help Z into the Explorer, but he used his upper body to grip the door frame and hoist himself inside. I closed the door and walked around. I walked Henry to his car.

"Don't sweat those folks," Henry said. "They're old and scared."

"I know who wants your condo," I said. "But he's worked very hard to keep himself hidden."

"You know where to find him?"

"I do."

"And if I know you, you'll just harass the shit out of him until he turns."

"I work in strange and mysterious ways."

"My ass," Henry said.

Henry looked to Z, sitting sullen and silent in the passenger seat of my SUV. He shook his head. "Worried about that one."

"Yep."

"These people need to pay for that, too."

"Yep."

"Damn shame," Henry said. "He's come so far."

16

I left Henry safely in Z's hands. Or Z safely in Henry's hands. Either way, I left them both at the Harbor Health Club so I might snoop, parking outside the Four Seasons for several hours. I counted cars, listened to the radio, and tried to keep up with spring fashions.

Several hours later, Jemma Fraser stepped under the portico, checked her watch, and waited for a car. A thick-necked man pulled around a black Lincoln Town Car and held open the door for her and an older man who seemed to be a doppelgänger for George Hamilton. Actually, the man was a few shades darker than George Hamilton, with thick leathery skin and highlighted brown hair. He grinned a blinding white smile at the doorman as I reached for a photograph of Rick Weinberg I had printed. Before I could be sure, he ducked inside the Lincoln and they drove off.

I followed. Traffic was sluggish, even for Boston, and the thick-necked driver took his time. He crossed over Tremont and took Washington away from Chinatown and up past Downtown Crossing and into the Financial District. I had the chance to listen to most of *Weekend Edition* on WGBH. Around Post Office Square, the driver executed a series of twists and turns and wound up at the entrance to the Boston Harbor Hotel. If there was any reason to leave the Four Seasons, the Boston Harbor Hotel would be it.

I found some street parking off Atlantic and dodged some cars on my way into the hotel. Ms. Fraser and the two men stood in the lobby talking, and I quickly turned to study an oil painting of yachts racing and some old nautical charts. The dark wood was well polished, and the brass gleamed. The hotel had embraced the aesthetic of the sea. I suddenly felt the need for a pipe or perhaps a can of spinach.

Ms. Fraser and company walked toward the large windows facing the harbor and all of Rowes Wharf. I wondered if they would mind if I joined them for breakfast. I thought about eggs Benedict and a mimosa over a quick discussion of threats and intimidation. I bet I could even work in racketeering over a bowl of fresh seasonal fruit.

Sadly, I was left alone to watch people come and go to a hotel brunch. I smiled and nodded. Past the maître d', I could see Ms. Fraser and the Tan Man chatting away, plates coming and going. Three Asian men in very expensive suits joined them. A silver bucket of champagne was placed by the table, the coffee cups filled and refilled. I was starting to dislike these people even more.

I had not gotten close enough to the Tan Man to make sure it was Weinberg. But if he wasn't Weinberg, he was pretty close. Part of the problem was that the only photo I could find was ancient. It seemed Weinberg had gone in for some recent tightening and tweaking, making something about his face and hairline seem a little off. I could just walk over and ask. Maybe get a thumbprint off his champagne glass like Nick Charles. Instead I sat back in the love seat and watched the double-tiered tourist boats sliding past the wharf. Jemma Fraser, the Tan Man, and the Asian businessmen continued to dine and drink.

"You got some kind of problem?" someone asked over my shoulder.

The driver moved into view. He took a

seat on a love seat across from mine.

"Do you mean with the world as a whole?" I said. "Or just with you?"

"I've seen you before," he said. "You were at the Four Seasons yesterday."

I had been at the Four Seasons for a few hours, reading the newspaper, studying the ads next door at La Perla. "Probably."

"And now you're here."

"You're good," I said. "Keen eye."

He looked odd for the Boston Harbor Hotel. He would have looked more at home grazing on the Serengeti. He had an eighteen-inch neck that was strangled by a burgundy turtleneck under a gray blazer. His salt-and-pepper hair was close-cropped. As he turned to the side, I spotted a gun at his right hip. It was a big gun. If he'd gone with something more fashionable, perhaps a .38, it would not have shown.

"So you gonna tell me what you're doing here?"

"I had been watching some very nice-looking people ready for a day of sailing," I said. "I was contemplating buying a pair of Top-Siders and a nice polo shirt."

"You know how many guys I know like you?" he said, leaning back in his seat and smiling. He found a comfortable spot for his elbows to rest on the back of the seat.

His arms were the size of a holiday ham. Ears thick with broken cartilage.

I waited.

"You know?"

"Know what?" I said.

"How many guys I know like you?"

"You were just about to tell me."

"See," he said, shaking his head in private amusement. "It's shit like that."

"I thought we were talking about sailing."

"And you were gonna tell me why you were snooping around Mr. Weinberg."

"I actually wasn't sure if it was Mr. Weinberg until you just told me," I said. "So thanks. Looks like he's been in the shop as of late."

The man shook his head again. He lifted his chin and studied me. "Oh, well." He reached out his hand. I looked at it, took a breath, and then shook his hand. "Lewis Blanchard."

"Spenser."

"Who you working for, Mr. Spenser?"

"A mysterious figure that is known only by the name Number Two."

"Jesus H."

"As a professional courtesy, just how did you know I was following you?"

"I don't believe in coincidences. I remember faces and especially that nose. How many times you bust it?"

"Several," I said.

"And you're following Mr. Weinberg?"

"I was actually following Ms. Fraser, and Mr. Weinberg entered the scene as a special guest."

"You know who Mr. Weinberg is?"

"I do."

"You know what he does?"

"He is a very important individual."

"Guys like you, you know, who harass him, have a way of getting hurt."

"Eek."

"So do I have to say it?"

"If I were you, I would say something like 'Shoo, fly, shoo.'"

"How about 'Get lost'?"

"Not as catchy. But direct."

"Okay," Blanchard said, standing. "You got about a minute before I walk over to the hotel dick and tell him you're giving some guests the hives. I don't even break a sweat."

"Can I ask you one thing first?"

Blanchard placed his right hand in his pocket. He smiled, waiting. "Sure."

"How much money is riding on this parcel next to Wonderland?" I said. "Because the more trouble you guys make, the more the price goes up."

His face reddened. "I don't know what you're talking about."

"Next time, send some better sluggers," I said. "They hurt a friend of mine. He was alone and they whipped him pretty good. They won't have the same luck with me."

"You off your meds?"

"Nope. Maybe you and Ms. Fraser should have a talk about intimidation tactics."

"That's not Mr. Weinberg's style."

"Okay." I stood. "Tell your employer that the price continues to rise by the hour."

"Mr. Weinberg is a very busy man."

"Don't forget important."

"I never do," he said. We stood in the marble waiting area and smiled at each other for a while.

"A pleasure," I said. Blanchard did not answer as I turned and walked to the hotel entrance. As I opened the door, he was still standing and staring. I caught my reflection in the hotel glass. Who could blame him for not forgetting this mug?

17

"How ya been, Spenser," Bernard J. Fortunato said. "Last time I seen you was in that shithole in Arizona."

"Potshot."

"Should have called it Shithole."

"That would do wonders for tourism."

I cradled the phone between my ear and shoulder and leaned back in my office chair. I stared out the window at the intersection of Berkeley and Boylston. A crew of workers were setting up some scaffolding around the old Society of Natural History building. A street musician played a guitar outside Starbucks. Will work for caffeine.

"You were very helpful," I said. "Considering your height impairment."

"Don't have to be that tall to point a gun."

"True. Don't need the gun, but could use your snooping abilities."

"Okay."

"Still charging the same rate?"

"From what," Fortunato said, "five years ago? What, are you nuts?"

"What is it now?"

He told me. I made a low whistle.

"Business really that good in Vegas?"

"I can't complain," he said. "I just bought a new hat."

"What could be better?"

"So what's the job?"

"I'm going to fax you a list of Massachusetts corporate names and ID numbers," I said. "I need you to cross-reference them with the secretary of state's office in Nevada to see if anything matches up."

"Sure," he said. "That's it?"

"One more thing." I leaned back in my chair. "You know Rick Weinberg, right?"

"You mean like personally?"

"Or professionally."

"You know the Pope?"

"No," I said. "But I hear he is a fan of my work."

"Well," Fortunato said, "you just don't pal around Vegas with Rick Weinberg unless you're loaded or famous. And I don't know about you, but I'm not either."

"I bet you have a following," I said.

"Sure, sure," he said. "I'm on the A-list with bookies, bartenders, and showgirls."

"Some of my favorite people."

"So what's the deal with Weinberg?"

"I want you to find out all you can about him," I said. "The list of companies I gave you should connect to his businesses in Nevada. He's setting up shop in Boston, and I want to know who I'm dealing with."

"Why?"

"He may be doing business with someone I know."

"We talking security codes or the time of his morning constitutional?"

"I'd like to know how he's connected and to whom."

"Guys like Weinberg turned Vegas into Disney World," Fortunato said. "He brought all the glitz and crapola and pushed out all the hoods. He's more interested in picking carpet samples than bumping people off."

"Come on," I said.

"I'm serious," he said. "I've heard rumors an old Vegas family got him started with his first casino. But that was decades ago."

"You ever heard of a guy named Lewis Blanchard?"

"Nope."

"Can you check him out?"

"Sure thing. I quoted my rate."

"How fast?"

"Check out some companies, make some calls?" Fortunato said. "Nothing to it. But

spell that guy's name again. Blanch-dick or whatever."

"Blanchard." I spelled it for him.

"And he watches out for Weinberg?"

"Yep."

"Then you know he's a pro," Fortunato said. "Don't be your usual self and piss him off."

"Too late," I said.

18

I sat in Z's Mustang early the next morning, again parked across from the Four Seasons at a nifty space along the Public Garden. The dark green exterior gleamed with fresh wax and the tan interior was pin neat. I tried not to drop donut crumbs on his freshly vacuumed floor mats but doubted my abilities.

"And what do we now know?" Z said.

Fortunato had faxed me overnight. I flipped through the pages sandwiched into a legal folder. "Cutting out ten pages of legalese and connect-the-dots, it says Weinberg owns Wonderland."

"Is this when an investigator is supposed to say 'Bingo'?" Z said.

"Precisely," I said.

"And without Henry's condo," Z said, "he's screwed for waterfront."

"Life's a beach."

Z just nodded. His breath smelled of Listerine and mints. But his bloodshot eyes couldn't hide that he'd been boozing. I did not mention it.

"And so, now properly armed with said information," I said, "we can approach Mr. Weinberg and company and bring them to the table for discussion."

"Is that our job?" Z said.

"Mainly I'll enjoy the satisfaction of telling Weinberg we have it on record. The negotiation is the lawyer's job."

"Your man in Vegas is good?"

"If he were taller, he would be quite formidable."

I handed Z the faxed papers, and he read them while I watched the steady motion of valet parking at the Four Seasons. The knuckles on Z's right hand were still swollen and black.

Twenty minutes later, we followed Weinberg's Town Car, Blanchard at the wheel, into downtown and dipped into the tunnel toward East Boston and Revere. By noon, we had tailed the two men back to a half-dozen empty lots. We watched them kick around one lot within walking distance of the defunct greyhound track. Weinberg was dressed down for the occasion, in work boots, jeans, and a navy coat made of canvas. A real blue-collar guy. Blanchard was dressed in a similar manner, only with a green coat that strained at his back and arms. He wore sunglasses and took glances in and around the property as Weinberg spoke to a guy with surveying equipment.

"Exciting," Z said.

We were parked within a mass of cars in the track lot. We made Claude Rains look conspicuous.

"Did I ever promise thrills from this job?"

"Yes," he said. "You did."

The marks on his face had turned from red welts to purple-and-yellow bruises. He studied his face in the rearview mirror.

"I'd like to kick that man in the balls," Z said.

"His right-hand man says they have no knowledge of the goons."

"Bullshit," Z said.

"Probably."

After a while, we left the men kicking around in the mud and drove back to Wonderland. Z and I got out of his car and wandered the wide expanse of the broken and weedy parking lot. In an adjoining lot sat a massive pile of rusted junk from beach amusements of days gone by. Parts of an old Ferris wheel, a heap of old bumper cars.

Even with a strong limp, Z kept up with me. The old grandstand stretched far and wide, looming over us as we approached several padlocked glass doors. A note on one door read THANKS FOR 75 GREAT YEARS. I stepped back and kicked in the door. The door was rusted and old, and came off the hinges. "Guess we found it this way," I said.

"Of course," Z said. He hobbled in after me.

The bottom level of the grandstand smelled of mildew and urine. Most of the fixtures had been stripped away, but you could see where dozens of televisions had once been bolted to the walls for off-track racing. There was still a sign over the bar and grill, and underfoot a chessboard of red and white tiles stretched in a slant up and out to the grandstand. At that exit, the doors had already been broken out. It looked as if some homeless had been camping there recently. There was evidence of a small fire and several boxes and filthy rags were piled against the wall. We walked outside, where we found a muddy track, which now sported waist-high weeds. Vines crawled over the lower seats, and birds had nested up in the rafters. I took a seat and stared out onto the old track.

"We had a casino in Box Elder," Z said. "Only reason folks stopped on Highway

337. Or to hunt elk in the Bear Paw."

I nodded.

Z looked around the decrepit grandstand. "Why would they call this Wonderland?"

"For all the grandeur and majesty."

"Where?" Z said.

"Used to be an amusement park," I said. "A long time ago."

"When you were young?"

"Way before that," I said. "I remember an old roller coaster and a Ferris wheel on the beach. They kept the name for the track, but the Wonderland park was long gone."

The space was big and open and oddly silent except for the sound of an air drill coming from a nearby warehouse. The wind made hollow sounds blowing through the broken windows, wavering the weeds and grass on the infield.

"Tough night?" I said.

"Nope."

"When Susan left a long time ago, I lost some of myself," I said. "I started drinking."

"I haven't lost anything."

"You got jumped," I said. "One held a gun. There will be other times. A lot more if you stay in this business."

"I'm fine," Z said.

There was a final edge in his voice. I nodded and listened to the wind for a while. I saw a tangled heap of metal dog cages and contemplated the fate of the old racers. I hoped they'd found a better line of work. Z touched his face and hobbled to the car.

We drove back to the nearby dirt lot in time to see the black Lincoln pull away. Blanchard drove inland, and we followed them around to three more sites. Susan would be flying home in a few hours, and I tried to contain my excitement, with little luck. In place of food, I tried to imagine our options for dinner.

"I'd rather be watching Ms. Fraser," Z said. "Nice legs."

"The same woman who sent thugs to Ocean View and in turn busted your teeth and knee."

"Yep," he said. "I like to look at her like I'd look at a prairie rattler."

"I take it a prairie rattler is deadly."

"Could be," Z said. "Depends on where you are bitten."

"And you had casinos as well as snakes on the rez?" I said.

"The casino came after I got my scholarship," he said. "When I went home, many people liked it. But what's not to like about a check in your mailbox?"

"I don't think anyone in Revere will get

that same deal."

"Maybe Henry will," Z said.

"One can hope."

"How long till you approach Weinberg?" he said.

I took a breath, watching the black Town Car a few lengths ahead. "No time like the present."

19

Blanchard pulled out onto Veterans Highway. Z and I followed through Revere Beach and Chelsea and back through the tunnel to downtown. The Lincoln drove south on Tremont and down past the Performing Arts Center and under the Mass Pike into Bay Village and further into the South End. We were silent. Z kept several cars back and did not change lanes unnecessarily.

"You do much parallel parking in Montana?" I said.

"Just between two buffalo."

"That come in handy?" I said.

Z said, "Frequently."

We crossed over Mass Ave and past the Northeastern campus. The South End soon became Roxbury and the brownstones and quaint boutiques soon became twenty-four-hour bars and convenience stores and soul-food restaurants. The Town Car took a hard left turn onto Malcolm X Boulevard and then slowed at an entrance to the community college parking lot. Z kept driving down the block, studying the Town Car in his rearview mirror. At the next light, I told him to double back and follow more closely.

"They see us," Z said.

"Yep."

"Next?"

"They saw us a while back," I said. "They're leading us."

"Where?"

"A rabbit hole."

The Town Car turned into the parking lot and stopped hard down a long row of cars. Z braked. Another car came up hard behind us and braked within an inch of the bumper. The Town Car threw it into reverse and Z maneuvered out. I placed my hand on the wheel and shook my head. The door of the Town Car opened and Blanchard got out. He studied the parking lot, straightened his jacket, and walked to the driver's window. He knocked on the glass and waited. Z looked to me. I shrugged. Z let down the window.

"You are starting to piss me off," Blanchard said.

"Give it time," I said. "It only gets worse."

Blanchard studied my face. I smiled. He glanced at Z's face and narrowed his eyes, seeing the bruises. Z did not smile.

"When I pull out," Blanchard said, "I don't want to see you in my rearview. I don't want to see this car in Revere. I don't want to see it parked across from the Four Seasons."

"Hold on, can you speak a little slower? I'll take notes."

Blanchard shook his head and the doors to the sedan behind us jacked open. Two toughs in slick suits and slick shirts piled out. We did the same. Z stood tall and cool, busted hands loose by his sides. I did not recognize the other men. Z studied them with no emotion.

"I'd like to talk to Mr. Weinberg," I said.

"I bet."

"About Wonderland."

"What about it?"

"Ask him," I said.

"My ass is starting to hurt, Spenser."

"My apologies."

I reached into my leather jacket. The hard guys behind me were itching to pull pieces they probably had never fired. I winked at them. Blanchard didn't flinch when I reached. He stood with arms across his chest and only made a motion to check his watch. Nice watch. Rolex Submariner. I handed him two faxed sheets. On both pages, a corporate name had been circled. One from Nevada. One from Massachusetts. And in a miraculous way, the two names and addresses matched and there was little room for discussion on what this all meant. He looked at the pages and lifted his eyes at me. He had wrinkles in his forehead and a five-o'clock shadow had started to show at nine a.m. "So fucking what?"

"Give it to Weinberg," I said.

"So he owns the dog track."

"Give it to Weinberg."

He crumpled up the paper and tossed it over his shoulder.

"I have more paper," I said.

"I bet you do."

"And a friend at the *Globe* who'd love to print that story."

"We all got friends."

"Should run 1A and all over the Web," I said. "You don't think that will make property values shoot up? He's gone to too much trouble to keep this quiet to blow the roof off now."

Blanchard walked away. He turned back around. He looked again at his Rolex.

I said, "Tell Weinberg I look forward to hearing from him."

Blanchard shook his head but grinned.

110

He turned back to the Town Car, climbed inside, and peeled off. The men in suits did the same.

"And now?" Z said.

"We wait."

"How do you know they will reach out?" he said.

"Because we've given them no choice."

"But how can you be sure?"

"We're talking Weinberg's language."

"What's that?"

"Money."

20

I picked Susan up at Logan at 6:30, and by ten we were redressed and sitting at her table at Rialto. There was a friendly interlude on Linnaean Street in an attempt to make up for lost time. And, of course, Susan needed at least an hour to shower and dress. It took me ten minutes. But after the interlude and the dressing, we finally sat down for dinner. "Stunning," I said.

"What did you expect?"

"Nothing less."

"You don't look half bad yourself."

"Thanks," I said. "It's the other half that's a real mess."

We toasted our adventures with a glass of Riesling for Susan and a Ketel One and fresh lime juice gimlet for me. The liquid shimmered in the glow of the table's candle. White curtains billowed about the velvet furniture.

"Pearl will expect some quality time tomorrow."

"Of course," Susan said, taking a small sip. "But I'm famished and have made a habit to never eat in an airport."

"Never?"

"Ever."

"The most nourishment I had all day was licking the bottom of a Dunkin' Donuts box," I said.

"And why was that?"

"Z and I were working a tail job."

"So you found a way to get him to work," she said.

I nodded.

"How is he physically?"

"He's walking on the leg," I said. "He probably should have surgery. But he should have had surgery after college, too. His face looks rough. His hands are busted up. All that will heal."

"But you think he's back on the sauce?" Susan said.

"Maybe."

"And did you ask him about it?"

"Yep."

"What did he say?"

"He wouldn't acknowledge it."

"Of course."

I picked up the menu, studying it for perhaps two seconds, and decided on the lamb chops with mashed sweet potatoes and Asian sautéed kale. Susan kept contemplating and further contemplated after we were read the specials.

"And another round," I said.

"I've barely finished mine." Susan squinted at me. She took another dainty sip. Given the same wine, I would already be into my third. The waiter arrived with another gimlet.

"And how is Chapel Hill?" I said.

"I like the campus better than Duke," she said. "Both are basketball-obsessed."

"What's wrong with that?"

"And good restaurants."

"Even better."

"There's a place called Crook's Corner that serves something called shrimp and grits and a wonderful barbecue plate," she said. "I didn't have the barbecue, but it made me think of you."

"And new friends?"

"There are some wonderful people on the faculty," she said. "But I look forward to returning to my practice."

"I'm sure your practice looks forward to your return."

"Theory is not practice," Susan said. "I like the practice."

"Me, too."

Susan touched the stem of her glass and smiled. The Rialto stereo played Dave Brubeck.

"And the situation with Henry?" she said.

I took a breath. "Evolving."

"Did you find the source of his troubles?"

"I did."

"And now?"

"We wait."

"Who was it?"

I told her about Jemma Fraser, Rick Weinberg, Lewis Blanchard, and Wonderland. Even a bit about catching up with Bernard J. Fortunato.

"And he'll offer a better price before being outed as the buyer in the *Globe*?"

"Definitely."

Susan looked bored. She let out a long breath, her lower lip protruding in a lovely pout. "Let's not talk business."

"Okay," I said. "May I then ask what kind of underwear you're wearing?"

Susan grinned. The grin was very full and very wicked. Her teeth were very white against her dark skin. She wore the thinnest of gold chains around her neck. "An absolute teenager," she said. I shrugged and sipped my drink. Susan placed her hand over mine.

21

I did not hear from Weinberg or his people all the next day. I checked in with my answering service several times while Susan and I frolicked with Pearl. We later shopped at Harvard Square and ate a late lunch at the Russell House Tavern, accompanied by a couple of Bloody Marys.

At five, I drove back to the Harbor Health Club and followed Henry home. He parked and went up to his apartment with a jug of red wine under his arm. There was no sign of trouble. I returned to my office to check my mail, hoping Weinberg or Blanchard had slipped a note under my door. No such luck. I picked up the bills I had found under the mail slot and sat at my desk. Night was just coming on, and I opened a window and sat down in my chair, contemplating dinner choices with Susan. We had talked about Grill 23, and although I did love Grill 23, I thought about Meyers and Chang in the

South End. I was inspired by the thought of Korean barbecue sloppy joes.

Jemma Fraser knocked on my door.

"I take it you didn't stop by with restaurant recommendations?" I said.

I opened my right-hand desk drawer and waited for Blanchard or another tough to follow her. But she closed the door with a light click and took a seat. I closed the drawer.

"Your office is exactly the way I expected."

"I'm saving up for a neon sign of a smoking gun."

"And I like your real voice better."

I shrugged with modesty.

"Fooled me," she said. She wore an immaculate cream-colored sheath dress that pinched in at the waist and accentuated the shape of her shoulders and tan skin. She wore a couple of gold bracelets on her left wrist. Her dark hair hung loose and straight around the shoulders.

Jemma looked around my office some more, eyes stopping for a moment on my Vermeer prints, and raised her eyebrows. "Well, you certainly have gotten Rick's attention."

I waited.

"He is not pleased."

"Heartbreaking."

Jemma sat very erect in my client chair, her knees together and neck held high. She smelled very good. I would expect nothing less with that accent.

"So Rick Weinberg is annoyed," I said. "What do we do about it?"

"He does not wish for his plans of development to be made public yet."

"His decision."

"But he does not wish to speak to the board about the property, either," she said. Jemma readjusted the gold watch on her inner wrist, awaiting my response.

"It's one or the other."

"I have come here to offer you an incentive of twenty thousand dollars to leave this alone and walk away."

I let out a low whistle.

She nodded. She smiled slowly at me, her eyes flickering over my face.

"Are you flirting with me?"

She dropped the smile and stared.

"Twenty grand to do nothing?" I said.

She nodded. She crossed her shapely legs. Nice shoes. Dark brown leather, very strappy and tall.

"Shall we have a drink to close the matter?" she said.

"Nope," I said.

"A man of principle," she said.

"I am not overly fond of anyone who would send some sluggers to harass old people."

"A misunderstanding."

"No kidding."

"They were supposed to make trouble, but never hurt anyone."

"They hurt my associate very badly."

"And did you not hurt the same men very badly a few nights before?"

I shrugged.

"So who is in the wrong?" she said.

"Keep the money," I said.

"Wonderful." She raised her eyebrows again. "Terrific."

"If you keep doing that," I said, "your eyebrows might stick."

The eyebrows dropped. Her red mouth pursed. She leaned in close. "You are making a huge mistake."

"Yikes."

"Rick won't be pleased."

"Double yikes."

"The offer was generous," Jemma said, standing. She smoothed down her dress and looked out my window at the lights across Berkeley Street.

"You will let me know," I said. "My offer is limited. And just in case you wondered, the information still gets relayed if I am . . .

um, incapacitated."

"I would expect nothing less."

I reached for one of my business cards and wrote my cell number on the back. I stood and passed it to her. She took it, turned on a heel, and huffed out of my office. Her heels made a great racket in the hallway as she disappeared.

Fifteen minutes later, Jemma called.

"Mr. Weinberg would like to invite you to dinner tonight," she said.

"Golly," I said. "What on earth will I wear?"

"So you'll come?"

"Can I bring a guest?"

"Your associate?"

"Nope," I said. "I assume Mr. Weinberg is picking up the check?"

"Naturally."

"Then I'll bring my shrink."

"Whatever you wish." She named the restaurant and the time.

I was left with a dial tone and an empty office. I smiled very big. What would I wear?

22

"So why exactly am I joining you for this business dinner?" Susan said.

"Because I said I'd go, I like your company, and I would also like your professional opinion on this guy."

"The same guy who sent hoods to rough up an old man and beat up Z."

"Don't let Henry hear you say that," I said. "Next thing you know, he'll find out he's short."

"So you want me to give you a professional appraisal of a Las Vegas casino mogul?"

"Yep."

"And how will I be paid for my time?"

"I'll explain later in great detail."

"I bet you will."

"And I bet he's nothing like you believe," I said. "Salt of the earth. Good, wholesome folk."

"Who employs hoods."

"If people didn't employ hoods," I said, "I'd be out of work."

Susan tilted her head and nodded. She picked up a lightweight coat and we walked down from my apartment. We decided to follow Newbury so that we could window-shop while we walked. Newbury bustled in the early night. The little cafés and bars were packed, the boutiques brightly lit. Susan wore an expertly fitted navy dress with a Grecian draped neckline and tan sling-back heels that made her legs look even longer. I wore a crisp white button-down under my J. Press blazer, super-creased dress khakis, and cordovan loafers buffed to a high shine.

Just an average couple on a night stroll, my S&W with a two-inch barrel barely felt behind my right hip.

"So you annoyed him until he invited you to dinner?" Susan said.

"Yep."

"One of your best skills."

"Weinberg can't have this news made public," I said. "It does and the condo board will be presented with fifteen offers bigger and better than his."

"Then why don't you make it public?"

"I want him to apologize to Henry and maybe to Z."

"Are you serious?"

"It is occasionally possible," I said. "And I believe he can come through with the money. He wants that property in a bad way."

We turned left on Mass Ave toward the Hynes Convention Center. A couple steps later, we found the Capital Grille. The restaurant was a chain, and we could have been in Kansas City, Milwaukee, or Tacoma. But in their defense, they served strong drinks and decent red meat. I happened to like strong drinks and red meat. There was a lot of polished brass and mahogany, and pictures of important-looking people, dully lit by Art Deco lamps.

A hostess walked us to a table in the back corner, where we found Rick Weinberg and a woman he quickly introduced as his wife, Rachel. Rachel Weinberg stayed seated and shook my hand. I introduced Susan. Rick smiled broadly and kissed her hand. He waved for the waiter, and drinks were ordered and served. We studied the menu and waited. Just old pals getting together for some laughs. I really hoped he didn't start by calling me Spense.

"So, Spense," Weinberg said after a few moments. He folded his menu and passed it to his wife. "That stuff, you know, with

123

those hoods, I want you to know that wasn't my idea. Someone working for me got a little carried away. It won't happen again."

I nodded.

"I'm sorry," he said. "It's bullshit. I know guys like you. I grew up in Philly. If someone pulled crap like that in the neighborhood, on a friend of mine, someone would get hurt. Am I right? Or am I right?"

"Is there a third option?"

"I just want you to know you don't have to keep busting my nuts," he said. "Okay?"

Susan leaned in. She took a careful sip of white wine. "And why would you want to deprive him of the pleasure?"

Weinberg laughed, a little too much for my taste. His teeth were bone white and massive. His hair was the darkest shade of ink, and the hairline showed strong evidence of plugs. I smiled at him. He smiled back. His wife looked unconcerned with our discussion, continuing to study her menu and then looking up, as if just realizing where she was, and said, "What the fuck? We're in Boston, I'll have the lobster."

Rachel Weinberg played with a strand of big chunky pearls that choked her neck. She had dark eyes and dark skin but very blond hair. She wore a lot of makeup and jewelry, and had bright red nails. As soon as she set down her reading glasses, she turned to Weinberg, who was still talking, and said, "Cool it, Rick. Let them eat first. Then lay on the bullshit."

I liked her.

"How about a steak, Spense?" Weinberg asked.

Susan gripped my knee under the table.

"You bet, Ricky," I said.

I took a sip of Blanton's over ice. Susan continued micro-sips of the wine. The Weinbergs both drank gin martinis. We had not been seated five minutes when the other guests arrived. A second table was adjoined to ours and then a third. And a fourth. There were more cocktails and conversation and introductions. Susan smiled and dazzled as if we did this every night of the week. I shook hands, meeting a city councilman, a character actor who played toughs in a few Ben Affleck movies, a couple local CEO types, and finally Tony Bennett. Bennett did not stay; he only came over to say hello with Ron Della Chiesa, a local jazz disc jockey I much admired.

Tony gave Susan an appraising smile. He looked at me and said, "How ya doin'." He hugged Weinberg and shook his hand warmly. He left in a wake of murmurs and pointing.

We all sat back down. Two waiters brought out the wine. I switched to beer, an Anchor Steam brought out with a frosted mug.

"Did I just hallucinate that?" I said.

"Yes," Susan said. "You did."

Susan started into small talk with the woman next to her in a way that a cat will play with a cornered mouse. The woman was dressed in a very sparkly silver dress that gave maximum exposure to surgically enhanced breasts. She was very tan and very fit. We learned that she had just returned from a week at an exclusive Caribbean resort to find she had missed recording two of her favorite reality shows. She owned a pampered bichon frise named Snowball. Her mate was an avid golfer. He also sported a Patriots Super Bowl ring.

"What position did you play?" I said. Susan tried to cover a quick laugh with a sip of wine.

"I'm friends with people in the organization," the CEO said. "I travel with the team and often discuss strategies."

"Tom Brady must take a lot of notes," I said. "I guess you played in college?"

The corpulent man with a florid face shook his head. "I had a trick knee."

"Ah," I said.

Appetizers arrived before any further

discussion with Weinberg, who sat at the head of the table and whose laughter echoed through the dining room. Lewis Blanchard sat in a booth toward the kitchen. The big man drank ice water and talked with the two toughs I had met earlier in the day. I nodded to him. He nodded back. I thought about ushering him over to see the CEO's Super Bowl ring. But by then most of the conversation had turned to the Actor. Weinberg stoked his performance, throwing back his head, teeth gleaming with laughter. The Actor told us all about a real tough he'd met while filming a movie. The tough was a guy I knew who had been convicted of accessory in multiple murders.

I never found much about him funny.

The waiter brought another beer. Dinner was served.

The CEO sent back his steak twice. He looked at me while waiting for his food to be cooked to perfection. It was one of those drunken, one-eyed stares of slow realization. "So what do you do?" he said.

"To whom?" I said.

Susan laughed again. Actually more of a snort. Only Susan could snort with such elegance. She was having a ball with the guests.

"What do you do for work," he said, raising his voice. "You know, for a living? What's your profession?" The conversation around us hushed a bit.

"I sell women's shoes at the mall at Quincy."

He shook his head, annoyed with the response, and swilled more scotch, never taking his bloodshot eyes off me. He pulled a paw around his well-endowed wife and gave a self-satisfied grin. It was not until dessert, when one trophy wife staggered to the john and the Super Bowl CEO abruptly left, that conversation resumed with the Weinbergs. The Actor had amassed a nice following at the other side of the table. The waiter had returned with a small brush and pail to remove crumbs.

"Would you like some brandy with your coffee?" Weinberg said.

I did. Susan was fine with a splash of Riesling.

Rachel Weinberg scooted up her chair and took a bite of cheesecake. "Rick, where do you find these fucking people?" she said. "Madame Tussauds?"

"Business," Weinberg said. I noted he was on only his second glass of wine. He sipped slower than Susan.

"Okay," Rachel said. She motioned to me with her wineglass. "Now, you want to explain why you've been busting my husband's balls?"

I waited for the brandy before I explained.

23

I drank brandy while Susan and Weinberg debated the ethics of gambling. The brandy was very good. The debate was a little heated. Rachel Weinberg and I followed, heads on swivel, and would occasionally interject some pithy comment. Some of mine were clever. But for the most part this was the Susan-and-Rick show. The Harvard shrink versus the Las Vegas billionaire. Weinberg did not stand a chance.

"What I offer is entertainment," Weinberg said. His voice low and gravelly, his hands clasped in front of him. Earnest. "It's about the experience. The fun. I don't just do slot machines and craps."

"But isn't that how you make most of your money?"

"Not true," Weinberg said. He picked up a wineglass and twirled it. "Most of our profits come from the hotels. The shows. It's pizzazz and glitter."

"But gambling is central," Susan said.

"It's part of the experience."

"I've had several patients who say it is the only experience," Susan said. "Not many leave your hotels winners."

"Don't you win if you have a good time?"

"Some might call that hyperbole," Susan said. She smiled the smile that could disarm North Korea.

"And you?"

"I'm mainly curious about your take on what you do."

"We try and discourage those kinds of people," Weinberg said. "That's not the clientele we want."

"Ah." Susan leaned in and opened her brown eyes wide. "And you are not concerned about those who say crime and vice will feed off the neighborhood? When it's public what you want, you'll be faced with countless studies of increased prostitution and drug use."

"I've been running casinos my whole adult life," Weinberg said. "A little wind doesn't scare me."

"Boston is not Las Vegas," she said.

Weinberg smiled and contemplated what Susan said while she sipped some wine. Rachel Weinberg cleared her throat and asked me why I thought the Sox were so goddamn

131

lousy this year. She wore a pair of diamond earrings as big as fists.

I shrugged. "It keeps a long and storied tradition going."

"Revere is a working-class town," Susan said.

"So is Vegas."

I smiled at Rachel. She rolled her eyes at me.

"I don't mean to be judgmental," Susan said. "Just a pragmatist, based on experience with addicts."

Weinberg nodded. He grinned and spoke low enough to give careful emphasis to his words. "But you know how many jobs I'd bring to that town? Doesn't that offset the losers? You know what this project will do to revitalize the beach? The customer we target isn't from Boston. We don't want local. We want the high roller. We want jobs and infrastructure. We want to bring back the original Wonderland."

"I hate to break it to you, but it was never much of a pleasure palace," I said. "Although I do have a soft spot for a hound named Momma's Boy. Came in six-to-one on a twenty-buck bet. Kept me bucks up that week."

"I can't stop you from leaking my plans," Weinberg said. He turned to me and finished his long-suffering glass of wine. "I don't blame you for being upset about some extremely unprofessional behavior by my employees."

"I'd use a much stronger term," I said.

"I can promise you I will deal with it," Weinberg said. "I can also promise you I will make a more-than-fair deal with your people. You open up Pandora's box with other developers and this thing will go tits up. I have to own that parcel to present a complete plan to the state board. You fuck me, and you will fuck your clients."

"Now, that's a motto," Susan said.

"He's not kidding," Rachel Weinberg said. "Can you get us a private meeting with the condo board? Let Rick do his shtick and see what they decide. You still want to go to the *Globe* and lay it out, go for it. But that's bad business."

"Bad business is sending leg breakers to harass residents and the people who protect them."

"Agreed," he said. "That's not my style. Mr. Blanchard is conducting an internal investigation of how that happened."

"I'd be glad to explain it to him."

"What can I offer you?" Weinberg said.

"I want what's best for my client," I said. Susan smiled at me. I think she was having a great time.

"Okay, then," Weinberg said. There was much laughter at the end of the table. The Actor separated his hands by a foot and announced, "Like a fucking horse." Laughter echoed throughout the dining room. Weinberg rolled his eyes and turned back. He looked appraisingly at me and Susan. He jabbed a thumb at me and said, "What's a nice Jewish shrink doing with a goy with a twenty-inch neck?"

"Actually, it's only nineteen and a half," I said.

"Would you believe he recites poetry?" Susan said. "He even appreciates art without prodding."

"No kidding," Weinberg said. "Seriously. What about real art? You like Picasso?"

"I prefer my guitars without noses."

"I just bought this fucking portrait Picasso did of his lover during the war," Weinberg said. He stated it as if he'd just returned from a Labor Day sale at Sears. "It's big and nuts. I'm going to design an entire casino around its colors. The shapes and energy of it reach out at you. I saved it, really. The asshole who owned it before put his fucking elbow through it. Can you believe that?"

"He likes to put art in the casinos," Rachel said. "We both think art is meant to be seen by the masses. Why put art in a stuffy museum? Let everyone experience it in an amazing setting."

"What was that broad's name?" Weinberg said.

"Who?" Rachel said.

"Picasso's mistress. The woman in the painting."

"Dora Maar."

"Yeah, Dora Maar. He ended up leaving her because she reminded him of World War Two. Crazy. It's just called *Woman Seated in a Chair*," Weinberg said. He smiled very big. "But it's a knockout. I collect all that shit. Miró, Basquiat, Soutine. But Picasso. Picasso is my man. I could have bought a jumbo jet for what I paid for it. But you know what? There are a lot of jumbo jets. Only one *Woman Seated in a Chair*."

I smiled at Susan.

"Plans call for an art wing at Wonderland," Rachel said.

"So there's already a blueprint?" Susan said. "That's confidence."

"I've seen this place in my head before the gambling law was passed," he said. "What you remember as a dog track, I think of as the original Wonderland. The place that inspired Walt Disney. One of the first

135

amusement parks in this country."

"I remember some crummy rides during the summer at the beach," I said. "And a peep show with a woman named Boom Boom Beatrice."

"This was at the turn of the century," Weinberg said. "It sat right where the dog track was built during the Depression. That's how the track got the name. Last year I started collecting all this shit from the original amusement park. I had my designers try to match the décor. It was all Art Nouveau, just gorgeous. This was in 1907, '08. Everything was constructed to match the drawings from the *Alice* book. The original engravings by Tenniel. Amazing. You must have felt like you were really going down the rabbit hole with these rides. Mushrooms bigger than cars. Disappearing cats with only the eyes. Rooms that would grow smaller and smaller as you walked into them. It was all like some crazy kind of dream."

"That sounds like Revere," Susan said. "A crazy dream."

"I even want the cocktail waitresses to be blond and dress like Alice. Only sexy. You know? We'll get chicks in bunny suits running through the casino every hour or so, holding on to a pocket watch like they got to take a piss."

"Performance art," I said.

"I know you two are being smart," Weinberg said. "But I happen to like smartasses. You'll see what I mean if I can present this all to the board. I can wrap in some incentives for them if we get the license."

"I would have thought that had been decided," Susan said.

"We have other problems," Weinberg said.

The waiter walked over and dropped off a variety of desserts on white linen. Lemon sorbet. Cheesecake. Crème brûlée. Some type of chocolate mousse within a chocolate cake.

"It's like falling into another world," Weinberg said, stabbing at the chocolate cake. "You can leave all the outside-world shit and baggage and fall down the rabbit hole."

"With Alice the waitress," I said.

"Server," Rachel Weinberg corrected. "Cocktail waitresses are tacky."

Susan grinned, took a single bite of the crème brûlée, and passed it to me. Susan had an iron will. I, on the other hand, had a large neck.

"I can't promise anything," I said.

Weinberg slapped me on the shoulder. He grinned and winked at his wife. She ignored him and tried a bit of the lemon sorbet.

Most of her brandy remained in her glass. The waiter swept away my empty glass.

" 'If everybody minded their own business,' " I said, " 'the world would go around a great deal faster than it does.' "

"Who said that?" Weinberg said.

"A powerful woman."

"Hmm," Weinberg said. He tossed an AmEx Black card on the table. "Smart broad."

Rachel smiled at her husband. Susan gave me a wicked grin. " 'Curiouser and curiouser.' "

24

"So you negotiated a peaceful and profitable resolution for the Ocean View residents?" Susan said.

"Z won't like it," I said. "Nor will it make sense to him."

"But it makes sense to you."

"It works best for Henry," I said, shrugging. "Z has to learn that the physical aspect of the job is separate."

"That kind of beating would be hard not to take personally."

"You don't negotiate with the hired help."

"And aren't you the hired help?" Susan said.

"No, ma'am," I said. "Just a simple interloper. Now that my work is done, I'll ride off into the sunset."

"Where's the horse?"

"Parked on level three."

Susan smiled, leaned in, and kissed me. We stood together for a long while outside security at Logan. People milled and swayed around us like a current. I had already handed over all three of Susan's suitcases at ticketing. And had tipped extra for hernias.

"You really think Weinberg will keep his word?" I said.

"I would be surprised if he went back on what he said," she said. "Might bruise his sense of ethics. However warped they might be."

"I think he's lying about not knowing about the sluggers."

"Cynic."

"You?"

She shrugged. "It's possible for employees in a large company to make decisions without the boss."

"Henry can decide what he wants to do," I said. "If the money is as good as I think, he's won the fight."

"Just promise me that we never have to dine with that freak show again."

"Promise," I said. "Two weeks?"

"Two weeks."

"And what am I to do with myself for two weeks?"

"Take Pearl for long walks, take in a few movies."

"Is it too late to learn how to darn socks?"

"Why does everything that comes out of

your mouth sound dirty?"

I grinned. Susan leaned in again and wrapped her arms around my neck. She smelled of lavender and good soap. I could feel my heart speed as she turned, blew me a kiss, and disappeared into security. Even with a heavy heart, I studied her backside until she was gone.

I sighed, walked back to my SUV, and drove in a light rain to the Back Bay and my office. The skies darkened and the rain grew heavy. My office reverberated with the gentle hum of the air conditioner. I opened my desk drawer and found a bottle of Black Bush. I lifted it to the light and twirled the bottle in my hand. The amber-colored liquid was enticing.

But instead I stood up, grabbed my Everlast gym bag, and headed to the Harbor Health Club. Sometimes a good sweat did more than the bottle.

Z was there. As was Henry. Z was already on to his second round of training. Henry had him working out without gloves or focus mitts. Z could do little more than shadow-box. As he moved and slipped, Henry shouted out dirty tactics applicable only on the street.

"Punch him in the throat," Henry said. "Elbow him in the temple. Take it to the

141

kidneys."

I gave them a wide berth and started out slow, wrapping my hands, jumping some rope, doing some stretching. By Z's fifth round, I started into the speed bag. And by his sixth and final round, I was feeling pretty good, knocking the hell out of the heavy bag. "Guy was a bleeder," Henry said to Z. "A fighter fights long enough and that scar tissue will open up like wrapping paper."

Z nodded, keeping his eyes on Henry as he spoke. Z moved slowly but deliberately, punching at his own reflection. His right eye was still swollen, and he moved with a limp.

"You don't want that life," Henry said. "I wouldn't wish a boxer's life on nobody. If you got the brains to get out, get out. Unless you know — or are crazy enough to think — you'll be a champ. There ain't a lot of middle ground."

I was on to the double-end bag, jagging and slipping, and timing the rebound of the weighted bag on elastic. Two and out. One and out. *Slip. Slip.*

"Look at Spenser," Henry said. "He got out when the getting was good."

The buzzer sounded. I got some water and tried to catch my breath. Rain tapped against a lone window at the back of the room. Z zipped his gym bag and hobbled toward the door.

"Henry's the best at biting ankles," I said. "Doesn't even have to bend down."

Z attempted to smile and kept going.

"You okay?" I said.

Z nodded.

"Can I buy you lunch?"

He shook his head. "I was going to wrap my knee and go for a walk," he said. "I need to work out some stiffness."

"You want company?"

"No," he said. "I'm fine. Need to think on some things."

Z nodded to me and headed to the showers. Henry walked up as I waited for the next round.

"How is he?" I said.

Henry shrugged.

"His heart's not in it," Henry said. "He's dragging ass."

I shrugged. "It'll take time."

"Now we'll see what he's made of."

"I know."

"You know more about a fighter by how he loses. Not how he wins."

"You're teaching him to fight dirty."

"Bet your ass," Henry said. "You should've taught him more."

"I did," I said. "But I think he froze in the

moment."

"Ain't no rules out there," Henry said. "Kick 'em in the nuts if nothing else works."

"I am a fan of that technique."

I took on the speed bag for another round and finished it off with a round of shadow-boxing and heavy back work. I wiped the sweat from a fresh towel that smelled of bleach and approached Henry. Half out of breath, I said, "Rick Weinberg wants to deal."

Henry smiled. The heavy bag still rocked on the chains, swinging to and fro, the spindle squeaking. The rain continued to tap harder on the lone window. Henry and I walked back toward his office.

"Can you set up something with the condo board?" I said.

"Yeah," Henry said. "But how will we know we can trust him?"

"I'll get Rita Fiore to keep him honest."

"You know the terms?"

"I know he'll sweeten the deal to each unit owner with a bonus if he gets the casino license."

"So we get zip if he doesn't get the license?"

I nodded.

"What did he say about sending out his gorillas?"

"He apologized," I said. "He said it wasn't his style and would investigate why it happened."

"Come on."

"It's what he said."

"How much you think he'll raise his price?"

"Don't know."

"What the hell do you know?"

"Susan met him. She thinks he'll shoot straight, too. But now it's up to you and the Ocean View people to decide."

"You done good."

"Shucks."

Henry unlocked his office door. Henry always locked his door when he roamed the premises. Someone might take his framed picture of Gina Lollobrigida. Z sauntered by the picture glass facing the gym, dressed in black jeans and a black silk shirt opened wide at the neck. His hair was combed straight back.

"You gonna tell Z that we'll deal?"

I nodded.

"He'll still want to find those men who cleaned his clock."

"The agreement is for the condo," I said. "Not for closing the books."

Henry smiled at that, the phone on his desk ringing. He let it ring. "What do you think would've happened to you if you and Hawk had kept boxing?"

"Fame and fortune?"

"And back rooms of spaghetti joints fighting over a C-note."

"Free spaghetti is nothing to sneeze at."

"Who told you to get in with the cops, get a trade?"

I looked to Henry. He nodded, took a seat at his desk, and propped up his tiny white running shoes. As he placed his hands behind his head and flexed his biceps, he muttered, "Damn straight."

25

I was on my first cup of coffee and taking Pearl for her morning constitutional when my cell rang. The rain had stopped, leaving a fine, lovely mist in the Public Garden. Pearl sniffed the moisture-dappled tulips as I answered.

"Spenser's pet-sitting service," I said.

"You wear many hats," said Jemma Fraser.

"I only have one client," I said. "She demands much of my attention."

"I see."

There was a long pause and a long sigh. "There is an offer on the table," she said. "Mr. Weinberg wanted me to present this to you. And to arrange a meeting with the board at Ocean View."

"And here I was hoping you missed my rakish wit."

"Shall we say an hour?"

"We shall."

We agreed to meet at the Starbucks across

147

the street, and she hung up. Or I suppose she might have said "rang off." I turned back to watch Pearl snuffle among the daffodils. Mission accomplished.

We returned to my office with twenty minutes to spare before the meeting. I spent the time cleaning my gun and reading the latest on the Sox's three-game series with Oakland. I was only halfway through when I reached for my jacket and walked across the street. Jemma was there, standing at a side table facing Boylston and adding sugar to a very frothy coffee. I smiled at her and nodded. I ordered a plain coffee and joined her at the bar.

"There's a Dunkin' Donuts on Exeter," I said. "I guess it's too late for corn muffins."

"Yes," Jemma said. She passed over a sealed legal-sized envelope. I felt like we were in a John le Carré novel. "It is."

She again wore the snug, stylish raincoat knotted at the waist. Brown leather riding boots artfully lifted her a few inches. She held sunglasses in her open hand. She tucked them into her purse before reaching for her coffee.

"Those heels put us on equal footing," I said.

"You don't like me very much."

"You hired some thugs to harass a good

friend, and in turn, beat up my colleague."

"Oh," she said. "Yes. Sorry about that."

"Somehow I doubt your sincerity."

I reached for the envelope. It was a bit like an impromptu birthday gift. Do I open it here or in privacy? I didn't want her to see my face if I was disappointed. "Weinberg says you acted on your own."

She sipped her coffee.

"Any response?" I said.

"Are we finished here?"

"I suppose I need to see what Mr. Weinberg has offered."

"He has attached contact information."

"Wouldn't that be you?"

She pursed her lips and studied my face. Her eyes met mine and then turned toward the open space along Berkeley. "Not anymore."

"A real shame," I said.

"I have been terminated."

"How long have you been in the States?" I said. "Shouldn't you say 'sacked'?"

"When Mr. Weinberg fires you, you have been terminated," she said. "My last bit of business was to deliver this to you. After that, I am done."

I nodded. "Truly sorry."

"Even though you got me fired?" she said. "Mr. Weinberg thought I might have crossed a few lines."

"Henry Cimoli would agree."

She studied my face some more.

I grinned at her and toasted her with my coffee cup.

"Best of luck with your clients." She turned on a heel and disappeared out into the soft rain. I took the fresh cup of coffee and the envelope containing the new offer and walked back across the street to my office. I almost felt bad for her. But not quite.

26

Rick Weinberg put on a great show. As he spoke, I waited for fireworks to shoot from his backside and an American flag to unfurl above his head. The condo board was all smiles. They didn't just accept him, they loved him. The deal was very sweet. I would need a CPA to help me configure all the zeroes. And there were free buffet vouchers for when Wonderland opened. No self-respecting AARP member would turn down vouchers.

Z and I sat in the back row of folding chairs. No thugs showed up. No threats were made. Rita Fiore sat in front of us, occasionally turning around to roll her eyes. She was no fan of the free buffet or a literary discussion of Charles Dodgson. "What a crock of shit," Rita whispered.

"But how's the contract?" I said.

Rita shrugged. "Our attorney says it's good," she said. "But I could do without the PowerPoint and Mickey Mouse nonsense. All we need to know is how much and when."

Weinberg wore khaki slacks and a light navy sweater over a white dress shirt with a rather long collar. His teeth were still nearly blinding at twenty feet. His voice was soft and gravelly, not pleading as much as trusting. If he talked any longer, I might have to hand over my wallet.

"We can all be winners here," Weinberg said. "You can be a part of the resurgence of this entire beach. It starts with a grain of sand. A dream."

Z looked as if he might fall asleep. His sizable arms were crossed over his chest, straining the fabric of his black T-shirt. That morning, he seemed more present but more silent than before.

Weinberg recognized Lou Coffone, board president, who sat beside him. Coffone stood and hiked up a pair of powder-blue pants toward his armpits with pride. Weinberg had the touch of making everyone he met feel important. A knowing smile. The two-handed handshake. Buddy, the old man who had lamented his keyed Cadillac days before, seemed to be fine with the world. His dyed black hair gleamed in the fluorescent light. He had his arm around his portly wife, who had exchanged the leopard-print muumuu for a blue pantsuit.

I leaned in to Rita. "Funny how a hundred grand can change attitudes."

"A hundred grand extra for every blue hair in this shitbox," Rita said.

"Worth Cone, Oakes, and Baldwin's time?"

"We are the biggest and best in Boston," Rita said. "Do you think I came here for the cheese and crackers?" She crossed her legs with a huff.

After the meeting ended, Coffone and Buddy braced me at the cheese table.

"It's unanimous," Coffone said.

"Yep," I said.

"Sweetheart of a deal," said Buddy Cadillac.

I nodded.

"You want some cheese?" Coffone said. "We got some of those good Ritz crackers."

"You guys are too good to me."

"Henry said we don't owe you nothin'," Buddy said.

"He's right."

"But the board feels like you need to be paid," Coffone said. He hiked up his pants as he spoke. "We knew you'd pull it off. Never doubted it for a moment."

"That's what kept me going during dark times."

"Weinberg, what a guy," Buddy said. "It's a sweetheart of a deal."

Coffone offered his hand. I shook it. What the hell. Buddy did the same, and I shook his, too. Henry looked at me from the far corner of the room. He stood tall, pointed to me, and winked. I made a gun with my thumb and forefinger and dropped the hammer.

Z stood by silently. His face registered nothing.

I walked outside and found Blanchard next to the black Lincoln, its motor running. He reached into a summer plaid jacket for a pack of Marlboros and thumped the box like a pro.

"Ever hear of the surgeon general?" I said.

Blanchard grinned and set fire to the cigarette with a stainless-steel Zippo. The lighter was engraved with the Marine Corps insignia. His buzzed gray hair showed pink scalp in the portico lights. He blew smoke out of his nose.

"How long were you in the Corps?"

"Twenty years."

"How'd you get into this?"

"Buddy of mine had a security firm in Vegas," he said. "Good hours. Get to carry a gun. You?"

"I like working for myself."

"I work for Weinberg because I trust him," Blanchard said. "Son of a bitch is charismatic as hell."

"Is he really going to pay girls to dress up like Alice?" I said.

"Why?"

"Thinking of investing in white pantyhose."

Blanchard exhaled. "Lots of stuff planned."

Z emerged from the front doors of the Ocean View.

Blanchard stared out at the weak light across the waves. He turned and watched Z walk with a limp.

"Sorry about the kid," Blanchard said. "That was not Rick Weinberg's doing. Or my doing."

I caught his eye for a good long moment. He held the stare and nodded. I nodded back.

Weinberg walked out the front doors of Ocean View. Blanchard scanned the parking lot and the cars parked along Beach Boulevard. Two other men, one on each side of the circular drive, stood guard. Both wore sunglasses and pressed tan suits. Blanchard nodded to his boss. Weinberg walked on.

"You guys put on a nice show," I said.

"It's no show," Blanchard said. "Two years ago, a couple ex-cons kidnapped the Weinbergs' daughter. They wanted five million."

"And what did they get instead?"

Blanchard tossed the spent cigarette onto the asphalt. He ground it with the heel of his shoe. Wind kicked up off the sound, and gulls floated in the soft gold light of the beach. "Five mil."

"Catch 'em?" I asked.

"Nope."

"Know who did it?"

"Part of the deal," Blanchard said. "Money was delivered and he got his kid back. No questions asked."

"I would have had some questions."

"Not Mr. Weinberg," Blanchard said.

"How about now?"

"There's always something," Blanchard said. "He is a very wealthy man. And in case you haven't noticed, Mr. Weinberg cultivates attention."

"Really?"

"He once had a helicopter drop him off on the highest point of this construction site in Vegas. There wasn't jack shit up there. Barely enough room to sit. But he wanted to show everyone he sat on the highest spot in the city. Even if it killed him. Shot the commercial intro from the copter."

"Sometimes I get woozy walking up Beacon Hill."

"Guy like you doesn't get woozy for shit."

Blanchard grinned. I shook his hand.

"See you around," I said.

Weinberg blocked my path to Rita and Z. He did not speak. He looked at me for a long moment, broke into a grin, and opened his arms wide. "Thank you," he said, and reached out to give me a bear hug. The hug was awkward, but Weinberg did not seem to notice.

27

Two nights later, at four in the morning, some unpleasant knocking at my door woke Pearl and me from a restful sleep. Pearl rushed to the door to bark loudly as I groaned and followed. I peered into the peephole to see two state troopers. Holding Pearl back by her collar, I opened the door. "I've paid most of those parking tickets."

"Commander Healy wants to see you," one of the troopers said. He wore the Smokey the Bear hat tilted across his nose. The other stood at the same height in the identical uniform of the Mass state police. Both were muscular, with square jaws and humorless faces.

"Sure," I said. "Want some coffee?"

"Healy wants to see you now."

I held on to Pearl's collar with two fingers. She showed her teeth. I didn't blame her. We both needed our beauty rest.

"Would you mind if I put on pants first?"
I said.

Ten minutes later, I sat in the back of a
state cruiser that headed east on Storrow
and then turned north into the tunnel. The
intermittent false light scattered over the
windshield, down deep under the earth, and
then up into the gaping mouth on the other
side.

"I can think of a better route to the DA's
office," I said.

"Headed to Revere," said the driver.
Neither trooper had introduced himself.
"Healy is there now."

"So someone is dead," I said.

The driver was silent and kept on heading
north on 1A.

"Does this have anything to do with Mr.
Cimoli?"

"Don't know the name," the other trooper
said.

I sat back and watched both sides of the
highway wedged by the docks along the
Chelsea River and the low hills facing the
ocean. The crisp, artificial lights along the
hills glinted in the black night. When we
turned off 1A onto Veterans, the flashing
red-and-blue lights led us the rest of the
way, on into the wide expanse of the old
dog track parking lot. Dozens of state police

and locals from Revere crowded the lot. There was an endless ribbon of yellow crime scene tape from the main entrance stretching all the way across the lot. Two crime scene tech vans were parked nearby, with television news camera crews shooting their every step.

One of the troopers opened the back door. He pointed across the hoods of the hundreds of parked cars I had seen the other day.

A gathering of Revere cops were the gatekeepers of the tape. I pointed to the troopers. A skinny woman wearing a Revere PD badge let me through without a trace of excitement. I guessed she had not been notified of my appearance.

"Wherever I go," Healy said from down a long row of parked sedans.

"There I am," I said.

"Lucky me," Healy said.

I followed Healy down the line of tightly parked cars waiting to be trucked off to parts unknown. We had to turn sideways to make our way through. Warm, sluggish salt air blew in from the sound.

"When I heard your name," Healy said, "I kind of had to laugh. You have a knack for this kind of thing. You know?"

Healy was a skinny, medium-sized guy

with clear blue eyes. He wore an off-the-rack blue suit with a red tie. His silver hair was buzzed into a crew cut.

"So," I said. "Who's dead?"

I continued to trail him down the length of parked cars and then turned left down another long aisle, where the techs were photographing and tweezing and doing whatever it is that techs do. Healy stood back from a car, not much of one, just a dark green Chevy Malibu. Only one of about five billion made. It looked innocuous enough. No bullet holes that I could see. No blood smears or satanic symbols. I walked behind Healy until he stopped and then held me back with the flat of his hand.

"When's the last time you've been speechless?" he said.

"Been a while."

"Just how did you get mixed up in the action with all this gambling shit?"

"Hired by a friend."

"Who?"

"Listen, Healy. I'm fine with showing mine if you show yours. But I'll have to explain to Pearl why you woke her master up early."

"You got a strong stomach?"

"I eat the sausage at Fenway."

Healy shrugged in agreement and led the

way with a flourish of his hand. The techs backed away, and two bright lights shone into the open mouth of the Chevy's trunk.

I did not say a word. I was speechless.

"Guy who watches the lot at night called it in," Healy said. "Ex-cop, and so is the dog. The dog went bullshit."

"I bet."

"You ever see anything like this?" Healy asked.

"Nope."

My breathing felt constricted. I could not take my eyes off the trunk.

"But you do know who that is?" Healy said.

"Yeah."

"Car is a rental," he said. "Rented it himself, in his name."

I nodded.

"A fucking mess."

"Yeah."

"Speechless," Healy said. "What did I tell you?"

He exchanged grins with the other cop.

"You tell his wife?" I asked.

"She's on the way," Healy said. "Flying in from Vegas. Bodyguard told us about you."

I nodded. "Does she have to ID the body?"

"Don't have the body," said the young guy

162

who brought coffee. "Just Weinberg's fucking head."

28

I watched dawn spread across the Public Garden through the big windows of the Four Seasons. Lewis Blanchard, Rachel Weinberg, Healy, and a state cop I knew named Lundquist sat huddled in a small group. The cops and I drank coffee. Blanchard and Rachel drank whiskey. After a while Healy nodded to the waitress and she brought him two fingers of Bushmills with his next cup of coffee. A housekeeper vacuumed back toward the bar, the only noise in the early morning. The air was silver and pale on the rolling green hills across Boylston.

"So no one saw Rick leave his room?" Rachel said.

Blanchard shook his head. His eyes were red-rimmed and soft. He looked as if he'd aged several years.

"He never takes a piss without Lewis," Rachel said. "He was obsessive about it."

Blanchard looked down at his hands. He rubbed them together.

Rachel Weinberg wore a pink Chanel tracksuit and very large black sunglasses. She may still have been crying, but with the sunglasses I could not tell. She looked much paler than she had the other night, washed of all color and makeup. Her bleached hair was knotted into a bun. Her hands rested on the gold handle of her oversized black bag. She answered all of Healy's questions while downing a large glass of fifty-year-old Macallan as if it were water. I drank my coffee black and listened. There was little I could say.

"We're pulling all the surveillance video from hotel security," Healy said. "There will be a record."

"Holy shit," Rachel said. "Holy shit. My phone is buzzing like a goddamn vibrator. Investors wanting to know where we stand. If Rick did something on his own and got himself killed."

"When was the last time you saw him, Lewis?" I said.

"Ten," he said. "Ordered a vanilla ice cream from room service. I made sure everything was okay. Rick didn't seem in the mood to talk. I told him good night, took off my shoes, and went to sleep in the

165

adjoining room. Rachel is right, Mr. Weinberg did not take crazy chances. If he wanted to go down to the lobby for a stick of gum, I was paid to go with him."

Rachel Weinberg took in a very long breath. Her face was impassive behind the sunglasses. "So much to do," she said. "All this shit. I could just kill Rick for this."

"We would like to make a list," Lundquist said. It was the first time he'd spoken in the last thirty minutes. He was tall and big, with light hair and apple-red cheeks, like he'd just stepped off some Midwestern farm. "Names of people who might want to harm your husband."

"Easier to start with the Las Vegas phonebook," she said. Rachel took a healthy sip of scotch. "My husband was a fair man. A direct man. But he was never what I'd call a loved man."

"I apologize for asking," Healy said. He looked down at the notebook in his hand. "But we have to cover everything if we want to help. I don't want to offend you, Mrs. Weinberg."

"You want to know, did he screw around?" Rachel said. "His personal habits?"

Healy nodded.

"Sure," Rachel said. "Rick has always loved the ladies. We had an understanding."

Blanchard looked up quickly from where he'd been staring at the notebook. She looked to him and nodded.

"Lewis knows," she said. "I knew. Everyone knew. I loved Rick, but I am not a fool. My husband was a real cock hound."

The housekeeper stopped vacuuming, underscoring the ugly word, letting it hang there in the crisp silence. The light in the Public Garden was infused with color, gold springtime tones on the greenery. Silver light lengthened into shadows that would soon disappear.

"I knew most of the women," she said. "Lew knew more. But hell, they wouldn't cut off his head. Jesus. Would someone get me another drink? These pills aren't working on their own. My God."

"We can take you to a doctor," Healy said. "Finish this up later."

"If I'm going to be doped up, better do it myself."

"There was a final message?" I said.

"Yes," Rachel said. "I played it for these men here."

"What's it say?" I said.

"Rick said, 'Fucking bastard,' and then hung up. Don't ask who he meant because I don't know."

"What time did the call come in?" I said.

"Ten-thirty Eastern."

"Did he have close friends in Boston?" I said. "Someone who may have seen him after he left his room. Or was forced?"

Rachel removed her sunglasses, her eyes naked and red. The waitress laid down a fresh scotch and took the old one away. Rachel looked to Blanchard. "Tell him, Lew. Tell them. What the hell does it matter? They need to know." Blanchard nodded. He leaned in with elbows on knees and hands laced before him. He looked a little unsteady. White scruff showed along his jawline.

"He was seeing Jemma Fraser."

I leaned back. I tried to seem shocked.

"And where is she now?" I said.

"Don't know," Blanchard said. "She can't be reached."

Healy nodded to Lundquist. Lundquist jumped up to make a call. If she was still alive, the staties would find her. Of course, they had yet to find the rest of Weinberg's body, but I'm sure the recovery remained high on their list.

"Did you know your husband fired her?" I said.

"That's not true," Rachel said. "He would have definitely told me. Where did you hear that?"

"From Jemma Fraser."

"Lying little bitch."

"She brought over contracts for the condo board," I said. "She told me it was her last act of business for Rick."

"She didn't give a shit about him," Rachel said. "She knew what she had and worked every inch. Men are such goddamn fools and don't know the reason."

"No argument, Mrs. Weinberg," I said.

"I can't stand it," she said. "I can't stand it. Rick and I have been together for forty years. My God."

Healy looked to Blanchard. Blanchard nodded back and stood and held out a hand for Rachel Weinberg. She took it, shaky as she stood, and walked a few paces before turning back to face me. She wavered on her feet. An old boxer, busted but unbowed. He helped her to the bedroom, returned, and sat down across from me.

"You will help us, Spenser?" Blanchard said.

I looked to Healy. I looked to Lundquist.

"Name your rate," Blanchard said.

I thought of a million reasons to say no. Mostly because I had been working for her husband's opposition. But that was old business, or maybe it was the same business. But I could not say anything else to him but "Yes."

29

When I got back to my apartment, I showered, shaved, and brewed a pot of coffee. I walked Pearl and filled her food and water bowls. Freshly caffeinated and smelling of bay rum, I drove over to the Paramount diner. Z was waiting for me outside. We walked inside, ordered breakfast, and sat at a high table near the rear of the narrow restaurant. I ordered huevos rancheros. Z drank black coffee.

"How's his wife?" Z said.

"In shock," I said. "But composed. In control. They asked me to help."

"But we can't," Z said. "Because of working for Henry."

"Those lines have been a bit blurred," I said. "It's all the same now."

"Not the same to me," he said. "These people are scum."

"Perhaps," I said. "But they need help.

And if we don't help, Henry could lose the deal."

"Since when do you care about money?"

"It's nice when my agenda involves a paycheck," I said. "I like to be able to keep the lights on."

Z drank his coffee. I took a forkful of huevos rancheros.

"And you liked Weinberg," Z said.

"Yes," I said. "Despite himself."

"You really think he was honest?"

"No," I said. "But I think he was good to his word."

"Which we value."

"Without it, you're like some kind of animal."

"Hemingway?"

"Holden," I said. *The Wild Bunch.*

"Haven't seen it."

"It's a Western."

"Westerns weren't too popular on the rez," Z said. "The good guys never win."

"Depends on your point of view."

"Only one right one, Kemosabe." The Paramount was unusually slow for a morning. We did not feel rushed to give up our table.

"So is the deal off?" Z said. "Because Weinberg is dead."

"His wife says it's business as usual," I

said. "But the company is going to be in a lot of turmoil and they'll need a swift resolution."

Z nodded.

"The bodyguard said I could name my rate."

"Naming your rate is a good incentive," Z said. "So we're back to Jemma."

"Would you mind watching her some more?"

Z smiled slightly. "She's a suspect?"

"I think cops call them a 'person of interest' these days."

"What do you call her?" Z said.

"A suspect."

Z nodded. A waitress came by and refilled our cups.

"Maybe they killed her, too," Z said.

"Thought had crossed my mind."

"But you like her for it."

"Maybe she knows more about what's going on," I said. "What do you think of Blanchard?"

"Smart," Z said. "Tough. But even when I was a drunk, I never lost my client. Even if I did not like what he was up to."

"What if the boss tells the bodyguard to get lost?" I said.

"A good bodyguard stays with the client no matter what," Z said. "It's your reputation if something happens."

"You speak from experience."

Z nodded.

"How could Blanchard have lost someone as animated and loud as Rick Weinberg?" I said. "Weinberg couldn't go to the toilet without making a Broadway production."

I watched a banner scroll at the bottom of a local television station. *Casino Mogul Slain.* I checked my phone. Wayne Cosgrove had called me thirteen times that morning.

"When did Jemma Fraser check out of the hotel?" Z asked.

"Late yesterday."

"Where is her car?"

I shrugged.

"Maybe the airport?" Z said.

"Police couldn't find a record of her flying out," I said. "I had my friend in Vegas check her home there. Nothing."

"Credit cards?"

"Staties are on it."

"Would they tell us if they found something?" Z said.

"Probably not."

"So whatever we uncover, we do on our own."

"They won't prevent work, but they won't help."

Z nodded. He could see over my shoulder

out the small window facing Charles Street and the Toscano restaurant. Without much enthusiasm, he said, "Looks like rain."

"You must have danced last night."

Z nodded. "Who would cut off a man's head?" he said. "That's some sick shit."

I nodded.

"What now?" Z said.

"I can do this on my own."

"If I can walk, I can work."

"How's your head?" I said.

"Thick," Z said. He smiled. I smiled back.

"Henry says only one man knows you better than you know yourself."

Z nodded. "Your competitor."

30

Every time I found myself in Lexington, I felt the need to invest in a tricorner hat. The Minuteman statue on the Battle Green, the crooked headstones for dead soldiers in the Old Burying Ground, and the many taverns where Washington might have set his wooden teeth for the night brought out the Colonial in me. Harvey Rose's house was a Colonial Revival, probably built a hundred years ago, considered practically brand new on Munroe Hill. Brilliant white and red-shuttered, the house had a second-floor terrace that looked out onto a small pond with blooming lily pads. The front door was also painted a basic red. Simple and unassuming went for several million in Lexington.

I speculated that Harvey Rose might be of help since he was Rick Weinberg's only serious rival on the casino bid.

A sprinkler lightly misted the flower beds

despite the gray skies. I rang the bell, and soon after a Hispanic house woman in a gray uniform opened the door. I presented her with my business card and stated I had an appointment with Mr. Rose. She nodded and left me with the door slightly cracked. Somewhere deep inside I heard voices, and another woman came to greet me.

She was very thin yet attractive. The kind of woman who had forgone the Botox and hair dyes and felt comfortable in her age. Her graying brown hair was tied up in a silk handkerchief, and gold hoops hung in her ears. The front of her jeans and designer T-shirt were covered in flour. She wore leather sandals decorated with Navajo beads.

"Harvey isn't here," she said. "May I help you?"

"I had an appointment." I lied, but it was a good one. He hadn't been at his office.

"He never meets anyone at home," she said. She hugged herself as she studied me.

"Don't tell me I made a mistake," I said. "Harvey told me to find him at home this morning. We were going to have lunch."

"I'm sorry, I need to check with someone," she said. "We don't have many visitors. Can you come back in an hour?"

"Let me consult with my personal assistant," I said. "See what I can do. Sure hate to disappoint old Harv."

She studied my face and my shoes some more. Women often study the shoes. I offered a smile fit for *People* magazine's Sexiest Man Alive. She smiled, unconcerned by my steel-toed boots, as I stepped away and checked my voice mail. Besides Wayne Cosgrove calling thirteen times, a former client called and wanted to dispute expenses. Apparently, some of my lunches had been excessive. I spoke to the machine for a few seconds, nodding back to Mrs. Rose until well satisfied.

"We're in luck," I said. "I can stay. Would you recommend a good local lunch spot while I wait?"

"I'm sorry, this is just very unusual," she said. "Given current events, I'm a little jumpy."

"I don't blame you for being cautious."

"It's just awful," she said. "God-awful. May I ask why a private investigator wants to talk to my husband?"

"I work for the Weinberg family."

She nodded. "There is that place on Massachusetts Avenue," she said. "Right across from the park and down from the movie theater. It's a decent enough deli."

I drove back downtown and found the

deli, and ordered the Paul Revere, roast beef with barbecue sauce, cheddar, lettuce, and tomato on an onion roll, with a scoop of potato salad. While I ate, I read a discarded copy of the *Lexington Minuteman.* Apparently, blueberry bushes were being replanted in historic Oak Knoll Farm, there had been a rash of streetlamp outages in the last week, and several accounts of BB guns shooting at windows and empty cars had been reported. The police lieutenant stated that most of the time these things turn out to be youths involved in random foolishness. I wondered if I could add that line to my business cards.

I read the *Minuteman* cover to cover and ordered a thin slice of cheesecake. I tried to think about anything but what I had seen in that trunk. If anything would qualify as pure horror, Weinberg's head was it.

Nearly two hours later, I drove back to Harvey Rose's newish Colonial and wound into the curve of the brick driveway. A large silver Mercedes SUV had been parked by the path to the front door. Two very unfriendly-looking men in sharply tailored suits stood on the steps. If they had been dogs, they would have most certainly been Dobermans. One had shaved his head nearly bald so that the stubble on his face was the same length. He was in his late twenties, medium-sized and hard-looking. The other was beefy, with thick brown hair and smallish eyes. His nose looked like it had been broken several times. I bet my life somewhere he had a tattoo that read MOM.

I got out of my car and met them halfway up the path.

"You Spenser?" said the bald guy.

"Yep."

"You come here to see Mr. Rose?"

"Yep."

The beefy guy eyed me. He stuck his hands in his pockets and turned to his partner. His mouth twitched a bit. The bald guy just stared straight at me, not appraising as much as telegraphing unpleasantness. "Mr. Rose doesn't know who the fuck you are," Beefy said.

"I take it you are paraphrasing."

"What?"

"Well, surely a former Harvard professor would never say 'fuck.' "

"What the fuck do you want?" said the bald guy. His hands hung loose by the edge of his suit jacket. I detected the bulge of a gun on his right hip.

"I have a few questions about Rick Weinberg," I said.

"You a cop?" Beefy said.

180

"I work for the Weinbergs."

"If you don't get the fuck out of here," the bald guy said, "we'll call the cops."

"The family would appreciate some co-operation from Mr. Rose," I said. "Given the circumstances."

They stared at me for a long time. No one made a move. I finally shrugged and said, "Look, guys, I know I'm pretty handsome. But give it a rest."

Baldy shifted his weight to his right leg, peeling back the edge of his jacket, showing off the butt of an automatic. It looked very expensive and shiny.

I complimented him on his gun. He closed his jacket.

I shrugged. I mimed a phone with my thumb and pinkie. "Call me," I mouthed, and walked back to my car.

So much for honor among thieves.

31

I never figured the Fenway HoJo for the kind of place Jemma Fraser would have chosen to meet the sluggers. I figured the sluggers had probably chosen a place they felt comfortable. So Z and I drove back to the Hong Kong Café that afternoon, Z finding the same spot where he'd sat the other night. I shook the water from my coat and ball cap and took a seat on the stool next to him.

There was a different bartender pouring drinks, a young Asian woman with her hair styled like a forties pinup. Her eyebrows were artfully drawn and dramatically arched. She wore a white tank top, a red hibiscus inked on her upper arm. The flower twisted and grew as she poured out a beer for Z and another for me.

I smiled pleasantly at the bartender.

"Nice tattoo," I said.

She smiled at me.

"Met a guy in here the other night had one I really admired," I said. "Had it drawn on his neck. Very classy."

She smiled some more.

"Really short hair. Balding, but with a mustache and goatee."

"You a cop?"

I shook my head.

"Just tattoo enthusiasts," Z said.

"Yeah, right," the bartender said.

"I was talking business with this guy," I said. "He seemed like a real straight shooter. I misplaced his phone number. We were going to take in a movie sometime."

"You guys suck for cops," the girl said.

"Do I look like a cop?" Z said.

"No," the bartender said. "But he looks cop enough for both of you."

I gave a modest shrug.

"We just need to speak to him," Z said.

"No drugs here," she said. "No way."

"He told me his life was the seminary," I said.

The bartender scrunched her mouth into a knot and shook her head. "You two are the worst cops I ever seen. You look like you should be pro wrestlers. Grow a mustache and you could be Pancho Villa."

"Not Mexican," Z said. "Cree Indian."

"Prove it," the bartender said. She crossed

183

her arms across her smallish chest and raised her artful eyebrows. Her face had been dusted with a lot of makeup. She looked sort of like a Kewpie doll.

"You want to test my DNA?" Z said.

"Say something in your language," she said.

He shrugged and said something in what I assumed was perfect Cree.

"What the hell does that mean?" she said.

"I asked, 'What is your name?' "

"Kym with a *y*."

"Kym with a *y*," Z said. He smiled. She smiled back. I let my apprentice take the lead. No reason to double-team her with charisma and charm. "We just need to talk to this man."

"About drugs."

"No," I said. "A woman he knows is missing. We need to find her."

"So you are cops."

"We are private investigators," Z said. He smiled. I could tell he liked saying it.

"C'mon." The bartender laughed and walked away. "That is so corny. C'mon."

"It's the best we got," Z said.

I drank some more Tsingtao. Rain hammered on the big bank of windows facing Fenway. Insignificant trees bent and shook in the wind. The day had grown dark, and no light shone from the stadium. I ordered a couple of spring rolls and glanced up at the television. More news about Weinberg's death on Fox 25. The room smelled of Asian spices and cigarettes.

"You want another beer?" Z said.

"I'm good."

"What if I ordered another?"

"You're a grown man," I said.

Z took a long breath. He stared straight ahead and glanced at his bruised reflection in the mirror. He shook his head. "I'm good, too."

I nodded.

"How long do we wait?" Z said.

"Long as it takes."

"You know I lied before?"

"About what?"

"What I said to that woman in Cree."

I waited.

"I told her she had the ass of a young elk."

"Is that complimentary?" I said.

"To a Cree woman. Very."

We both finished the last of our single beers. We waited. We watched more of the news crawl about Weinberg's death. He had been in town to meet with casino investors. Police have not given official cause of death but were treating it as a homicide.

When I turned from the bar to the entrance, the black man Z had fought walked into the room. He smiled and pointed at Kym with his index finger. Mr. Popular. She stood motionless, mouth open, slowly shaking her head. Z stiffened and removed a boot from the railing. He set it down on the floor. His eyes met the man's. Z braced the edge of the bar with the flat of his one hand.

The man stopped mid-stride, looked at Z, and closed his mouth. Z took a step toward him.

The man ran. Even on the injured leg, Z was quick. I left some cash with a nice tip and followed. The man had disappeared from the front lot. Z darted for one corner of the motel, and I ran around the other. When I got to the back parking lot, the man was trying unsuccessfully to scale a chain-link fence topped in concertina wire. Even without a hard rain, this would have been a difficult task. But the rain had made the metal slick and unstable, and the slugger had found himself trapped in the razor wire, one foot hanging over the HoJo property and the other on Van Ness Street and the back of Fenway.

Z yanked him from the fence, flesh and clothes ripping, and knocked him to the wet ground. The man tried to stand, but Z hit him hard in the throat, sending him to his knees. I kept running. Z kicked the man in the face, and as the man tried to regain his footing, Z punched him in the face. There was a flurry of rights and lefts, and then the man toppled to his back. Z was on him, pinning him to the ground, fists pummeling until I pulled him off. The man was bleeding badly.

"Fuck," the man said. "Fuck."

He had curled into a ball, waiting for more. I reached for his gun, a cheap .45, and his wallet, The man had a New York driver's license issued in the name of Bryant Crowder. Bryant had given up trying to escape. He had the word MISUNDERSTOOD tattooed across his neck.

I stared down at him. "Ain't it the truth," I said.

Z had his hands on top of his head and was catching his breath. He looked like he wanted me out of the way. I held up a hand and shook my head.

"We're looking for your friend, Jemma Fraser," I said. "Where is she?"

Bryant wiped the blood from his lip. "Who the hell's that?"

A lot of rain trailed off the brim of my cap. I shook my head. "See, sluggers like Bryant here will always answer with ignorance. Obviously, they come by this trait naturally."

"Jesus," Bryant said. "He broke my fucking ribs."

Z looked at him. "Easier to fight with a gun on me."

Bryant grinned a little. Z stepped up and kicked him again.

"Where is Jemma?" I said.

"Don't know the bitch."

I closed my eyes and shook my head. "Such a mouth."

"Woman hired you to shake down those old people in Revere," Z said.

"Damn. It wasn't no woman," Bryant said. He was breathing heavily. "She just told us where to go and what to do."

"Okay," I said. "Who hired you?"

Bryant tried to push himself up off the ground. Z moved in closer, his face an inch from Bryant's. Z did not wear a pleasant expression.

Bryant shook his head. "Mr. Weatherwax."

I nodded. "Come on, Z."

"Not finished."

"You are for now."

Bryant smiled a bit. "Got you once," Bryant said. "Get you again."

Z nodded but punched him hard in the throat before standing. Bryant curled into a ball, choking. I walked back to my car in the rain. Z followed.

"You know who he's talking about?"

"Jacky Wax," I said.

"Who is he?"

"Dope dealer, pornographer, killer, extortionist."

"Man of many talents," Z said.

We got into the Explorer and headed out. The windshield wipers worked overtime.

"You good?" I said.

"Better," Z said.

32

I wondered if Jacky Wax still remembered me. I wondered if some people still called him Jacky or if he used John Weatherwax. I hoped he was still Jacky Wax, a name befitting the manager of a Boston landmark such as the Purple Banana. The strip club was in the South End, not far from Tufts medical school. An artfully drawn neon banana shined under dark skies as Z and I trod through a few puddles to the front door.

"Used to work a club like this in L.A.," Z said.

"Lots of job satisfaction?"

"Nice for the first week," Z said. "Strippers are all crazy. Hooked on drugs. The boyfriends are usually losers who either sit at home all day or deal. A man can only look at naked women for so long."

"I am willing to test that theory."

"Trust me," Z said. "Music is bad. Dancing is bad. Places always smell like smoke and puke."

"Not the Purple Banana," I said. "This is a class place. Jacky Wax is a class gent."

"How do you know him?"

"Used to work for a guy named Mr. Milo."

"And who is Mr. Milo?"

"One does not utter the name Mr. Milo in these parts," I said.

We paid the twenty-dollar cover and walked inside. A dozen or so oiled, nubile bodies worked gold poles in rainbow light. Men in crumpled suits and loose ties sat alone, fanning out dollar bills. A couple held hands in a back booth by long black curtains leading to somewhere called the VIP room.

I sat down at a table facing a giant golden birdcage while Z made his way to the bar. Two women ran their hands over each other to some music that sounded like Madonna. Of course, all bad music sounded like Madonna to me. Z placed two Budweisers in front of us, reached into his wallet, and slipped a dollar bill into the cage. One of the women picked it up with her teeth. The other woman helped her turn upside down and slide down the pole, which was not so much sexy as it was awkward.

We drank warm beer and turned from the cage to watch the main stage. A bony girl with straight blond hair came out in little else but tall fur boots. The boots looked as if they'd come from a skinned yeti. Next, a black girl with a short Afro and enormous breasts did a lot of twirling and tumbling to some pinging electronic music with a thumping electronic drum.

"You think the DJ could play 'Night Train'?" I said.

"What's 'Night Train'?"

"Probably haven't heard of pasties, either," I said.

I hadn't finished half my beer when a top-less waitress appeared and asked if we wanted another round. I shook my head. Z did, too.

"Is Jacky around?" I said.

"Mr. Weatherwax?"

"I knew it," I said. "Now he sounds like the brand name for a boot cleaner. Yes, Mr. Weatherwax. Tell him Spenser is here."

"Spenser?"

I nodded. "With an *s*, like the English poet."

Z waited. A young girl dressed as Poca-hontas stepped onto the stage and twirled around the golden pole. "Maybe I should let you two talk," I said.

Z shrugged. "Different tribe."

Halfway through the song, Jacky Wax ap-proached our table. He smiled and revealed

192

his crooked yellow teeth. He was tall and thin-shouldered, and wore a tailored gray suit with a lavender dress shirt and pink tie. The pink tie was held in place by a ruby stickpin. When he sat down, I noted he wore very pointy black short boots that zipped at the ankles.

"You're looking good, Jacky," I said. "Get that suit off the back of a truck?"

"This is fucking Gucci," he said. "Cut by a tailor with the hands of a surgeon."

"This is Mr. Sixkill," I said. "My associate."

Jacky did not take his eyes off me. "I heard you was dead."

"Maybe your watch had stopped."

"Funny," Jacky said. He took his eyes off me for a moment to look in the birdcage. He nodded with approval. "So what brings you to the Banana? Lose another whore?"

"The Fine Arts Museum was closed," I said.

"Ha," Jacky said. He crossed his legs as a waitress brought him a drink that looked like grenadine and club soda.

"Looking for Jemma Fraser," I said.

"Who?"

I leaned in. "The woman who needed a few thugs for a shakedown."

Jacky scratched his cheek.

"You need me to call Mr. Milo?" I said.

"Oh, that Jemma."

Z grinned.

"You know that many?" I said.

"I was just trying to help the broad."

"How do you know her?"

"Came recommended."

"By whom?"

Jacky shook his head.

A couple of girls walked over to Z. One massaged his shoulders. Both wore bras and panties and high fishnets. He told them he was broke. They scattered.

"Associate?" Jacky said.

"Yep."

"You getting old?" he said. "Need someone to pick up the slack?"

"Nope."

Jacky shrugged, then rolled his shoulders. "Don't know what to tell you. Ain't my problem if you got it in for the broad."

"Come again."

"When she come to me the second time, she was shitting a brick."

"Why?"

"Protection," Jacky said. "She said someone was trying to fucking kill her."

"They may have succeeded."

"Not my problem," he said. "Not now."

Z turned from the stage and leaned forward to listen. The acoustics were not grand in the Purple Banana.

"She say who wanted to hurt her?" I said.

"Say, I could use a big guy like that," Jacky said, looking at Z. "Work the door. Scare the knuckleheads who try and hump the furniture."

"Not my kind of work," Z said.

"What is?" Jacky said.

Z nodded toward me.

"Too bad," Jacky said. "You looked smarter than that."

Jacky studied Z. He then turned his attention back on me, slowly smiling. "I heard Hawk was out of town."

"Maybe."

"I'd watch your back if I were you," he said. "These ain't nice people."

Jacky looked over Z's shoulder. He then craned his neck behind him to another stage, another girl. He looked me up and down, took a deep breath, and leaned in. I met him halfway. "This ain't nothing like the local crews you're used to," Jacky said, whispering. "I don't want no part of this crap."

"Why's that?"

" 'Cause I prefer to keep on breathing," he said. "Too much money. Too many guns."

"From Vegas?"

Jacky snorted. He shook his head with pity and walked away.

33

"Z been in another fight?" Henry said. "His knuckles were busted again."

"Yeah," I said. "But this time he came out on top."

"Good," Henry said. "Good."

"If I hadn't pulled him off the guy, I think Z would have killed him."

"Not good."

"Nope," I said. We both stood outside our own cars at the Ocean View. The storm had brought in a heavy surf. And even in the diminished rain, the waves rocked across Revere Beach. Henry locked his car and we walked toward the condo.

"Where's Z now?"

"Looking for the woman who sent the thugs," I said.

"Not satisfied?"

"Not in the least."

"You think this broad killed Mr. Weinberg?"

"I'd like to find out what she knows," I said. "So would the staties."

We reached the glass doors to the condo. I held one open for him.

"Might've finally expanded the boxing room," Henry said.

"And a sauna?"

"Don't push it," Henry said. He smiled.

"The fight today wasn't much of one," I said.

"Then what the hell was it?" Henry said.

We stood in the empty lobby together on the silent terrazzo floor. I searched for the word. "Rage," I said.

"What's wrong with being pissed off?" Henry said. "If it works."

I shook my head.

" 'Cause it's what you think made him drink before?"

I nodded.

"Because of what happened before he ended up here?"

I nodded.

"No family, people that he knew wiped their ass with him?"

"Yep."

"But he's not drinking?" Henry said.

"Susan said he needed to work," I said. "So we're working. He's handling things."

"But you're concerned about the after?"

"I am."

Henry nodded. He walked to the elevator and pushed the up button.

"But how long can you look out for the kid?" Henry said.

I tilted my head. "Long as it takes."

"Yeah," Henry said. "Me, too."

The elevator dinged and the door opened. Henry walked inside. I stayed in the lobby.

" 'Cause he's one of us now," Henry said, pressing the button to his floor.

"Yep."

34

When I returned to my apartment, Wayne Cosgrove was waiting at the front door. I unlocked the door, and without a word, Wayne followed me up to the second floor. I went to the kitchen, Pearl curiously sniffing at Wayne, and reached for a couple beers in the back of the refrigerator. I popped the tops. I handed Wayne one. He did not say thank you, only took a sip and said, "Okay, what the hell's going on?"

"I left you a message."

"Wasn't much of a message," Wayne said. "You said you would be in touch when you can."

"Ta-da."

"I have editors breathing down my neck while all the television stations are doing live shots in Revere," Wayne said. "And the one guy who can shed some light decides to get shy on me."

"You seem annoyed."

"I have two whole file cabinets marked 'Favors for Spenser.' "

I sat at a bar stool where a long counter separated the cooking from the dining. Pearl sat at Wayne's feet. She tilted her head and waited for him to speak. I drank some beer and nodded. "I promise to tell you the whole story when I can," I said. "But right now I'm really not sure I have anything for you. I can't prove any of it. And what I think I know doesn't make sense."

"How about off the record?"

I nodded. I got up and poured out some morsels for Pearl. She sniffed the bowl and walked back to Wayne. "Have you eaten?"

"I've been waiting for you for the last four hours."

"Nice to be in demand."

"The last time we spoke, you wanted to know about casinos in Revere," he said. "You asked me about Rick Weinberg buying up condos on Revere Beach."

"True."

"And now someone has cut off Rick Weinberg's head and left it in Revere."

"Yes."

"And now I hear you're working for Rachel Weinberg?"

"How about some fried chicken? You being a Southerner and everything. I have some kale, too. I can sauté it in sesame oil with some lemon."

"That might get you arrested down south."

I pulled out some chicken parts from the refrigerator and patted them dry with some paper towels. I reached for some black pepper, kosher salt, and garlic powder. I found a well-seasoned cast-iron skillet Susan had given me and filled it with peanut oil to set on the stove.

"You should feel honored," I said. "I don't fry chicken for just anyone."

"I bet you'd be frying it for yourself just the same."

"Probably," I said. "I did just receive an ominous warning from the manager of the Purple Banana."

"What did he say?"

"He reminded me Hawk was out of town," I said. "You mind spicy?"

"Nope," Wayne said. He walked to my refrigerator and helped himself to a second beer. He was in a threadbare blue oxford button-down and a brown knit tie. I was pretty sure he was in the same jeans and boots from the other day.

I poured some milk into a bowl, cracked some eggs, and added a nice dose of Crystal hot sauce. The mixture was whisked to an orangish pink. I mixed the spices with the flour and tested the oil with a pinch of it. Not hot enough.

"So you connected Weinberg to the condo sales?" Wayne said.

"I did," I said. "And I had a nice deal negotiated for the residents."

"And then someone kills him."

"And perhaps shadows the deal."

"But you're still working it?" Wayne said. "I don't get it."

"Rachel Weinberg was so impressed by my relentless nature and perhaps by kind words from a state police captain, they hired me."

"You got to be kidding me."

"Nope." I drank some beer. "Weinberg's right-hand man asked me himself."

"And before his untimely death, what did you find out about Weinberg?"

"That he really liked the works of Lewis Carroll."

"And all your work is in the shitter."

"His wife doesn't think so," I said. "She's moving ahead with what she is calling Rick's final dream."

"Poetic," Wayne said. "Can I use it?"

"Talk to her."

"I tried," Wayne said. "Her people in Vegas hung up on me."

"Let me see what I can do."

Wayne smiled for the first time since he walked in my door. Maybe he was thinking of the fried chicken. I tested the oil. Still not hot enough. It took a while to get the pan just right. You don't get the oil hot enough, and your chicken turns out greasy.

"If the property deal is still good, will your people still sell?"

"Probably."

Wayne nodded. He finished the beer. He walked in front of my windows and placed his hands in his old jeans. "So who killed him?"

"That's where things get fuzzy."

"How fuzzy?"

"The back of a grizzly?"

Wayne shrugged. "Some cops I know think it was the Mob wanting to stop legal gambling on their turf."

"You make it legal and that cuts into most of their business."

"Is that what you're hearing?"

"What I suspect," I said. "I just don't know if it's local or imported."

I tried the oil again. The flour sputtered and hissed and started to brown. I started in on the chicken. I dipped each piece in the flour and spices, then bathed them in the hot-sauce-and-egg mix, then rolled them back into the flour, and finally set them into the hot oil.

My efforts earned another beer. I started in on my second. Wayne was on his third. He got a phone call from the desk at the *Globe* and excused himself for a few minutes to argue with a copy editor. When the desk was satisfied, he came back to the kitchen with his empty beer.

"That's a message killing," Wayne said.

"Mario Puzo would have loved it," I said. "Or whoever writes his books now."

"But you're not so sure."

I nodded. "Almost everything in this case is screwy."

"Why don't you just quit?"

"Henry Cimoli asked for help," I said. "And he's already counting his money."

"So all we know is that not twenty-four hours after Rick Weinberg secured a very elusive piece of real estate for his dream casino, someone whacked him."

"Yep."

"But we don't know who or why," he said. "But we suspect it's connected to organized crime either in the city or in Las Vegas."

"That's about all of it."

"What's next?" Wayne said.

I pulled out the browned chicken pieces and set them on paper towels. I forked the chicken breasts still in the milk and started the process again. I heated a wok for the kale and began rinsing the greens.

"You're a Yankee," Wayne said, turning his nose up at the kale. "Ever heard of collards?"

"Heard of grits, too," I said. "And Tallulah Bankhead."

Wayne watched me as I cooked. "Something bothering you?"

"There's a woman who worked for Weinberg," I said. "She had just been fired. But I think she may be dead, too."

"What about other employees?" he said. "Surely there were others close to him."

"I actually went the other way," I said. "I reached out to Harvey Rose today."

I added some sesame oil to the wok and started chopping the kale.

"What did he say?"

"His people hung out the 'Do Not Disturb' sign," I said. "Or, more precisely, said 'Fuck off.' "

"I wrote his first profile when he was still teaching at Harvard," he said. "I could call him. Set something up. Hell, I interviewed him today on the obit on Weinberg."

"What did he say?"

"Off the record and for your ears only, he says he may pull his name from the casino license bidding."

206

I tossed the kale into the wok and started stirring fast. Two beautiful heirloom tomatoes from the Fresh Market sat on the ledge over my sink. I reached for some plates. I found a couple more beers. Maybe bourbon for dessert.

"Did he sound scared?" I said.

"Wouldn't you be?"

" 'Maybe everybody in the whole damn world's scared of each other.' "

Wayne smiled and shook his head. "Never trust a detective who reads."

I grinned and added the chicken and greens to his plate. I sliced up the purple tomato on the side. "Food for thought."

35

If Harvey Rose was trying to make share-holders feel money wasn't being wasted on office space, he had succeeded. The following morning, I found his Boston headquarters were housed in a run-down three-story in Newton that hadn't seen a renovation since the Nixon administration. It was built of brick-and-beige panels with rusted air conditioners jutting from aluminum windows. From where I parked in a back lot, there was a great view of the Mass Pike and a U-Haul dealer. I walked to a back door and found an intercom and security camera. I punched the speaker button and waved to the camera. The deadbolt slipped open.

Inside were a bunch of office types trapped in no-frills cubicles. Phones buzzed, keyboards clicked, and worker bees did whatever they did for Harvey Rose. I walked down a narrow hallway until I was greeted by the bald guy I had met at Rose's house.

Today he wore a blue pin-striped suit and a lot of cologne.

I sniffed. "Wood smoke?"

Rose's guard did not respond. He just motioned with his bald head to a stairwell we followed to the second floor and a large open room with drafting boards and blueprints tacked on corkboards. On a long table that sat twenty, there were open laptop computers, countless boxes of files, and legal notepads. The beefy guy I had also met in Lexington followed us, glanced at me, and joined his pal at a folding table. He leaned back in his chair, suit jacket open and holster purposefully exposed, and eyed me with a slow indifference.

The bald guy picked up a hand of cards and tossed some chips into the pot.

"I could order a couple pizzas, pick up some beer," I said.

They did not answer. The fat guy tossed down some cards. Somewhere in a back room, a toilet flushed and out walked Harvey Rose. He was several inches below six feet, chunky, and wore black dress pants with a wrinkled white dress shirt with French cuffs. A blazing red designer tie hung loose and careless around his neck. Remnants of lunch or breakfast spotted the shirt. He had not shaved, and his eyes were dark-rimmed and bloodshot.

"Mr. Spenser?"

I nodded. He studied me as we shook hands, before slumping into an office chair. He leaned back against a headrest. His eyes darted around the room.

"Wayne Cosgrove is a good reporter," he said. "He's always been fair with us."

"And me as well."

"It's been a tough twenty-four hours." Rose pulled a pair of half-glasses from his breast pocket and glanced down at a cell phone. "First, we learn of what happened with Rick, and then someone broke into our offices. They stole several files and fifteen computers."

"Anything else?"

"Whoever broke in knew what they wanted."

I nodded. "And you believe this had something to do with Rick Weinberg's murder."

Rose shook his head, placed the cell on the table, and stared up at the ceiling. He folded his hands over his chest and took in a great deal of air. He nodded as if agreeing with the direction of his thoughts and looked over the glasses. I felt the sudden urge to reach for a pen and notebook.

"There's been illegal gambling here since

the Pilgrims got off the *Mayflower*," Rose said. "But the emergence of the gaming industry in Massachusetts signals the death knell to the underworld. We have numerous studies from the FBI that point to no less than fifteen criminal enterprises working in greater Boston."

I whistled. "Just fifteen."

"As you know, there are plenty more," he said. "They hate us. We are changing everything they know. They can't compete with modern business. Bartenders still keep leather ledgers under the register, for God's sake."

"Did you and Rick ever discuss possible threats of doing business in Boston?"

"Rick and I haven't spoken in years," Rose said. "The nature of competition. But we were businessmen, not gangsters. What happened is sickening and barbaric."

"A long way from Harvard Business School."

Rose nodded. He may have straightened up in his chair by an inch.

"How does one go from Cambridge to Vegas?"

"Money," he said. "Opportunities for my family not afforded in academia."

"Not to mention free tickets for Wayne Newton."

Not amused, Rose laced his hands in his lap and waited for me to finish speaking. A technique he had no doubt perfected on grad students.

"So you think the same people who burgled you last night killed Weinberg?"

"I don't like coincidences."

"But Weinberg's death would also open opportunities for others wanting the Commonwealth's golden ticket."

"Excuse me?"

"One of three casino licenses," I said. "Or, as someone duly noted, a license to print money."

"Wayne Cosgrove said you needed some basic background," Rose said. "But if you think I had something to do with Rick's death, I need to call a lawyer."

"You're not the only casino group in the running."

"We prefer the term 'gaming corporation.'"

"Ah."

Rose rocked back and forth in the chair.

"Did you happen to know an employee of Rick Weinberg's named Jemma Fraser?"

"Of course," he said. "She used to work for me. She went for more money with Rick. Something I did not hold against her. How could I? I had done the same thing."

I leaned back in my office chair. He leaned back in his. A warm breeze blew through an open window and ruffled papers. We continued to duel in swivel chairs. "And what exactly did she do for you, Mr. Rose?"

"You can probably tell I'm not a gregarious man."

I was quiet.

"She did for me as she did for Rick." Rose paused. "Jemma was the face of the company. In short, her job was to dazzle clients. I crunched numbers while she did dinners and presentations. I did math. She made impressions."

"That she did."

"Don't let her looks fool you, Mr. Spenser," he said. "She is one of the sharpest, toughest women I've come across. She has brokered deals for casinos across the country. Frankly, I didn't think we stood a chance working against her."

"Even on your own turf."

He nodded. "They came in late," he said. "It was a surprise."

"How did you feel about Weinberg challenging you for the license in your home state?"

"Rick and I were not peddling the same product," Rose said. He stopped rotating the chair. "He was a dreamer."

"And you?"

"A realist."

" 'The greatest way to live with honor in this world is to be what we pretend to be.' "

"Rick Weinberg wanted to build marble palaces and museums. I just want to open a clean, smoke-free place where an old couple can play slots and blackjack and get a discount buffet. Good parking."

"Rick Weinberg said experience is everything."

"Rick did not understand his consumer," Rose said. "He projected himself on his customer. He sold what he himself wanted. I have computers tell me who is buying my product. The high roller from Tokyo is a myth. I want the retired schoolteacher from Haverhill. I want a parking deck and shuttles to run from retirement homes."

"If you ruin bingo night, you might piss off some nuns."

"Another unfortunate reality of the gaming industry." He shifted in the chair again. He took a deep breath and met eyes with the beefy bodyguard across the room. I imagined my fifteen minutes were coming to a close. "Why, may I ask, did you want to know about Jemma Fraser? Do you think she's involved?"

"I think she may have been with him," I

said. "Or maybe she's scared and hiding."

"Jemma is a smart woman," he said. "She's not one prone to hysterics."

"Maybe not," I said. "Although a beheading might rattle her a little."

"Did the Weinbergs tell you their daughter had once been kidnapped?"

I nodded.

"I would want to know more about that situation."

"What do you know about that situation?"

"Only that it was a rough time for them."

I nodded. Rose put hand to chin and nodded back. He folded his hands again across his chest and waited for me to speak. What the hell. I took the bait.

"I heard you may withdraw your bid," I said. "Close up shop."

"We have had plenty of threats," he said.

"From whom?"

"We don't know," he said. "Anonymous e-mails. Calls from disposable phones."

"Cranks?"

"We're not sure." Rose straightened his wrinkled tie. Two buttons on his dress shirt were open, exposing his soft, hairless stomach. "But I have spent the last ten years prepping to open a casino in Boston. I have done countless studies and compiled all the data that will make sure it happens according to our plans."

"Even without the needed land?"

"We have our own properties," Rose said. "Our casino isn't as grand, but it will complement the East Boston lifestyle."

"Beer and clam buckets."

Harvey Rose stood and offered his hand. "Whatever it takes, Mr. Spenser."

36

Outside, an unmarked state cop car sat idling next to my Explorer. Healy and Lundquist climbed out. Lundquist nodded to me and walked around the car to the driver's side. Healy walked over to where I stood and said, "Where's Z?"

"On assignment."

Healy shrugged. "Let's take a ride."

"Get me home before curfew?"

"Drive," Healy said.

I unlocked my SUV and Healy got in on the passenger side. Lundquist backed out and drove off. I followed him to the pike and toward downtown. Healy was quiet until we got in the flow of traffic.

"We found the rest of Weinberg," he said.

"Where?"

"Floated up by the Tea Party Museum," he said. "A bunch of schoolkids saw it. They'll be in therapy until they're fifty."

"You want some coffee?" I said.

"Why the hell not?"

I put on my blinker and passed Lundquist. He followed me and did the same. We got off by BU and found a Dunkin' Donuts on Buick Street. I parked in front of a hydrant.

"Lawbreaker," Healy said.

"I prefer rebel."

Lundquist sat in the car on his cell phone. I followed Healy inside and we ordered a couple of coffees. The endless varieties of donuts called to me like sirens. I resisted.

We took the coffees to one of those little ledges where you can stand and eat. We watched the college kids shuffle past us on Buick, backpacks heavy on their shoulders.

"What did Rose say?" Healy said.

"Not much," I said. "The man has no sense of humor."

"The problem is that you think you're funny, Spenser," Healy said. "A guy who taught at Harvard would find you juvenile."

I shrugged.

Healy drank some coffee. A Boston PD car pulled behind my Explorer with its lights on. Lundquist got out and reasoned with him. The prowlie took off.

"Perks," I said.

"Did Rose give you any suspects?"

"He thinks it's related to organized crime."

"Gee," Healy said. "Wish we'd thought of that."

"So that narrows it down to some key players."

"Ukrainians, Irish, Italians, Vietnamese, or some new crew we never heard of."

"My associate and I spoke to an upstanding member of Boston society yesterday," I said. "He hinted it was the Mob. But he didn't say if it was hometown or imported."

"Yeah," Healy said. "But you and I are thinking the same thing."

"Chocolate glazed?"

"Gino Fish."

"Does a beheading sound like Gino to you?" I said.

"Doesn't sound like the Girl Scouts."

"Who else?"

"Maybe something the Ukrainians would do," Healy said.

"True."

"You've dealt with those creeps."

"Yep."

"Not nice folks."

"Nope."

"We don't have jack," Healy said. "I'd like to talk to Gino anyway. If he isn't involved, he will sure as hell know. He can throw a rock from his front porch to Wonderland."

I nodded.

"And you being such good buddies with him and Vinnie Morris," Healy said. "Might have a better chance with an unofficial visit." He sipped his coffee and stared out the big plate-glass window.

"I am judicious about using my in with Gino."

"This would be the time."

I nodded. A man in a hairnet walked through a swinging door with a loaded rack of fresh glazed.

"You call us when you find out?"

I nodded.

"Christ, don't be the Ukrainians."

"You told Rachel Weinberg about the body?" I said.

"Headed that way," he said.

"Bad choice of words."

"Hell, she already knows. The news crews beat us there."

"You think a glazed might brighten my day?"

"Go for it, big guy," Healy said. He slapped my back as he left. I watched from the other side of the glass as he and Lund-quist drove off. My SUV looked very exposed out by the meter.

37

The King Suite had an impressive sitting area with comfortable plush chairs and a big green-and-gold sofa. There was a built-in bookshelf filled with leather-bound books, framed botanical prints, gilded knickknacks on the coffee table, and a mantel over what I presumed to be a working fireplace. A baby grand piano sat by a bank of windows with a sweeping view of the Public Garden. Flowers, sympathy cards, and a fruit basket sat on the baby grand, covered in red cellophane. No one spoke. Rachel Weinberg and Blanchard sat across from each other. Rachel smoked. Who was going to tell her it was against the rules?

I took a seat. Rachel was dressed in another velvety jogging suit. Blanchard sat remote and cross-legged in a plush chair. He wore dark green dress pants and a white dress shirt with no tie. He leaned forward, hands laced in front of him, staring intently at the ground. A uniformed cop sat in the master bedroom, drinking coffee.

"What did Harvey say?" Rachel said. Her voice was rough, as if it was the first time she'd spoken in hours.

"He said he was very sorry," I said.

"Bullshit."

"You doubt his sincerity?"

"He's not normal," Rachel said. "Don't get me wrong. He's a very, very intelligent man. But he's missing something. It's like he was born without a personality."

"That would account for him not thinking I'm funny."

Blanchard looked up from his hands. He lifted his eyebrows and then looked back down.

"Can I get you anything, Mr. Spenser?" she said.

I shook my head. "Do you mind me asking about your daughter's kidnapping?" I said. "I know it was a few years ago, but could it be related?"

Blanchard shook his head. He looked to Rachel, and Rachel nodded back to him. She looked much older and paler without any makeup.

"That has nothing to do with what happened," he said. "That's an unrelated matter."

"Business rivals?"

"No," Blanchard said. "Opportunists. A few jailbirds who thought they'd been touched with inspiration while in the can."

"You seem confident they're no longer a threat," I said.

Blanchard and Rachel again exchanged glances. Rachel frowned. She let out a long, disinterested stream of smoke. Blanchard said, "They've been removed from the grid."

I lifted my eyebrows and nodded. "Harvey Rose said he's had recent threats," I said. "Same here?"

"We have had a few," Blanchard said. "But nothing we took seriously."

"What about now?" I said.

"Nope."

"How were they received?"

"Crank calls," Blanchard said. "Threatening e-mails. But we figured it was some local yokels. If there had been a serious threat, I would have been all over it with the cops."

"Rose took them seriously."

"Because it makes him feel important," Rachel said. Her cigarette was spent. She started a new one. The cigarettes were very thin and very long. Her lighter elegant and gold. "Rick had to deal with all kinds his whole life. Whoever killed him was a coward. Rick grew up in Philly. He would have responded personally to a real attack."

I nodded.

"Was Rick's relationship with Rose contentious?" I said. "Did he think Rose could end up with the license?"

Rachel shook her head. Cars cut between the Garden and Common on Charles. The white lights coming and red taillights going looked pretty in the night.

"Because he controlled Wonderland," I said.

She nodded.

"Harvey Rose said he had other properties in East Boston."

"Not on the beach," she said. "If he said so, he's lying. The beach was all Rick's idea."

The door in the other room opened and closed. The cop, a short and stocky black man, walked into the sitting area. A small man in a Four Seasons uniform wheeled in a cart and set up dinner. I spotted some pasta and scrambled eggs. A fruit plate and shrimp cocktail. There was a large bottle of Johnnie Walker Blue and a pot of black coffee. Blanchard continued to stare at the ground. He finally stood and walked to the large bank of windows and looked out onto the Common. No one approached the food.

The waiter poured out a cup of coffee and added ice to two glasses. He lit a few candles, set a carnation into a vase, and left the room. The cop led him out.

"You two eat," Rachel said. "I don't know who sent this up."

"You did," Blanchard said. He smiled weakly. "You said you were hungry."

"I did?" Rachel said. "Not anymore. Are you hungry, Spenser?"

I was. But I politely declined.

"Pour me a drink?" Rachel said. She stubbed out the cigarette.

I poured some scotch over cracked ice and topped it off with a little soda and passed it to her.

Blanchard continued to stare out the window. I heard the cop in the other room talking on a cell phone.

"We had been married forty years," she said. "Holy Christ."

"Has anyone been able to figure out why Rick left in the middle of the night?"

"The police said no one called the room," she said.

"And his cell?"

"Was lost with him," Rachel said. She took a healthy swallow. The ice rattled in her glass. Her throat moved as she drank more. "Did you hear they found his body?"

I nodded.

"He was a good man, Mr. Spenser," she said. "He was not perfect, but he was very good."

I nodded. "That accounts for a lot."

"Did you know I married the son of a bitch twice?" she said. "We met in college. Got married as kids and divorced after twenty years. We remarried two years later after he had a fling with a cocktail waitress. He bought me a Cadillac that Frank Sinatra had owned as a wedding gift. He was crazy and wonderful."

She began to cry. I was quiet for a long while. She stood up quickly and went to the bathroom, where I heard gagging and the toilet flush. She came back as if nothing had happened. She brushed at her eyes and gritted her teeth. "Cops said they couldn't find him on hotel security cameras," she said. "How is that even possible?"

Blanchard walked back toward us. He poured himself coffee and sat down. He rubbed his bristled chin in thought. "Anything on Jemma?"

"Nope."

"Did you ask Rose?"

"He said they had not been in touch for some time."

He nodded in thought. "Maybe that's

true," he said. "Maybe not."

"Did Rick ever mention problems with organized crime here?" I said.

"The Mob?" Blanchard laughed and shook his head. "He said most of the Italians were in prison or dead."

"Maybe, maybe not," I said. "I'm being told those who remained resented you guys opening up gambling in the Commonwealth."

"If they did," Blanchard said, "they did not make themselves known to us."

"When you came to Boston," I said, "where did Rick reach out for local support?"

Blanchard again consulted with Rachel. Rachel had her bare feet tucked up under her. She nursed the scotch. As she swallowed, she rolled her index finger, telling Blanchard to get on with it.

"We bought up most of the land through anonymous buyers," Blanchard said. "That last condo was the sticking point. It was a pain in the ass because people still lived there. They were old and difficult. The other parcels, the goddamn dog track and all the other spots, were empty. We had been working that deal for five years."

"So all his meetings were about land," I said.

"Most," Blanchard said. He sipped some coffee. "Politicians, too. You know the drill, got to grease the wheel."

"Was there one wheel that needed more grease than others?"

Blanchard's face remained impassive. "I can't discuss that," he said. "That's one thing Rick would want to keep private."

I looked to Rachel Weinberg. Her eyes roamed over mine. She closed her eyes and took another sip.

"If I'm to help you," I said, "I need to know all of Rick's business. Not just what you put on the books. Or what you think I should know."

"This could get ugly," Rachel said. "Rick would not want it."

"It's not pretty right now, Mrs. Weinberg."

"We have obligations," she said. "Promises."

"Some people don't know I have a middle name," I said. "But it's actually Discreet."

"This was one area that Rick dealt with personally," she said. "He insisted on it. I don't even know all the details."

I looked to Blanchard. He just drank more coffee.

"Handing out gold only makes friends," Rachel said. "It doesn't make enemies."

" 'Nothing gold can stay.' "

"What?" Blanchard said.

"Just thinking out loud."

"Confidential matters have to remain confidential," Rachel said. "Nothing has changed. Business continues. We have to keep Rick's wishes."

"I need to know who got the payoffs," I said.

Neither answered.

"I know this whole thing is ugly and horrific, Mrs. Weinberg. If it were me, I might not have the energy to get out of bed. You asked me to help, and I am trying. But I can't get you answers if you treat me like the hired help."

"That's enough, Spenser." Blanchard stood up.

I asked again. Blanchard pointed to the door.

I shrugged. Begging would only demean my stature as a professional investigator. I said my good-byes, walked past the cop, and let myself out.

38

My phone buzzed in my jacket pocket while I was cutting through the Public Garden on the way back to my apartment. "Where are you?" Jemma Fraser said. She sounded out of breath, as if maybe she was walking.

"Standing on a bridge and watching tourists feed ducks."

"I need you."

"My significant other may disapprove."

"I'm being followed," she said. "Someone is trying to kill me."

"That would put a damper on an evening."

"I'm fucking serious," she said. "I need help."

"Where have you been, and who is trying to kill you?"

"I'm at Copley Place," she said. "And I have no idea. This man has been following me for the last hour. The mall is closing and I'm afraid to leave."

"Talk to a security guard."

"And then what?" she said. Still walking. Still out of breath. "I don't want to end up like Rick."

"So you've been hiding?"

"Wouldn't you?"

Ducks paddled under the stone bridge. An older black man hoisted a little girl up into his arms. She tossed some broken crackers into the water. She smiled. The old man smiled. He let her back down on the bridge and they walked on hand in hand.

"Why me?" I said. "Why not call Blanchard?"

"Blanchard hates me."

"He thought you might be dead," I said. "Rachel Weinberg did, too."

"For an ace detective, there is a lot you don't know," she said. "Will you come or not? All the shops are closing. My credit cards have been frozen. I have no money. Nowhere to go."

"I must have the word 'sucker' removed from my forehead."

"I can help you."

"Do you know who killed Weinberg?"

"Please."

"Were you with him before he died?"

"I am on the second level," she said. "God, there are two of them now."

"Go to the bar at Legal," I said. "They'll be open late. Nobody will make a move there."

"Please hurry."

The phone went dead. I wished Hawk was back in town. I wished Z was full strength and Vinnie and I were on the same team. But before them there was just me. And self-reliance was a hell of a thing.

39

Inside Copley Place, I passed the J. Crew, Kenneth Cole, Calvin Klein, and Armani Exchange. I walked alone, listening to a Muzak version of "April in Paris." But I was well armed and well dressed. Only a fool would try to shoot a man in his best sport coat. I spotted no ruffians lurking about. I heard no mysterious clacking on the marble floors. Harry Lime, where were you?

As promised, Legal did not let me down. The restaurant had a smattering of patrons. Most of them at the bar. Jemma sat at the far-left corner near the kitchen. A gray-haired man in a black suit with a loosely buttoned black shirt leaned over her with a sharp leer. As I walked up, he turned to eye me. He turned back to Jemma and said, "I bike, kayak in season, do a lot of outdoors training."

The bartender placed a martini in front of her.

"Hello," I said.

The guy in the black suit gave me a steely stare. He sipped a glass of white wine and continued to talk as if I were a figment of his imagination. "You have great legs."

"Thank you," I said. "I do a lot of squats."

"I wasn't talking to you, buddy," he said. He took a dramatic sip of his wine. He turned his steely gaze back to Jemma. He was a bit wobbly on his feet, closing time his specialty. I stood close to him and whispered sweet nothings in his ear. He took his white wine and left.

"God," Jemma said. "What did you say to him?"

"It would only make you think less of me."

"Profane?"

"Extremely."

She reached for the fresh martini on the bar. Legal, like all the Legals I have dined in, was a lot of dark wood and brass. They had a nifty neon sign shaped like a cod. I ordered a Sam Adams to keep with the program. Jemma's hand shook enough that she needed them both to steady the glass.

"Where are they?"

"I don't know," she said. "When I walked in here, they didn't follow me."

"I know all the best late-night spots."

"I am scared shitless."

"Why do things like that sound better with an accent?"

"They were waiting for me," she said. "They were the men who came for Rick."

"How do you know?"

She sipped the martini. It was served dirty, with extra olives. The bartender brought me my beer.

"I don't know," she said. "How would I know?"

"You said you saw Weinberg before he was abducted."

"I did," she said. "But I don't know where he went or when he left the hotel."

"What time did you see him and where?"

"He came to my room," she said. "He was drunk."

"Time?"

"Early," she said. "Right after dinner. Maybe nine?"

"Where was Blanchard?"

"Obviously not with him," she said. "Of course."

"But of course."

I drank some beer. "Are you hungry?"

"God, no," she said. "I'm shaking like a leaf."

"There is a feast in the King Suite at the Four Seasons," I said. "Maybe we should stop back by."

"You're kidding."

She shook her head. She drank a sizable portion of the martini. She looked at me for a moment and then at the neatly aligned bottles of vodka. When she finished the drink, I signaled the bartender.

"Why did Weinberg come to see you?" I said.

"Why do you suppose?"

"To further his discussion on talking rabbits and disappearing cats?"

"He wanted to get into my knickers."

"I guess that would hold more interest," I said. I judiciously took another sip.

"Were you and he . . . ?" I said.

"Can't you say it?"

"I don't want to be indiscreet."

"Were we fucking?"

I inhaled and held my words.

"Rick and I enjoyed each other's company," she said.

"But that night?"

"No," she said. "No. Not that night."

"And why would he make a pass after firing you?" I said.

"He said he was sorry," she said. "He wanted to explain his decision to me."

The martini was served. I sipped my beer and studied the scene. I saw no one sauntering out in the mall carrying Thompsons.

"What did these men look like?"

"Swarthy," she said. "Young."

"Sounds like the title of a Mexican soap opera," I said. "Had you seen them before?"

"I said no."

I took another small sip. I put down the glass and lightly tapped the bar top with my fingers. "So, going back," I said. "When you thwarted Rick's advances, how did he react?"

"He put on his pants and left."

"Did he arrive pantsless?" I said.

"He took them off when he walked in."

"Quite an entrance."

"He was very drunk," she said.

"Did he say where he was going?"

"No."

"You said there is a lot I don't know," I said. "Like what? Besides Weinberg needed tips on seduction."

"I promise to tell you," she said. "But by all means, please get me out of here."

I studied the room again. Silver Hair had paid his tab and was escorting a new friend from the room. A man eating a lobster roll finished and dabbed his greasy lips with a napkin. He turned his attention to key lime pie and coffee. I did not see a single individual who was young, swarthy, or menacing. The waiter announced that the kitchen

237

was closed and it would be last call.

My night was going well.

"So where to?"

"I have no money."

"I will pay."

"I have nowhere to stay."

"Will you help me?" I said.

"Yes," Jemma Fraser said. Her eyes were big and brown and pleading. She had freckles across her cheeks, giving her a kid-like quality up close. I signed the check and she grabbed for her purse.

"If you come with me," I said, "I can promise to keep my pants on."

40

Marlborough was very quiet and pocketed in shadows and squares of light from the red-brick buildings and brownstones. The orange-white light of the streetlamps glowed intermittently from Arlington onward, toward Dartmouth and beyond.

I looked east to west and did not hear a sound. A black sedan of some type passed and continued down the one-way street. I watched as the taillight glowed and the car hung a right on Berkeley. I took a breath and opened the passenger-side door. Jemma was silent and a bit wobbly on her tall heels as she got out of the Explorer. Cars lined nearly every inch of the street.

"Are you okay?"

"Yes."

"Can you walk on your own?"

Nod. I helped her anyway.

There was a light click of a door opening. And then another. I nearly did not hear it. I reached for Jemma's hand and hustled her across the street as two men approached us. They were both young and swarthy and blocked the steps to my apartment. They both wore dark suits with dark dress shirts and no ties. The word "eek" came to mind but did not feel appropriate. I could ask them if they would let us through or comment on the nice spring night. Or we could turn tail and run. Unfortunately, I did not think Jemma could get far in six-inch heels and full of three vodka martinis.

No one said anything.

One of the men walked down two steps and shoved me with the heel of his right hand. He was thick and muscular, like a competitive weight lifter. But I had expected it and widened my stance. The other reached for Jemma and grabbed her by the elbow, dragging her to the open door of a sedan. I reached for her wrist with my left hand and clocked the young man with an overhand right. He wavered. Jemma screamed. His pal jumped on my back and started to pound my head using the bottom of his fist as a hammer. I spun him toward the glass door and rammed him against it. The glass shattered and he fell halfway into the vestibule. The other man had reached out for Jemma again, pulling her into the car by a handful of hair. He threw her inside and slammed the door shut. He was halfway around the hood of his car when I slipped a forearm around his throat and pounded his head with my left hand. He fell to the ground and I got a knee in the base of his skull, pushing his face flush to the street. I grabbed a handful of his hair and knocked his head against the bumper of the sedan.

When I looked up, his partner was over me, holding a .45 automatic.

He had narrow black eyes, a dumb stare, and hair artfully gelled to look like he'd just woken up. I let go of his partner's hair and stood. He stepped carefully around me, shards of glass tinkling from his suit jacket to the ground. He was bleeding. His narrow dumb eyes watched me as we circled, trading places. *Do-si-do.*

His friend was having a hard time standing. Dumb Eyes watched me, unsure what to do, keeping the gun outstretched in both hands. He held the .45 like cops in the movies did. It was so close I could touch it. And I did. I pulled forward and twisted it away from my body just as he fired. The sound of the gunshot elicited another scream inside the car from Jemma and caused her to honk the horn repeatedly. I tried to twist the gun from his grip, the barrel turning away from me, muscling it enough to keep it pointed away but unable to pull it from his hands. Lights clicked on up and down Marlborough. The horn kept honking.

His partner on the ground reached out and grabbed for my leg. The whole thing was as undignified and unpretty as it gets. I kicked at the man on the ground and nearly got the .45 from the other's hand. I head-butted him and knocked him back a step. He would not let go, gritting his teeth and using both hands. I held the gun with one hand and reached around his neck to pull him down in a headlock. His partner bit my ankle.

It was that kind of thing.

Jemma honked the horn some more. Someone new screamed. I thought I heard Pearl barking from up in my bay window. The gun went off again.

And then it was all quiet. Jemma honked the horn two more times, and then, seeing her attacker was down, crawled outside and behind me. The ankle biter was bloody but unbowed as he got to his feet and behind the wheel of the black sedan. The key warning dinged inside until he slammed the door and started the engine.

I was catching my breath in the headlights.

The other man lay busted and bleeding against the curb as the car squealed out and headed west at about ninety. I put my hands on top of my head like a sprinter, my right hand still clutching the .45.

"He's dead," Jemma said. "Bloody hell. He's dead."

I closed my eyes and lowered my hands, placing the .45 on the ground. The man lay in the street, his dumb, narrow eyes staring into nothing. Police sirens sounded in the distance. There had probably been a few 911 calls. I wondered how my neighbors felt about me now.

"Jesus Christ, Spenser," she said.

She started to cry. I put my arm around her and waited for the cops.

They arrived thirty seconds later. Thirty minutes later, a patrol officer told me that Sergeant Belson requested my presence at headquarters.

"Terrific," I said.

41

I was brought to a slick room with a slick laminate conference table at the police headquarters in Roxbury. Everything about Boston Police Headquarters was slick. It reminded me of a conference center in an airport Hyatt. I waited at the table for maybe thirty minutes before Frank Belson walked in wearing a damp raincoat along with another homicide cop named Lee Farrell. Belson said Quirk was on vacation.

"I didn't know Quirk took vacations," I said.

"I think he spends the time rearranging his tool shed," Farrell said.

Farrell set a digital recorder on the table. He wore an old pair of Dockers and a red-and-white-striped golf shirt. It was very wrinkled. When he sat, he exposed navy socks worn with moccasins.

"Are you sure you're gay?" I said.

"I played Celine Dion all the way here," he said.

"Yeah?"

"Sounded nice with the siren."

"I thought all gay men had style."

"No," Farrell said. "We just like other dudes."

"Ah."

Belson took off his raincoat and sat at the head of the table. His always bluish-tinged jawline was now black with a full day's growth. He probably shaved with a weed whacker. The rain and dampness of his clothes had deepened the smell of cheap cigars on him. It was fortunate that the city had instated a no-smoking policy when they opened the new digs.

"So," Belson said. "Tell us about the stiff."

"Well, they forgot to introduce themselves while trying to kill me."

Farrell snorted. Belson gave him a hard look and Farrell broke into a small grin.

"Can I see your belt?" Belson said. "Like to know where you're adding all those notches."

"They tried to take a woman by force," I said. "When I tried to stop them, they pulled a gun on me. When I tried to disarm the man, he pulled the trigger and shot himself. The other one ran."

"And you didn't know them?" Farrell said.

"Nope."

"Never seen 'em?" Belson said.

"Nope."

"Who is the woman and why were you with her?" Farrell said. He had pulled out a legal-sized yellow pad. He kept eye contact while jotting down notes. It was quite a talent.

"Jemma Fraser," I said. "But you know that. You just came over from talking to her. That's why you left me for thirty minutes without coffee."

Belson shrugged. "So the broad worked for Rick Weinberg, and since the son of a bitch was found without his head," he said, "she needed some protection."

"He didn't show up without his head," I said. "It was just his head that showed up. They found the rest later."

"And this broad was missing."

"Woman," Farrell said. "You straight guys wonder why you don't get laid more." He tapped his pen on the paper. Since the last time I'd seen him, he'd bulked up a little and shaved the blond mustache. He looked much younger and healthier.

"She said she was being pursued," Belson said.

"That's what she told me, too," I said. "I

246

met her at Copley Place and drove her back to my apartment."

"Did you not believe her at first?"

"Nope," I said. "Would you?"

Belson let out a long sigh and then leaned back in the slick office chair. He set a pair of scuffed brown loafers on the edge of the table and stared up at the ceiling. "What'd this Fraser woman tell you?"

"She was about to tell me something of importance before those two tried to throw her into their car."

Belson nodded. He looked to Farrell. Farrell's eyes looked over me, and he waited a beat. "Nobody has told you, then."

"Told me what?" I said.

"Jimmy Carlucci is the dead one," Farrell said. "We think he was working with his brother, Tommy. You don't know the Carlucci brothers?"

"Sounds like a used-car dealership."

"They were a couple of young hotshots," Belson said. "Real up-and-comers in the life. You know?"

"Quirk always served me coffee before bringing bad news."

"We've spoken to the DA," Farrell said. "We don't have to hold you, in light of the Carluccis' record."

"Okay," I said. "So it's you that knows

247

these guys."

"Yeah," Belson said. "I've known these shitbirds since they were stealing ATMs out of bars in the South End. They used to run with this half-Irish, half-Cuban fuckup. Named Carlos or Carlito. Shit, I don't remember. But their pal ended up in a little alley off Tremont. They wedged his body in a one-foot space and covered him up with garbage bags."

"You make the case?"

Belson shook his head.

"Frank, you're leaving out the best part," Farrell said. He rubbed the wide place under his nose as if he still had the mustache. "You want to tell him, or do I?"

"No, wait," I said. "I love the suspense."

Belson stood up and stretched his legs. He felt for his shirt pocket and pulled out a wet cigar that looked like he'd extracted it from a cat box. He stuck the limp, brown mass in the side of his mouth. "You just aced Gino Fish's nephew."

"You're gonna need some help," Farrell said.

"I have someone."

"Hawk?"

"My protégé."

"Where's Hawk?" Belson said. The cigar vice locked in his jaw.

"Miami."

"You sure you want to bet your life on that Indian kid?" Belson said.

I didn't answer. Z was not Hawk.

"Call him," Farrell said. "Because I'll lock you up myself if you try and leave here by yourself. Christ, it's three a.m."

"Where's Jemma?"

"Next room," Belson said.

"She's coming with me."

"Of course, why not make the target even bigger," Belson said. He walked to the door. "Terrific. For someone who quotes poetry and shit all the time, I wonder about your common fucking sense."

"You're not alone."

Belson made a sound that was somewhere between a grunt and indigestion. He shook his head and left the room, not bothering to close the door. His steps were soft and silent on the industrial carpet. Farrell turned back to me. "You doing okay?"

I shrugged.

"Was it bad?"

"I don't ever like this part," I said.

"On the bright side, you did not let them shoot you."

"There is that."

"It always makes me feel rotten, too," Farrell said. "You realize, it's okay for a man to feel that way."

"Thanks, Lee," I said. "And now I promise not to tell Susan about your outfit."

42

"You want me to come inside with you?" Z said.

I shook my head. I stood with him outside the steps to my apartment. A soft, warm wind shot down Marlborough Street. There was crime scene tape on the edge of the street. The super had replaced the broken glass on the door with plywood. It was still very dark. I had left Jemma upstairs with Pearl.

"I can sit on your place till morning."

"Not necessary."

"People will come for you," Z said.

"Not until I get the talk," I said. "I'll wait to hear from Vinnie. He'll set up a meet with Gino. Gino would want a polite sit-down first."

"Before he kills you?"

"Being a good bad guy comes with a lot of etiquette."

"On the rez, someone has problems, they

just shoot you."

"Simpler," I said. "But less elegant."

"I'm staying anyway," Z said. Without another word, he walked toward his car and closed the door. Marlborough contained many dark pockets and long shadows out from the iron streetlamps. I went upstairs and found Jemma cross-legged on the floor. She was rubbing Pearl's belly. Pearl didn't seem to notice my entrance. Her tongue lolled from her mouth and her eyes had rolled up in her head.

"I'll make up the bed with fresh sheets."

"I can sleep out here," she said. "On the couch."

"Against the rules."

"Whose rules?"

"My own."

"I see," she said. She stood and walked toward the kitchen. "May I have a drink first?"

I displayed the contents of my modest bar. I offered her an assortment of beer and a half-bottle of Riesling I had kept for Susan. She joined me in some Blanton's, served neat. I drank half and started work on the sheets in the bedroom. I changed out the pillowcases and turned off the overhead light. An old brass lamp on an end table created a nice homey glow.

I looked out the window. Z's Mustang was still parked on the street.

"There are plenty of towels and soap in the bathroom," I said.

"I would very much like to shower," she said. She helped herself to another bourbon. I continued to stand while she sat perched on a bar stool.

I got an extra pillow and an old quilt from my linen closet. I could hear the shower running as I turned on the television to see if the shooting made the replay of the late news. It was not easy sharing the couch with Pearl. She liked to stretch out. But her soft breathing and groans made me tired. The adrenaline finally began leaving my system. I turned off the television and then the light.

I heard the shower stop.

My eyes were closed, ears still ringing from gunshots, when she padded into the room. Being vigilant, I opened my eyes. She was in the kitchen, wrapped in only a navy blue towel as she poured out more bourbon. Her body was as taut and impressive as Z and I had surmised. Her wet hair had been combed straight down her back. She took a sip of booze, eyes closed and throat working. She noted my staring and inched toward me. She looked younger without the makeup. The soft, natural droop of her breasts was noticeable as she clutched her towel with one hand, the bourbon in the other.

"Spenser."

"Yes."

"You don't have to sleep on the couch."

"Thank you," I said. "But Pearl might get lonely."

"We can both sleep in the bed," she said. She sat on my coffee table. "There is no harm in that. I promise not to bother you."

"You might give in to my raw Irish magnetism," I said. "Plus, I snore."

She drank some more and wiped her mouth. She smelled of Susan's good soap and shampoo. The little light in the room came from a crack by the bedroom door. Pearl turned and huffed in her sleep. Jemma was doing a very poor job holding on to the towel. Her chest and shoulders were very freckled. Her legs were muscular and smooth.

"I can't stand to think of a man your size sleeping out here."

"I've slept in worse."

She was quiet for a while. A few cars passed out on Marlborough. I heard a siren from far away and the laughter of people walking under my window. She touched my hand.

"I can't stop thinking about tonight," she said. "The way the man looked, bleeding out on the street."

"Have another," I said. "And you'll stop thinking about everything."

"I'm quite scared."

I opened my eyes. "You could tell me what happened to Rick," I said. "What don't I know?"

She took a breath. Waited a beat. "It's quite complicated."

"I think I can handle it."

She put down her glass and dropped her forehead into her right hand for support. Her towel dropped even more. I began to try to recall the roster of the '69 Red Sox.

She reached out and squeezed my fingers.

"Rick double-crossed some very important people."

"Okay."

"He let me run so much, but then would keep me in the dark about so much else."

I waited. I did not want to blurt out "Who's getting the slush fund?" if she was about to point to the maid or Colonel Mustard in the kitchen.

"He had made friends at the State House," she said. She stood up and padded back to the kitchen. She poured out more bourbon. After I scraped her off the floor in the morning, I would have to restock.

"This person, whoever it was, is how we got the gaming initiative passed," she said. "And they were to work out details with the local Mob."

"For a tribute?"

"More like a percentage."

"Who would know the name of the politician?"

"Rick."

I placed both hands behind my head. I looked up at the ceiling in contemplation. Jemma walked back and sat down. As she moved, one of her breasts was exposed. I do not think she noticed, or perhaps she did not care.

"What about personal papers, computer files, messages? What does Rachel know?"

She kept shaking her head. "Something of that importance was known only to Rick," she said. She steadied her drinking elbow on her knee and took a sip. "Please come to bed."

"Alas, my heart belongs to another."

"I don't want your heart." Her accent had slipped a bit.

Carlton Fisk, Carl Yastrzemski, Sparky Lyle.

"You think he was killed because of this politician?" I said.

"Good God," she said. "Can we discuss

this later?"

I sat up from the couch and placed my bare feet on the floor. I massaged my temples. Pearl did not stir.

"Have you ever heard him say the name Gino Fish?"

"No," she said. "I would definitely remember that name."

"Can you help me find the politician?"

She shrugged. She looked at me for a long moment and smiled. Then she tucked her wet hair behind her ears and stood. She looked down at me with a sneer just in time to trip over a footstool. She thudded in a heap, naked and sprawled on an antique rag rug. I did my best covering her in the damp towel and dropped her in my bedroom. I turned off the table light and walked back to the couch.

Tony Conigliaro, Rico Petrocelli, Reggie Smith.

43

Bright and early the next morning, Vinnie Morris walked into my office and took a seat in my client chair. Z was on the couch, with Pearl's head resting in his lap. We were drinking coffee and discussing the night's events. Although Vinnie had not called, the visit was not unexpected.

"Nice to see you," I said.

"Congrats. You're number one on Gino's shit list."

"With or without a bullet?"

"That's up to you," Vinnie said. "Reason I'm here."

Vinnie was dressed, as was most often the case, like Ralph Lauren's oft-neglected Italian cousin. He wore a trim-fitting blue blazer over a crisp yellow dress shirt and pink tie, with lightweight charcoal pants and buffed wingtips. His hair had been recently barbered and swept back with a light sheen. His nails were manicured. The pink tie was knotted with a single Windsor at his throat.

"I'm sorry about Gino's nephew."

"We'll get to that in a second," Vinnie said. "How the fuck did you get involved in this casino crap?"

"Would you believe sheer luck?"

Vinnie rubbed an invisible dirt spot off his wingtips. Z and I both wore sweaty workout clothes. I hadn't been able to sleep, and I had run steps at Harvard Stadium while Z had walked the track. My thighs felt like Jell-O, but my breathing was calm. Relaxed. I folded my arms across my chest and leaned back in my chair. "Some sluggers were trying to push Henry Cimoli around."

"That didn't have shit to do with Gino."

"Says who?"

"Says me," Vinnie said.

I looked over Vinnie's shoulder. Z lay back relaxed on the couch. He took a sip of coffee, listening but silent. Sunlight slanted across my wooden floor and over half of Vinnie's face.

"Jimmy and Tommy were just trying to scare the broad," Vinnie said. "Not kill her."

"Attempted kidnapping."

Vinnie shrugged.

"Why?" I said.

Vinnie kind of laughed, mainly just blew

some air out of his nose. He sat erect in my client chair and leaned back to stare at the ceiling. I again glanced over at Z. Z patted Pearl's head with one hand; the other hand put down the coffee and disappeared at his side. Z did not know Vinnie Morris.

"Gino wanted me to tell you to back off," Vinnie said. "I told him that was a waste of breath. But he wanted to say it anyway. So there you go. I fucking said it."

"What's Gino say about Rick Weinberg being smoked?"

"The headless horseman?"

I nodded.

"Not our business," Vinnie said. "Gino said you'd ask. And I said I'd tell you we were not involved."

"You saying that or Gino?"

"Me."

Vinnie widened his eyes. He shuffled in my client chair. He scratched his cheek.

"I'm sort of working for Rick Weinberg's widow," I said.

"What the fuck does 'sort of' mean?"

"I was asked to help, but now she's being evasive."

"Lot of that going around," Vinnie said. "Big money makes people cautious."

"Where has Gino put his money?"

Vinnie shrugged and yanked his head

260

back. "That the big fucking Indian I keep hearing about?"

I nodded.

"A real-life fucking Indian," Vinnie said.

"Say hello, Z."

Z said: "How."

"Fucking funny," Vinnie said. "Is being a smartass part of the training?"

"Just a fortunate side effect," I said.

"Are we clear now?"

"What about Gino's nephew?" I said.

Vinnie stood and straightened the sleeves on his blazer. He found a bit of fuzz on his lapel and flicked it away with his finger. "He's not taking this thing personally," he said. "Between us, he never liked the numbnuts anyway. But on the business end, he says it was an unfortunate misunderstanding."

"Why did Gino want Jemma Fraser?"

Vinnie shrugged. "Who shot first?" he said. "Just curious."

"Not my gun," I said.

Vinnie nodded.

"You know I won't back off."

"No fucking kidding," Vinnie said.

"I need to see Gino."

"Like I said, he doesn't blame you for what happened, but he doesn't want to talk

261

to you, either. How the fuck would that look?"

"I am interested in why someone wanted to clip me."

"He didn't know you were involved."

"Now he does," I said. "Police think he may have aced Weinberg as a message."

"You really think that's his style?"

"To be honest, I've never really thought Gino had much of a style."

Vinnie walked to the door and set his hand on the knob. "I told Gino if something goes down between you and him, it's between you and him. I'm on the fucking sidelines."

"I appreciate that, Vinnie."

"But I'd consider it a personal favor not to put me in a bind and to back the fuck off," Vinnie said. "You got to realize this is about shit tons of money. Lots of big-time players want a piece."

"You ever meet Rick Weinberg?" I said.

"See you around, Spenser."

"Or Harvey Rose?"

"Nice name."

He opened the door halfway. He looked down at the place where the sunlight spilled across the office floor. "No matter what you do, things will shake out the same," Vinnie said. "That's what I came here to tell you."

"And that if I stop poking around, Gino won't turn me into a hunk of Swiss cheese for shooting his beloved nephew."

Vinnie looked over to Z and grinned. "Stick close to this one. He's quick."

He closed the door with a light click. I propped my running shoes on the edge of the desk and leaned back in thought. Z's hand came back out from under a pillow. He set a .44 by his leg and nodded. "You better watch your back with that guy."

"Wait till you meet my enemies."

44

Jemma had triple-locked the door and it took a moment of assurance before she let me into my apartment. Pearl trotted in first. I followed triumphantly with breakfast. I had stopped off at the Flour on Washington and bought some cinnamon-cream brioche and lemon-ginger scones. I filled a bowl of water for Pearl and set about making coffee.

"Do you feel better?" she said.

"Nothing like running steps to sweat off guilt."

"He pulled the gun on us."

I nodded.

"I borrowed one of your T-shirts," she said. "I hope that's okay."

"Just don't take the one from Karl's Sausage Kitchen."

Pearl lapped up all of her water. I again refilled the bowl. I waited for the water to boil and measured out eight heaping spoonfuls of coffee into the press. When the water started to bubble, I poured it over the grounds. While it steeped, I squeezed some oranges and set the juice on the kitchen counter.

"First-rate," she said.

"How's your head?"

"Horrific."

I went to the bathroom and returned with two aspirin. I mashed the plunger on the press and poured us both some coffee. Brioche and scones were set in the toaster oven on low while I stirred just a little cream and sugar into my mug.

"I apologize for last night," she said. "Quite embarrassing."

"Don't apologize," I said. "Blame Kentucky's finest."

"I'm sure you saw more than you were bargaining for."

"I averted my eyes."

Jemma smiled and took a sip of her coffee. "Quite embarrassing."

"You had a lot to drink," I said. "Attempted kidnapping often leads to anxiety."

She smiled. I drank some orange juice and took the scones and brioche from the toaster. I set them into a gingham cloth napkin and then into a basket.

"Truly first-rate," she said.

"But there is a price to be paid," I said.

She put down her coffee and set her elbow on the edge of my kitchen counter. Pearl sat at my feet and stared up at me, waiting for a sampling of goodies from Flour.

"I need you to explain in as much detail as possible exactly what the hell is going on," I said. "I feel as if I'm in a maze."

She nodded. She let out a long breath, looking as elegant as possible in a BU T-shirt and cut-off sweatpants. "You more than deserve it," she said. Her face flushed. "More now, knowing that you weren't willing to take any of the other spoils."

"I barely remember," I said.

"Liar."

"I may recall a birthmark in the shape of Winston Churchill."

"Most men would have made the most of the situation."

"Most men don't have what I have."

"The woman in all of your pictures?"

"Yep."

"She is quite beautiful," she said.

I nodded.

Jemma smiled slightly as she shook her head and reached for a brioche. She took a healthy bite and washed it down with some coffee. I ate a scone and drank some coffee while standing at the counter.

"What do you think is happening?" she said.

"I think a lot of very powerful people are battling it out for a license to print money."

"That's most of it."

"What I don't understand is why they would come for you," I said. "You don't work for Rick Weinberg anymore."

She nodded. "That's partially true."

"And the other part?"

Her eyes roamed over my face. A light breeze washed in from the window over my sink. I waited. "I did not tell you the other reason Rick came to see me," she said.

"Okay."

"He wanted to figure out the company's next move," she said. "I had not been fired. We only said that so the people in Revere would sign the agreement."

"Makes sense."

"You don't believe me."

"No," I said. "I believe you very much."

"Rick was in a very good mood. He knew we had made the deal and that Wonderland would be a reality."

"So you are now in charge of the project in Revere?" I said.

"And Las Vegas, and Biloxi, and now Macao," she said. "I now run the whole company."

"Envolve?"

"Weinberg Entertainment," she said. "In the event of Rick's death, I take over as CEO. The board insisted on a clear line of succession."

"What will Rachel Weinberg say?"

"Nothing." She squinted her eyes in surprise. "She voted on the promotion like everyone else on the board."

"I guess she forgot to tell me you were taking over."

"I imagine she had other things to worry about."

"She was more concerned about you and Rick having an affair."

"She knew I was shagging her husband."

"Yikes."

"Well," Jemma said. "We're both adults."

"Somewhat."

"Well, that's what adults do."

"Shag each other?"

"Understand the difference between love and sex," she said. "Rick and I had been intimate for some time. I'm surprised she didn't tell you. She was completely complicit with the arrangement."

"She did," I said. "So now what's Rachel's role with the company?"

"She remains on the board," she said. "But I am the CEO."

"And the list grows." I nodded and took a breath.

"What list?"

"People who would want you dead."

"Aren't you skipping the most obvious?" she said. Her legs looked tan and muscular in my cut-off sweatpants. Certain details were crucial to my profession.

"Let me go back to my notes," I said. "I'm starting a flow chart."

"Harvey Rose is one of the most ruthless, calculating bastards I have ever known," she said. "With Rick dead, I am the only one left between him and getting the license for East Boston."

I nodded.

"Have you checked in with your friend at the condos lately? I would expect an offer, if only to block the sale."

"Do you think Harvey had Rick killed?"

"Perhaps," she said.

"And tried to have you killed?"

"Perhaps," she said. "I can make arrangements for my own protection. I can't impose on you further."

"I've spoken to my associate," I said. "He can guard while I make inquiries."

"Is he as good as you?" she said.

"I think one day he'll be even better," I said.

"With less ideals."

"We share the same ideals," I said. "Z just hasn't found the right woman yet."

"A stalwart lover," she said. "I hope your girlfriend knows this."

"I think she suspects it."

45

"You would like the food down here," Susan said. "They serve a lot of cornbread and have swell biscuits."

I could hear restaurant sounds around her. She had stepped away from a table and the sounds became more slight.

"I took a drunk woman home last night," I said. I leaned back in my office chair and crossed one jogging shoe over the other. "She got naked as a jaybird."

"Good for you," Susan said.

"And this morning, I brought her breakfast."

"Even better," she said. "If you had made her breakfast, I might become resentful."

"She had great legs. Very tan and muscular."

"Why else would you take her home?" Susan said.

"That and two men tried to kidnap her at gunpoint," I said. "I had to intervene."

"Are they dead?"

"One."

"She must have been frightened to death. Or is she used to this kind of life?"

"Can't say," I said. "She's from Vegas."

"Ah," Susan said. "The Brit who used to work for Rick Weinberg."

"She says she's now the CEO of his company."

"And what does Rachel Weinberg say about that?"

"I don't think she knows," I said. "I've tried to reach her, without success."

"Does your Brit admit to the affair?"

"She said Rachel and Rick had an open marriage."

"Professionally, I do not condone or refute an open marriage," she said. "I have patients who find it not only freeing but sexually stimulating."

"Ick."

"You would not find it sexually stimulating to think of me with another man."

"Did you miss the part where I just killed someone?"

There was a long pause on the other end of the phone. My chest swelled with the sound of her breathing. "Have you spoken to Hawk?"

"I'm starting to develop a complex," I

said. "Every time something dangerous happens, you want me to call Hawk."

"Just looking out for you."

"I call Hawk only in case of emergency," I said. "I break that glass sparingly."

"Where is Z?"

"Close."

"He is not Hawk," she said.

"Hawk would argue that nobody is."

"He may be right."

"Z stumbled a bit after the beating," I said. "Physically and mentally, but he's making a comeback."

"Is he drinking?"

"Not to excess."

"As much as he tries to emulate you, you can't change ingrained behavior overnight. It takes time. And often, therapy."

"He works hard on his own," I said. "I hope he'll come back even better."

"Has he wavered on wanting to be like you and Hawk?"

"Nope."

"Could I interest him in a solid career as a social worker or a stable office job?"

"I don't believe so."

"And if he's going to do this, we both have to watch him stumble and fail."

"It's never pretty," I said.

"Before I met you, did you often fail?"

"Meaning did I often have the crap kicked out of me?"

"Yes."

"But I never liked it much."

"Perhaps until Z is one hundred percent, you find better help."

"Few options," I said.

"Vinnie?"

"I will explain later."

"And dare I ask about the naked woman?"

"I plan to drop her at the Boston Harbor Hotel," I said. "Z will watch her. But first I'll make sure she puts on some clothes."

"Did she really look that good naked?"

"I'm not sure," I said. "I had my hands over my eyes."

"Hmm."

"But she is no lithe, flexible Jewess."

"No shit," Susan said.

"Z seems very excited about his new gig," I said. "I think he put on some cologne."

"Be careful," she said. "After what he's been through, he may be very susceptible to her advances."

"And that would be bad?"

"You yourself seem not to trust the woman."

"I don't one bit."

"And may I remind you, Z can be quite impressionable."

"True."

There was another long pause. Susan sounded lovely breathing way down south. "Not long," she said.

"Every minute," I said.

"Safe," she said. "Please be safe."

46

Many boats filled the Boston Harbor that afternoon. Sailboats, speedboats, and water shuttles cut across the choppy, dark water. The day was bright, beautiful, and cloudless. There was a heavy wind as Henry and I stood outside the health club for a chat. The wind ruffled his white hair as he stood rock-solid in satin running pants and a tight-fitting white T-shirt. The shirt had the logo for Harbor Health Club on the pocket.

"Put me on the shirts," I said, "and you'd sell more memberships."

"You need to work your legs more," Henry said. "Do more squats."

"I had a tip that there may have been another offer on the Ocean View."

Henry leaned against a piling. The air smelled heavily of salt and dead fish. No amount of posh condos and restaurants could eradicate the smell. But the wind was strong and cool, and felt good against my face.

"Yep," he said. "Just heard myself. Five hundred grand more than the original."

"They had a deal."

"Tell that to Lou Coffone," Henry said. "He'd screw a dog for a nickel."

"Hard times."

"They want to hire another lawyer to deep-six what we signed."

"Will they?" I said.

"What do you think?"

I leaned against a separate piling, my back to the harbor and the wind. The day was warm enough to leave my jacket in the car. I wore a navy T-shirt with Levi's and my dress running shoes. I held the edge of my T-shirt down with my right hand so as not to let the wind expose my .38.

"I need to tell Rachel Weinberg what's going on."

"I think her husband was stand-up," Henry said. He chewed on his cheek and nodded. "Do it."

I nodded.

"Z told me about what happened," he said. "Fucking Gino Fish's nephew?"

"I have it on good authority Gino wasn't overly fond of him."

"Does that matter?" Henry said. "Jesus,

277

I'm sorry I pulled you into this crazy fuck-ing mess. I just wanted to keep my place. I like it out in Revere."

"Z seems to like it here."

"And I want the kid to stay," Henry said. "Part of his training is being able to live where he works out. We still got some work to do."

I nodded. A bright, warm wind kicked off the harbor. We watched the Logan shuttle dock at the wharf and the bright-eyed tour-ists setting foot on land. A man dressed as Ben Franklin met them, ringing a handbell. Henry pushed off the piling as if doing a one-handed push-up.

Ben Franklin kept ringing the bell. "Didn't you used to go to school with him?" I said.

"He was in the grade up," Henry said. "We thought he was a pussy 'cause he wore them socks."

"I'll explain to Rachel what's going on," I said. "Try and set something up with the board."

"Tell her something for me," Henry said. "Okay? Tell her that I ain't a part of this. I shook hands with her husband. It was a done deal. I don't even know who the hell these people are who want to buy it now."

"Guy named Harvey Rose."

"Harvey who?"

"Rose."

"How did you find that out?"

"Sometimes a raven is just like a writing desk."

"You need to get some fucking sleep, Spenser," Henry said. "Before you go nuts."

"Too late," I said.

47

In the spirit of true cooperation, I called Wayne Cosgrove as I drove back to my office. "How can we connect Rick Weinberg with any officials of our great Commonwealth?" I said.

"Now we're a 'we'?"

"Did I not share whiskey with you?"

"I had to stake out your place."

"Can I help if I'm popular?"

Trees had started to leaf in the Common; red and yellow tulips waved in the light spring wind. My windows were down. I played some Gerry Mulligan. If there hadn't been so much ugliness and Susan Silverman had been by my side, all would be right with the world.

"I read the report on the shooting," Wayne said. "Jemma Fraser, formerly one of Weinberg's inner circle, was with you."

"Maybe not former."

"What do you know?"

"Can you try and track down something on Weinberg and his philanthropic touch with local politicians?"

"I live to serve."

"Ms. Fraser is now CEO of Weinberg's company," I said.

"How do you know?"

"Advanced investigation techniques," I said.

"She told you."

"Yep."

"And Mrs. Weinberg?"

"She may not like it," I said. "But she voted on it. She's stuck with Jemma."

I passed the Angel of the Waters statue at the edge of the Public Garden. Traffic slowed at the light and I continued on west toward Clarendon. "You could search out some of Bill Brett's party photos?" I said.

"Or I could look through donation records of some politicians I might suspect of shady dealings."

"The reason I love you, Wayne."

"How about a quote on the shooting last night?"

"Pow," I said. And I hung up.

I parked in front of a Marshalls discount store and walked the rest of the way down Boylston. I was halfway down my hall when I spotted something not quite right. My

281

door was wide open. Perhaps it was Z. Perhaps Hawk had come back early. Maybe it was Angelina Jolie, waiting to give me an early birthday surprise. Always the cynic, I pulled the .38 from my hip and kept it down by my right thigh.

I crept close to the door. I waited. I listened for the sound of paneled floors creaking, or the smell of smoke. After a couple minutes of feeling silly, I gave up and walked inside.

It was empty. But not as I'd left it.

My file cabinets hung wide open. Desk drawers had been removed, shaken of their contents, and dumped on the floor. Sofa cushions had been ripped open and thrown on the floor. Even my Vermeer prints had been pulled from their frames and carelessly flung about. At least I knew we were not dealing with a lover of the Low Country masters.

I checked my overturned right-hand drawer. I found my .357. I checked my top filing cabinet. I found my Bushmills. I sighed with relief.

I could call Frank Belson or Healy. They would both tell me to go cry in my soup. If someone was ratting around my office, they would have worn gloves. I knocked on the door to the design showroom across the hall. I asked two very tall, very attractive women if they had seen anything unusual.

They said no.

I asked if they knew what evil lurks in the hearts of men.

They stared blankly at each other.

I knocked on the door to a commercial real-estate firm and on the door of a two-person marketing team. Same answer without the second question.

I went back to my disheveled office. I picked up my Vermeer prints, set them back inside the frames, and hung them on the proper nails. I stood back in a pile of loose letters and files and noted the print on the left was crooked.

I closed the door behind me, opened a window, and poured some Black Bush into a coffee mug. The wind off Berkeley kicked up and stirred some papers and files. I set the phone back on the cradle. Stuffing exploded from the rips in the sofa. My printer lay cracked and useless in the corner. I lowered the blinds. I drank some more Bushmills while I studied Vermeer. A young woman caught while taking a music lesson. Holding sheet music, she seemed shocked by the interruption of the artist. Her tutor unaware.

I threw back the whiskey, left the papers

where they lay, and locked the door behind
me.

48

Henry and I met Rachel Weinberg and Blanchard the next day in Revere. Lou Coffone and his geriatric crew had chosen a one-story cracker box off 1A called the 3 Yolks. A place that proudly advertised eggs at both breakfast and lunch. Rachel was dressed in an ornate white blouse with lapels that spilled over a black jacket. Her pearl earrings must've choked the oyster. While we waited, she dabbed at the partially wet table with a folded napkin. The table was well-worn Formica and the booth padded in orange vinyl.

"Who needs the Four Seasons?" I said.

"Me," she said.

Outside a row of plate-glass windows, I spotted Z standing next to my Explorer. He said he would rather keep watch while we talked. Keeping watch meant he did not have to listen to another speech by Coffone and Buddy.

"Why here?" Rachel said. "We could have met in town." She crumpled up the wet napkin and left it for the waitress.

"Old and set in their ways," Henry said. "They're scared shitless because of what happened. This place is familiar and safe."

Rachel raised her eyebrows. "Unless you're worried about salmonella."

"The whole thing did start a little dicey," I said. Henry nodded.

"That was unfortunate," Rachel said.

"Perhaps we should call Jemma Fraser?" I said.

Rachel's face colored. "Why?"

"Since she's now running Rick's company."

Rachel looked me over and then nodded. "Unfortunately," she said.

"Would have been nice to know," I said. "Given the circumstances."

"Her current position is tenuous," she said. "These people trusted Rick, and they will trust me."

"It would have been nice to know," I said.

"Her position will be short-lived."

I nodded and decided on two eggs with rye toast. Henry eyed me as I ordered. He smiled at my selection. Rachel and Blanchard ordered only coffee.

Coffone and Buddy walked in a few minutes later. Coffone wore a yellow polo shirt again embroidered with the Ocean View logo and the word *President*. His white hair had been swept back boldly, face pink with a fresh shave. Buddy was hunch-shouldered and unsmiling in a gray tracksuit and thick white tennis shoes. Schlubby and potbellied, in shoes fastened with Velcro.

"Mrs. Weinberg wanted to hear the board's concerns," Henry said. "I thought it best to do it in person."

Coffone nodded gravely. Buddy studied the menu and fingered at a tooth.

"It's kind of gotten complicated," Coffone said. "We don't want to make any major changes until we find out what's going on."

"What's going on is that someone killed my husband for trying to do business in Boston."

"I'm sorry about Mr. Weinberg," Coffone said. "But that contract can be contested. We liked your husband a lot. And we liked his plans for the Ocean View. But now, I mean, hell. It's all very different. He's no longer a part of this. A person doesn't know what to think."

Rachel Weinberg leaned her head back. She took in a deep breath. "Bullshit," she said. "You want to sit around with your dicks in your hands until you see who's going to take charge for the widow. Or are you fishing for more money?"

I enjoyed the company of Rachel Weinberg.

"This has been a bad shock to all of us," Coffone said.

"I'm sorry my husband's brutal murder has been so hard on you," Rachel said.

Buddy looked up from his menu. He signaled the waitress and asked for a western omelet with french fries. He continued to work at whatever was in his tooth with his little finger.

"If the picture cleared up," I said, "would that make a difference?"

"Like if whoever did this was locked up?" Buddy said.

"Exactly, Buddy," Henry said.

Coffone shrugged. Buddy followed.

Blanchard drank coffee. He turned his head very slightly, studying Z, who was outside, leaning against my SUV. Z had his arms across his chest, watching traffic zip by on 1A. No judge had ever been as sober.

"I can legally hold you to the agreement," Rachel Weinberg said.

"Lot has happened." Coffone gave a smile befitting a condo board president. "People have been killed. Ma'am, I'm sorry, but we have consulted with a new attorney."

Henry looked at me. He had not been notified.

"Has anyone at the Ocean View been approached in the last few days?" I said.

"Since Big Chief got his ass handed to him?" Buddy said.

I just stared at Buddy. I waited. Buddy craned his head to the kitchen, looking for his western omelet. There was great clamoring in the kitchen. The cook rang a bell.

"Nobody," Coffone said. "But we're all scared to death. Nobody even wants to go to the store or get their dry cleaning. We just kind of want to be left alone now."

"Holdouts," Rachel said under her breath.

Coffone nodded. "What would you do? This is the only thing we got left. What we get from this deal is how our children and grandchildren remember us."

Rachel Weinberg rolled her eyes. She grabbed her purse and stood. Blanchard pushed his chair back and waited. "This is the last goddamn thing Rick wanted to see through," she said. "Think about that legacy."

Coffone opened his mouth.

Rachel Weinberg held up a finger to silence him.

"Excuse me, but I'll be gone for two days," she said. "Now that my husband has been reassembled, I have a funeral to plan and attend. I hope your nerves settle by the time I get back."

Rachel Weinberg walked out. Blanchard widened his eyes and followed.

Henry and I sat there with Coffone and Buddy. Everyone stayed quiet while we ate.

"Should have ordered the hash," I said.

49

"Are you Busy?" Wayne Cosgrove said.

"Extremely," I said, phone cradled against my ear.

I had spent the afternoon cleaning my office, refiling files, and looking in catalogs for a new sofa for Pearl. The Vermeer prints now hung razor straight.

"So I guess you don't have time to find out what I found out about Weinberg's political donations?"

I put down the dustpan, and sat at my chair with the phone. Z looked up at me from the cushionless sofa, reading a copy of *The Ring*. The blues and purples on his face had faded to a yellowish hue.

"On the official contribution list, I found pretty much the expected," Wayne said. "He greased the palms of everyone he should. Right and left. He gave a few thousand here and there. Senators, congressmen. Council folks in Revere. Usual suspects."

"Okay."

"But being the true muckraker I am, I also looked into contributions given to super-PACs in the Commonwealth," he said.

"Which I understand is legal."

"A candidate can take as much money as he or she wants from a super-PAC, but the Supreme Court says all donors must be made public. And late last year, through his front Envolve Development, it looks like Weinberg gave nearly a half mil to a super-PAC run by the brother of Joseph G. Perotti."

"Great Caesar's ghost."

"And you might ask what Perotti has to do with casino licenses?"

"Mr. Cosgrove, just what does Joseph Perotti have to do with casino licenses?"

"As speaker of the house?"

"Yep."

"Everything."

"Aha."

"Damn right."

"What's your bar tab running now?"

"You've gone from a bottle of Blanton's up to a bottle of Pappy Van Winkle."

"The seventeen or the twenty-three?"

"I like my bourbon ancient."

"Done."

"Just wait," Wayne said. "I followed up.

Dug deeper. Quarterly reports were just filed for Perotti's super-PAC. I did not see Weinberg's name or anyone related to Envolve."

I waited. Z had set aside his boxing magazine and listened.

"But I did see a more-than-generous contribution from someone else," Wayne said.

"Harvey Rose?" I said.

"Which means our illustrious speaker has jumped ship."

"Did the donation confirm that?"

"What do you think?" Wayne said.

I thanked Wayne and hung up. I looked to Z. He sat up straight and set his cowboy boots on the floor. Pearl looked from me to him, waiting for a word. I wondered if Pearl knew much about super-PACs.

"Seems like we now know the missing link."

Z nodded. "Who?"

"A politician," I said. "Shocked?"

"Cree takes everyone on faith. Especially white politicians. Why would they lie?"

"This one sold out Rick Weinberg before he got killed," I said. "Be good to know why."

Z stood up. "Why don't we go ask?"

I smiled. "Let's."

50

Z and I spent the afternoon on Beacon Hill.
I showed him the Hall of Flags, Doric Hall, and the murals opposite the main staircase. The State House was indeed grand in marble, mahogany, and brass. I took interest in murals of the Civil War and our war with Spain. Z studied the rotunda mural of John Eliot preaching to the Indians and the giant stained window of an Indian in a grass skirt. It read "Come and Help Us." Z was not impressed.

At about four o'clock, the House broke for the day and I found a spot to rest my elbows on a filigreed iron banister.

Forty minutes later, Joseph G. Perotti, house speaker, emerged from his office. He made his way down the marble hallway with official clicking of his official shoes. He was discussing a matter of great importance to a flustered young woman in a navy pantsuit. She held many files in both arms. Perotti was empty-handed.

"Speaker," I said.

He smiled. He offered his hand. Politicians often do goofy things like that to strangers.

"I am one of your proud constituents," I said. "Duke Snider."

"Glad to meet you, Duke," he said. He shook my hand with both of his. Z continued to watch with detached interest down from the third-floor railing. An imposing statue of Roger Wolcott had his back.

"May I have a moment of your time?"

"I'm already late," he said. "My secretary sets my appointments."

"Is that how you met both Mr. Rose and Mr. Weinberg?"

Perotti stopped his happy skip down the marble steps. He turned to me. Perotti was a rotund little man with thinning gray hair and a brushy gray mustache. He wore rimless glasses in gold frames. I waited and he told his aide to meet him at the bottom of the steps. Perotti leaned in. "You fucking people from the *Globe*," he said. "I just got through answering questions for that son of a bitch Wayne Cosgrove, and now you brace me on my way out."

"Bracing?" I said. "Nope. Only asking. I'm not with the *Globe*, but I'm sure Mr. Cosgrove will appreciate your comments."

"Who are you, then?"

"Just a constituent interested in the fate of some land in Revere."

"What do you want?"

"When did you tell Rick Weinberg you switched teams?"

Perotti shook his head. His face grew red as he peered down the marble staircase to his young aide. He nodded very quickly. She trotted off. Time was short. Perotti began to move again, holding on to the rail, trying his best to escape me.

Z watched from above.

"Were you brokering a deal with Gino Fish," I said, "or on your own?"

"I don't know any such person."

"Everybody with an office in the building is aware of Mr. Fish."

"Not me."

"But you were to broker a deal," I said. "Pave some roads."

"Bullshit," he said. "Bullshit."

Perotti rested for a moment at a landing near the bottom of the stairs. He wiped his brow with the flat of his hand. He was potbellied and winded. The aide had returned with a couple of house security guards. They began to approach. I looked up; Z had disappeared.

"All I want to know is why Rick Weinberg was killed. I leave you out of it."

"I never met the man," he said. He grasped the railing again and continued his descent.

I followed.

"What else did Harvey Rose offer?"

"You are insane," he said, just as we hit the last step. Each security guard grabbed one of my arms. They asked what I had done. I looked to Perotti, and he blanched. I ripped free of one of the guards and raised my fist high in the air. "Free the Sacred Cod."

"Sir," a guard said.

"Insane," Perotti repeated.

He and his aide clacked off. The guards escorted me out of the building. Z was waiting for me on the steps where Beacon meets Park. He had found a comfortable spot on a bench. "Why'd they let you go?"

"Perotti told them I was just an ordinary nut."

"Which means he has something to hide."

"Yep."

"And he will jostle the source."

"One can hope."

Z pushed himself off the iron bench. I could tell he was still in some considerable pain. He walked down Beacon and back toward my office. The day had warmed, and we removed our leather jackets as we strolled. It was hard to be dignified when you had just proclaimed to worship a fish.

51

I met Lewis Blanchard that night at the
Bristol Lounge. Happy hour was over and
the bar had thinned of patrons. We found a
small table only a few steps from the taps
and drank cold Sierra Nevadas as we discussed details of Rick Weinberg's funeral.

"She wanted me to stay here," he said. He
toasted me with his second beer.

"Punishment?"

"Didn't say that," Blanchard said. "She
said she trusted me to continue working in
her absence. I should have been there. I
should have gone."

I nodded. "A lot riding on Wonderland."

"And now with the white-hairs spooked,
holy crap," he said. "You think they're holding out?"

I shrugged. "I think they may be genuinely
scared shitless. And a bit greedy."

"Gaming commission will want detailed
plans in a few months," he said. "In a couple

weeks we got to pony up a half mil for the registration fee."

"Nonrefundable," I said.

"If we can't get this parcel, how are we supposed to get all of Revere behind us?" Blanchard said. "I want this for Mr. Weinberg. I really do. I mean, Christ, he used to come here as a kid. His dream was to bring back Wonderland. So much work to go to waste. Who wants that putz Rose to get the license?"

I nodded. I drank some more beer. I got to it. "Lewis, do you know who Joe Perotti is?"

"Holy Christ."

"Nope," I said. "He's the house speaker of this great commonwealth."

"How'd you find out?"

"Mr. Weinberg left a trail of very large bread crumbs."

"Rachel is going to be pissed."

"You don't owe him," I said.

Lewis leaned back in his chair and rubbed his hand over his jaw, nodding. "We need him," he said. "Who else knows?"

"He'd promised to push Wonderland through."

"Yes," Blanchard said. "The reason why Rachel didn't want him involved in your investigation. Holy crap."

"Did you know he accepted twice the amount of Rick's donation from Harvey Rose?"

Blanchard's mouth opened and hung there for a few seconds.

"You really didn't know."

"Perotti had been elusive lately," Blanchard said. "He was the main reason Mr. Weinberg was in Boston. He was trying to nail down Perotti on terms."

"Percentages?"

"I don't know the details," Blanchard said. "Like we said, Mr. Weinberg preferred those terms to be worked out direct."

"Did Rick ever say where this money would be funneled?"

"Nope."

"Mention the name Gino Fish?"

"I know who he is," Blanchard said. "I know he was the one person who had to get behind all this if it were to happen."

"Did he?"

Blanchard shrugged. "Was yet to be determined."

I leaned back. I drank some more beer. A man in a tuxedo and a woman in a sparkly dress sidled up to the bar. The woman was giggling. The man had a smug look as he patted her backside. If I patted Susan's backside in public, I'd meet her left hook.

"What can you tell me about Jemma Fraser?"

Blanchard grinned. He leaned forward. He had recently cut his receding silver hair. The cuffs of his blue oxford had been rolled back to the elbows, showing off thick forearms. He looked like he'd broken his knuckles plenty of times. "What do you want to know?"

"Is she to be trusted?"

Blanchard grinned some more. "Hell, no."

"You find her recent replacement as CEO a bit shady."

"You don't?"

"I find some of the family dynamics tricky."

"You mean that Mr. Weinberg was shagging her while he got the board to approve the contingency clause."

"That's the one."

Blanchard tilted his head. He crossed his legs. Two men having a nice business drink after a day making sales. The waitress returned and asked if we'd like another round. We did.

"Let me say I don't think Jemma had Rick killed," Blanchard said. "I think she had more to gain with Mr. Weinberg doing what he was doing."

"What was that?"

"Taking care of Jemma."

"And what if Harvey Rose is now taking care of Speaker Perotti?" I said.

"We're fucked."

"Officially speaking."

"Yep," Blanchard said. "He is the key to whoever gets the license."

"You mind if I ask you something?"

"Shoot," Blanchard said.

"Was it Jemma's idea to send the leg-breakers to the condo?"

"Absolutely."

"And Rick did not know."

"He fired her, didn't he?"

"Actually," I said. "No, he didn't."

"Whatta you mean?"

"Jemma said they lied about the firing to keep the Ocean View board thinking in the right direction."

"Shit, sounds like something she'd do," Blanchard said. "She can't stand not winning. Not at anything she does. Hell, she learned everything she knows from fucking Harvey Rose."

"I know she used to work for him."

"Not just work for him," he said. "He was her mentor at Harvard. He fucking made her."

"Holy smokes," I said.

"Goes back a long time," he said. "A really

303

deep, twisted relationship. Mr. Weinberg said he hired Jemma because she thought just like Harvey Rose. But was a hell of a lot better-looking. He used to say things like that."

52

When I arrived at the Harbor Health Club the next morning, Jemma Fraser was working out with Z. He had brought her into the boxing room to show her the fundamentals of the jab. Dressed in a white tank top and black satin shorts without shoes, she smiled attentively at her trainer. She looked to be very fit.

"The toughest and loneliest sport in the world," I said.

"Breathe," Z said to Jemma. "Don't hold your breath."

Jemma took a deep breath and did not turn. She kept on attacking the bag with sloppy yet significant punches. Z smiled and walked toward me. His hands were expertly wrapped in red tape.

"I tried to call," I said.

"She wanted to leave the hotel," Z said. "And she wanted to learn some self-defense stuff."

I was still dressed in street clothes with my Everlast workout bag over my shoulder. Today was a day for weights, not boxing. I needed to put some thought on the recent developments.

"Henry wants to see you," Z said. He canted his head toward the office and turned back to Jemma. She had yet to acknowledge my presence as she worked out a simple left jab over and over. Her brown hair was tied up in a high ponytail. Z had forced her into a steady, even sweat. She had her breath working and her concentration was all on the bag.

I strolled into Henry's office, dropped my bag at my feet, and said, "What's the haps?"

Henry was paying bills, half-glasses down on the end of his nose. There was a stack of envelopes on his desk and an old-fashioned ledger bearing Henry's distinctive scrawl.

"You see Z is working with Mata Hari?" Henry said.

"He says she needed to learn some self-defense."

"Z's the one who needs to watch out."

"He's a smart kid," I said. "He'll keep it professional."

"At that age, I couldn't even spell 'professional.' "

I sat down. I had once counted nearly

sixty framed photos of boxers, wrestlers, and weight lifters on the wall of Henry Cimoli's office. Many of them were long gone, and the pictures were bent and faded. Henry took off his glasses and tossed them on the table. He rubbed his eyes. "Got to say, Z looks better."

I nodded.

"He's lost the limp," he said. "Got real zing and pop in the punches."

"Maybe he's showing off."

"Nah," Henry said. "He's back on center."

"Just what did you say to him after the beating?"

"I told him when a fight is over, it's over."

"He carried that rage with him."

"He doesn't think what happened to him is finished," Henry said. "I told him to put it on the shelf for a bit. Use it when you need it. Being mad all the time screws up your head and tires you out."

Henry walked to a shelf by his lone window and rattled some vitamins into his hand. "You know, I boxed for twenty-nine years and never hated nobody."

"Never?"

"Nope."

"Different on the street."

"It is, but it isn't," Henry said. "Throw out the rules. But a fight is a fight. Bein' mad clouds your brain."

I changed into my workout clothes and launched into a circuit on the machines. I started off with my upper body, shoulders, chest, triceps, and then onto back and biceps. I jumped from one exercise to the next, giving myself no rest or downtime. I finished off working my legs and lower back. I counted off two minutes on the clock and repeated the circuit two more times. I used heavy weights, taking it up to twelve to fourteen reps on most exercises. On the last cycle, I felt fatigued but strong. I was past the point of showing off in the gym or maxing out with weight. I was interested in endurance and strength. Someone may be stronger or faster, but they couldn't outlast me. Nobody could outlast me. Except maybe Hawk. Hawk could outlast Atlas.

As I headed to the shower, I glanced into the boxing room. Z was still there with Jemma. He was teaching her to throw a hook, hands on her hips, showing how they should flow loose and easy. He rotated her hips again and again. She smiled and giggled.

I dressed in my street clothes and left without a word. I was driving back to my office when Healy called.

"I got something I want to show you."

"I have been warned about conversations that start that way."

"We got two shitbirds we're pulling out of a Dodge Charger parked in Chelsea," Healy said. "Both shot in the head. Whoever it was got close enough to whisper in their ear with a .22 pistol."

"Anyone we know?"

"Seems these guys are from out of town," Healy said. "Tourists in from Las Vegas. Both of them with records as long as your arm."

"Lovely," I said.

53

I sat with Healy in the passenger seat of his unmarked unit. We had a pretty good vantage point to watch the detectives and crime scene techs work. I was never really sure what the techs did these days, but Rita Fiore assured me they focused mainly on confusing juries. The coroner had already removed the bodies by the time I arrived. Now there were several yellow cones placed in spots where evidence had been found.

"No shells, of course," he said. "But we should find a nice .22 short bouncing around in their skulls."

"Who are they?"

"James Congiusti and Anton Nelson," Healy said. "AKA Jimmy Aspirins and the Angel of Mercy."

"Inspired."

"Jimmy Aspirins because he takes care of the Mob's headaches —"

"Naturally."

"And Angel of Mercy because who the fuck knows. Nelson is a demolitions guy. Federal agent I called in Vegas says Nelson once blew up a dentist's office because he pulled the wrong tooth."

"What was Jimmy's specialty?" I said.

"Crazy son of a bitch used a cordless drill into people's heads."

"And what were their ties with our beloved Commonwealth?"

"Zip," Healy said. "This looks like an encroachment."

"Of which someone was extremely resentful."

Healy nodded. We had the windows down in the sedan. Parked along Shawmut Street, we had a lovely view of an endless row of sagging and paint-deficient triple-deckers. Empty trash cans, busted and turned upside down, lay along the curbs. Chain-link fences guarded front yards as big as area rugs. Another gorgeous day in Chelsea.

"What are you hearing?"

I shrugged.

"May I remind you that I have saved your ass on many occasions?"

"My ass is eternally grateful."

"I'm getting a lot of pressure from the hill on this one," Healy said. "I can't turn something on Weinberg and I start hearing

311

whispers of my retirement."

"And then what do you do?"

"Watch soaps with the wife and drink light beer."

"Did I not put you in touch with Weinberg's second in command?"

"Belson put us in touch after the shooting."

"A mere technicality."

"Didn't get us anywhere."

"At least we know this thing is being stoked from Vegas," I said. "But I'm not sure who is allied with whom."

"Whom?"

I nodded. "Have you spoken to Harvey Rose?"

"This ain't my first day on the job, Spenser."

"What did you think?"

"I think he's a schlub," Healy said. "I think he resented Weinberg, but I don't think he's the kind of guy who knows people like Jimmy Aspirins exist."

"Maybe."

"What do you know?"

"I know the Sox are sucking this year," I said. "And that Charles Mingus is the finest double bass player that ever lived."

"I'll tell you what I think," Healy said. "I think there is a whole group of hoods in

312

Boston who don't want a casino to ever happen. They can't get it into their thick heads that it's happening whether they like it or not. But every day they continue to screw with the process is another day of big profits."

I shrugged again.

"Jesus. What?"

"Or maybe they want a piece of the action," I said. "And they are not evolved individuals when it comes to business negotiations."

"Three men dead," Healy said. "And we got zip."

"Be nice to know who is negotiating exactly what."

"You got something on that?"

"Gino Fish has removed his welcome mat."

"And your other hoodlum friends?"

"That's no way to describe some of the city's most valuable resources."

"Hoodlums."

"At least they come honest," I said. "It's the ones in disguise that concern me."

54

Dean Agarwal kept a neat and tidy office, as neat and tidy as one would expect of the head of Harvard Business School. A pal of mine named Bill Barke had made the introduction, Bill being a one-phone-call guy, and that afternoon I found myself drinking coffee with the dean in Morgan Hall. Agarwal was a professional academic, the framed paper hanging on his wall telling me he'd been educated in Bombay, London, and Cambridge. I noted from his bookshelf that he had authored several books with titles such as *Leadership in the 21st Century, Leadership Through Economic Crisis,* and *Leadership and Building Trust.*

Agarwal was a dark man, slight of frame, with a very shiny bald head and thin, trendy glasses. He was warm and polite, and spoke with a British accent overlaid with subtle tones of India. His hands were small, but he had a firm and assertive grip. He wore a light khaki suit and looked a bit like Vijay Amritraj, only with much less hair.

"Harvey Rose was one of our great stars," he said. We sat a short distance from a large desk in a cluster of chairs set about a table with good china and a coffeepot. "I taught organizational behavior to many glum students. Harvey would attract hordes to courses that were somewhat unorthodox at the time. He said the key to corporate success was simple if you understood how to accurately predict consumer behavior. Many of the faculty frowned upon his methods, feeling they bordered on emotional manipulation, but one could not deny his genius."

"Did he strike you as a future casino mogul?"

"Frankly, I never saw Harvey leaving the safe haven of academia," Agarwal said. "On paper, Harvey is spectacular."

"And in person?"

Agarwal reached over to the table behind us. With a small spoon, he extracted two cubes from the sugar bowl and plopped them into his coffee. He smiled and took a sip. "Less than," he said.

"I've had the pleasure."

"And now you are running a background check on him?"

"In a matter of speaking," I said. "I work

for the wife of the late Rick Weinberg."

"Surely she doesn't think —"

"No, she does not," I said. "But part of my job is to check into the backgrounds of those who did business with Mr. Weinberg. I hope to learn a little bit more about his world and perhaps find some clues."

"And even better with a competitor?"

"Some argue that Harvey Rose was running second."

Agarwal took another sip and placed the cup on the saucer. He leaned back into a lemon-yellow Queen Anne chair. "If Harvey had entered the competition, then he had found a formula to win."

"I believe his odds have improved recently."

Agarwal smiled. "And had Harvey not taken his current position and left the business school," he said, "this would be his office."

The dean had a nice view of Shad Hall and some tennis courts. I added two sugars and a little bit of cream to the coffee.

"Besides being a mathematical genius," I said, "why would a Las Vegas company hire a fairly bland figure like Harvey Rose?"

"The system."

I drank some coffee. I waited for more.

"Surely you have heard about the Rose

system," Agarwal said. "It was quite the buzz in all the journals."

"I only keep up my subscription to *Guns and Ammo.*"

"Harvey was the first to say the gaming industry was no different than any other form of retail," he said. "He applied the same approach to the consumer as he would if he was working for JCPenney. What I would call a very macro point of view. Star Gaming hired him as a consultant and were so impressed with the results, they offered him the CEO position. What he's done for them is really quite genius."

"And what is that?"

"He got his best consumers to tell him everything," Agarwal said. He smiled, pleased with the tidbit of information. "True genius. He gave everyone who came into his casino something called a Star Card. The more you played, the more points you would get. You could follow your card online and win dinners and trips. But you could also win a windbreaker or a Frisbee. He wanted everyone to add up their points."

"I once earned a beer stein from S&H Green Stamps."

"One and the same," he said. "The prizes at the base level were worthless. But the data he was able to collect was priceless. He could track an individual every time he or she set foot in a Star Casino. He used a massive data bank to build computational models that predict the behavior of every consumer. Especially their ideal."

"The Star Card."

"Precisely," Agarwal said. "Profits soared. Casinos raked in billions. He has doubled the number of Star Casinos to thirty or more."

"Because of a formula?"

"Harvey can stand back and take an unemotional appraisal of a business situation. His moves and reactions are purely mathematical."

"And this is revelatory?"

"Very."

"Do you recall a student who was here when Harvey Rose taught?" I said. "A woman named Jemma Fraser. She was or is a British citizen. I don't have the dates."

"We do have certain privacy standards."

"Of course," I said. "But just to verify she was a student."

"That should be easy enough to find out."

He opened the door to an anteroom and requested the information from his secretary. He promptly closed the door and returned to our grouping.

"The name seems familiar, but I can't

place it."

"She was one of Mr. Rose's protégés."

Agarwal shook his head and surreptitiously looked at his watch. The door opened and the secretary appeared with a computer printout. She smiled at me as she walked out.

"Ah," he said.

"You know her?"

"Vaguely," the dean said. "I think she worked with Harvey in some capacity."

"Can you tell me more from her student record?"

"I'm sorry, but I cannot share academic information, Mr. Spenser."

"I'm looking for more personal," I said. "Do you know someone who knew her?"

He held the paper loose as he thought. He fluttered the paper in his fingers, studied the information in hand, and then called his secretary again. The door opened, and she appeared. This time she did not smile at me. I felt we were keeping her from something.

"Can you find out if Stephanie Cho is teaching today?" he said.

The secretary nodded and the door closed. Agarwal nodded.

"A lead?"

"I believe I have someone you should meet."

"Goody," I said.

55

"Of course I remember Jemma Fraser," said Stephanie Cho. "We called her the Duchess because of the accent and the attitude. She always wore these killer tall riding boots. God, that was a while back."

"Who is 'we'?"

"Other MBA students," she said. "I'm pretty sure she attended Oxford and worked for some private equity group before coming to the States. Knew everything and thought everyone else was a lesser being. All the men, and some of the women, were crazy about her. But she didn't really mingle. We had some classes together. Can't say I liked her very much."

We sat together at a table outside Spangler Hall, the student union of Harvard Business School. I had bought Stephanie a tall iced mocha. I had decided against more coffee and drank bottled water. Now out of sight of the dean, I again sported my Brook-

321

lyn Dodgers cap and slumped a bit in my chair.

"Do you remember the classes?"

Stephanie Cho thought for a moment. She was a pretty girl, a bit heavyset, with blunt-cut black hair and a wide face. She wore a short-sleeve cowboy shirt that fit tightly around her chest and upper arms. She tapped her front tooth as she thought. "Machiavelli, for one."

"That was a business class?"

"It has a fancier title than that, something like 'Machiavelli and Computational Models for Consumer Behavior' or some kind of junk," she said. "It was Harvey Rose's signature class. We all read *The Prince,* and Rose would relate the text to using data to get your consumers to do what you want them to do."

"As in the ends justified the means."

"Computational models are not educated guesses," she said. "Using data of past behavior, a well-built model allows its user to accurately predict what consumers will do in any given situation, often more accurately than the consumer assesses his or herself."

"And what does that have to do with *The Prince*?"

"It reduces everything to a data set," she

said. "If you think of your consumers as data sets and not people, it allows you to completely disengage from morality. Data sets are amoral. If the data says low-income consumers are more likely to spend that extra fifty bucks than middle-income consumers, then you target them. You don't care if they can't pay the rent or go to the doctor."

"Ah."

"And as the model gets better and better, it becomes a manipulation tool. Based on past behavior, you can set up the optimal circumstances that pretty much guarantee the outcome. It almost destroys free will. We can know that they will, and how they will, and for how long, and under what conditions."

"Yikes."

"What did you think we discussed here?"

"Love thy neighbor?"

"Yeah, right."

"How about Jemma?" I said. "Did she ever discuss Professor Rose's lack of ethics?"

"I doubt it," she said. "But I really didn't know her very well. Sometimes I'd see her out for beers or at parties. That was rare. But mainly she was stuck up Rose's ass."

"A true believer."

"More than that," Cho said. She took a sip of the mocha. "I think she had a thing for him."

"For Harvey Rose?"

"I know, I know," she said. "Right? He was one of those professors who couldn't match his socks. Had ketchup stains on his shirt all the time. Uncombed hair."

"I'm not so good with ketchup myself. Worse with salsa."

"So you know, he wasn't exactly the kind of professor that made women swoon," she said. "I think he found Jemma's devotion very flattering. Especially with her style. And that gorgeous accent."

"Was there preferential treatment?"

"Well, he hired her immediately when he left Harvard."

"Do you think they were intimate?"

"I have no idea," Cho said. "God, I hope not. I mean, that's why you come here. To be independent, to impress employers into leadership positions. Not to screw your way to the top."

"Do you recall anyone else she was close to?"

Cho shook her head. "I really can't. I'm sorry. We all knew her. But she was very, very aloof. I can ask around."

"Did she have family in the States?"

"I had the impression she was here just for the education. All I can remember are those clothes of hers. Wore very fancy stuff that was a bit out of place. Inappropriate for nine a.m. classes."

"And the riding boots."

"Always wore them."

"And her without a horse."

"You have to understand we don't have traditional graduate assistantships here," she said. "You are not required to have an internship, either. But we all pretty much do. I had one with Prudential and later with Bain. You work with a company and then you're assigned a professor as a mentor."

"And Rose was Jemma's mentor."

"And mine, too, and plenty of male students'," she said. "I just don't recall him taking that active a role in my off-campus work."

"Do you remember what Jemma did?"

"I think she pretty much interned with Professor Rose," she said. "Some of the students did that. But it was preferred that we left campus and worked in a real business setting. I just recall her always being in his office. Almost like his secretary, or a personal assistant. I thought the whole arrangement a bit weird. Maybe it was because I was always wearing sweatpants while

Jemma was in haute couture."

"You should see me on Saturday nights."

"You seem very odd for a cop," Stephanie said. She pulled her legs up and wrapped her knees with her arms. She stared at me, looking very much like a little girl, a bit quizzical. Her blunt-cut hair ruffled a bit in the spring breeze.

"I could not stand being a cop," I said. "That's why I work for myself."

"That's what I want," Stephanie said. More wind kicked up on the common and you could smell the river. "My parents were first-generation. My father thought life was work. He believed that every day you must take a hard path to be a good man. You don't seem that way."

"I am often late for work."

"My parents are very proud of me," she said. "But they don't understand why I left my job. And why I don't take what I learned and put it in practice. I could never tell them I'm quite content to teach."

"Makes sense to me."

"You know, Professor Rose came back here last fall to speak," Cho said. "He told us to be unemotional and detached in our decision making. He said you only need to know the who, what, and when, not necessarily the why."

"I've been teaching an associate of mine the same thing."

"Computational models?"

"Hoodlum ethics."

56

Z met me at Danehy Park in Cambridge at sunset. People jogged along paths, and dogs frolicked about. I had decided to sort out what I learned by throwing the tennis ball to Pearl. She had spent much of the last week cooped up, which tends to make a hunting dog psychotic. So we worked out her issues by letting her sprint for the ball and return it. My arm had grown tired and I tossed the ball to Z. Pearl, tongue lolling from her mouth, showed no signs of fatigue.

"I heard about the two dead men," Z said. "They part of the new team?"

"Healy thinks so," I said. "Heavy hitters from Vegas. Someone wanted to make sure they were not welcome."

"Maybe they were hired by Weinberg's people," Z said. "To come for the killers."

"Or maybe they killed Weinberg and got their due."

Z threw the ball over a rolling hill. Pearl

disappeared for several moments. She appeared triumphantly with the tennis ball covered in slobber and blades of grass.

"What is Jemma saying?" I said.

Z shrugged. He watched Pearl intently.

"She won't talk about Weinberg," he said. "It makes her very upset."

I nodded. Z tossed me the slobbery ball. I wound up and threw it to the moon. Pearl was off like a rocket.

"How does she treat you?" I said.

"Fine."

"I found out today that she had been an intern for Harvey Rose," I said. "Ten years ago at Harvard Business School."

Z nodded.

"That was something she had not told me," I said. "You?"

Z's face was impassive, and he shook his head. Pearl returned. I rocketed the ball again. This time a black Lab broke into stride with Pearl but was no match for her. She beat him by three car lengths, and upon return, she teased him with the ball, nudging it to his mouth.

"Watch your step," I said.

"She's very scared and alone."

I nodded.

"She said I make her feel safe."

I nodded again.

Z took the ball from Pearl and threw it far and wide. His face was slick with rain as he stared up at the rolling hills and picnic tables. Pearl and the black Lab nuzzled each other. Pearl was faster and stronger, but for some reason, she dropped the ball in front of the Lab. I reached for the ball and threw it as far as I could.

"We had sex," Z said.

"Uh-huh."

"The other night," he said. "She wanted me to come up to the room. She was naked."

"Hard to resist."

Z shrugged.

"I don't know much about this woman," I said. "But the more I know, the less I like."

"Because she was Rose's protégée?"

"That she didn't mention it."

Z nodded.

"She asks me a lot about you," Z said. "Wants to know what you know. She asks me a lot about Rachel Weinberg, too. And wants to know about your meetings with Healy."

Pearl returned. She looked happy and winded. A man in a red windbreaker called for the Lab, and the Lab trotted off. I placed my hand on Pearl's head and attached her leash.

"What else?" I said.

"Jemma says you took advantage of her the other night."

"By saving her life?"

"After," he said. "She said you poured her a lot of drinks and that things happened."

"She tripped on my rug and I put her to bed."

"She said she does not remember it all," Z said. "But she remembers you crawling on top of her in the night. And doing things."

"You would think that I would remember, too."

"I told her that I couldn't trust you anymore," Z said. "I said that you were a liar and a man without honor."

"Gee, thanks."

Z broke into a grin. "I said I was through with you," he said. "But I would act as if we were still friends and pass along information."

"Some sidekick."

Z shrugged. He was still smiling.

"Perhaps you can find out why she kept her relationship with Harvey Rose secret?"

"If you slept with that man, wouldn't you lie about it?"

"Most definitely."

We walked back to our cars, taking a

winding path covered with pebbles and stones. The air seemed to swell and expand, the dark, full clouds pregnant with an oncoming storm. Z walked to his car while I stopped at my Explorer.

"She does believe those dead men were coming for her," Z said.

"Maybe so."

"She has a lot of fear in her," Z said.

"You would know," I said.

"How long do we keep this up?"

"Me as the Lone Ranger?"

Z nodded.

"When we come to a fork in the road, we both take it."

57

Despite my best efforts, nothing new was learned for two whole days. Pearl seemed unconcerned, as she had taken the entire new couch while I walked across Berkeley for a tall Starbucks coffee. I tossed her a bit of a blueberry scone, and she caught it in midair and swallowed it whole. I spread out a copy of the *Globe* on my desk, going right for the sports section. It was early in the season, but many were already calling for the Sox manager's resignation. Many also doubted the salaries of several marquee players. Perhaps my job was more stress-free. Then again, ballplayers seldom dodge bullets.

After reading the box scores and checking in with *Arlo & Janis,* I got right into the ac-cumulated mail. I was shocked to find a check from a previous client. And not so shocked to see a check I had sent to Mattie Sullivan torn in half and returned in a new envelope. I received an amazing offer from a local pizza chain, two for one. I put that aside. I found out I was preapproved for a credit card. That I tossed in the trash. I saved the largest envelope for last.

I slit open the edge with my thumbnail and out dropped what seemed to be a basic key fob. But on further analysis, I realized it was a flash drive. The envelope was otherwise empty. My address was computer-generated on a basic Avery label. Of course, there wasn't a return address.

I clutched the flash drive in my hand and tried it out in my computer. My computer spoke to the flash drive, and in a couple seconds, a fifty-eight-page Excel document opened, filled with rows and columns of neatly aligned numbers and figures. At the top of several columns were names of many area banks. Running along the side of the document were dates of transfers. Gadzooks.

Being a trained detective, I noted this might mean something. Being someone who did not have a degree from Harvard Business School, I knew I needed a bit of help. I reached for the phone and called Wayne Cosgrove as I copied the Excel file to my hard drive. He did not graduate from HBS but would know someone who could translate.

"Hold for subscriptions," Wayne said.

"I just received this neato electronic thingy in the mail," I said. "It appears to highlight many banks' wire transfers and payments over the course of the last six months."

"Good for you."

"Many payments of note go to a deluxe slush fund for Joseph G. Perotti."

"And how did you come by this information?"

"On this neat thingy," I said. "Sent in the mail."

"Just showed up in your mail?"

"I do believe someone has been searching for it," I said. "My office was torn apart a few days ago. Someone believed I had something of value."

"Maybe you had other stuff they wanted."

"They left the coffeepot, a .357, and my Vermeer prints."

"Ah." The buzzing phones and tapping keyboard sounds of the city newsroom came from the other end of the line. "When can I see it?"

"It says Perotti, but who knows if it's genuine or who sent the funds."

"You may be a trained investigator,"

Wayne said, "but I am a trained muckraker. I know people who could read that thing if it was encrypted from the original Mandarin Chinese."

"Good to know those people," I said.

"You bet."

I hung up and whistled for Pearl. But Pearl was already at the door, waiting for me to slip the choker over her neck. She must have heard the conversation and known.

"The game is afoot."

Pearl stared and tilted her head.

"Tally ho," I said.

Pearl was not impressed until I rolled down the passenger window on our way to the *Globe* newsroom in Dorchester. I placed the drive into an envelope and handed it over to Wayne at security. For what seemed like ten hours but was more likely two, Pearl and I took in the sights around Dorchester. I let her off the leash at an empty Joe Moakley Park and we strolled along the beach.

I finally met Wayne at a reporter gathering spot called the Harp and Bard and left Pearl in my car with the windows cracked. The bar was a newish pub with dozens of new televisions hanging from metal beams in the ceiling, along with old Bruins and Celtics flags. Wayne sat in a dark corner of the bar, studying an open folder.

A sign advertised a karaoke contest every Thursday at five p.m. Prizes awarded.

"We stick around long enough and we can enter," I said.

"Oh, yeah," Wayne said. "What would you sing?"

" 'The Girl from Ipanema.' "

"Glad to know you're keeping up with the times," Wayne said.

I ordered the club with a Bud Light, and Wayne ordered a burger with a side of Jameson. After the bartender walked away, he shuffled his papers and looked at me.

"This appears to be some pretty damning stuff," he said. "It shows direct payoffs going right to Perotti. Some of it is legal, but most of it isn't."

"Terrific."

"But proving is another matter," Wayne said. "I know what this says. But we don't know if it's bullshit."

"And how can we find out?"

"A court order."

"Or go through the cops."

Wayne nodded. The bartender reappeared with my Bud Light and Wayne's whiskey.

"Jesus, Spenser," Wayne said. "Bud Light?"

"It's not even noon," I said. "Same as water."

"But Bud Light," he said. "I thought more of you."

I shrugged. Wayne shook his head and rattled his whiskey around the ice. He looked down at his notes and then up at me. "You do understand what you are meant to see here?"

"Enlighten me."

Wayne Cosgrove's face morphed into a very serious expression. He tapped at the sheets of paper littering the inside of the file. "Two of these companies making the payoffs belong to Gino Fish," he said.

I drank some beer and nodded.

"Who do you think sent it?" Wayne said.

"I have a few ideas," I said. "But I don't know for sure."

"You think Fish believes you have it?" Wayne said.

"Perhaps," I said. "I know that Harvey Rose had a break-in recently. They stole several computers."

"Wow." Wayne tossed back some of his drink. "If this can be verified, I would have a hell of a story."

"And what would I have?"

"If we could connect Harvey Rose and

Gino Fish to Perotti, the shit would hit the fan."

"Still doesn't get me any closer to finding out who killed Rick Weinberg."

"Not my job." Wayne drank a bit more, settled into his booth, and sighed. "I sure would like to know who laid this in your lap. And who the hell wants to screw Harvey Rose so bad they break into his office and steal those files."

"That list is growing shorter by the minute."

"You want me to hold on to the drive?" Wayne said.

"I assume you made copies."

Wayne handed me the drive, and I placed it in my jacket pocket.

"If something happens to me —" I said.

"I will write a glowing obit about a man who refused to conform to the times."

"And maybe turn over this information to the state police."

Wayne smiled and signaled the bartender for another round. "Oh, and that, too."

58

Gino Fish did business out of a brownstone on Tremont Street, in the South End. A plate-glass window next to the door read DEVELOPMENT ASSOCIATES OF BOSTON. You had to walk down a few steps to get to the door and enter a room walled in red brick. A handsome young man in his twenties greeted me at a small desk. The room was the same; the young man was new.

"What happened to Stan?" I said.

"He retired."

"Put out to pasture?"

The young man smiled. He looked like a J.Crew model in a slim-fitting navy suit worn without socks. A large diamond sparkled in his left ear.

"Tell Mr. Fish Spenser is here."

"Does he know you, Mr. Spenser?"

"We're old pals."

That may have been stretching it a bit. But the young man kept smiling as he disappeared behind a purple velvet curtain. After a few moments, Vinnie Morris appeared. He didn't say anything, only looked me up and down.

"What do you have going on back there, a puppet show?" I said.

"Yeah," Vinnie said. "Punch and Judy."

There was a larger room behind the purple curtain and more exposed brick, with worn floors that probably were made from the *Mayflower.* The light was dim and colored by Tiffany lamps. Tasteful antiques filled the room, including Gino Fish. Who was more antique these days than tasteful.

"To what do I owe the honor," Gino said.

"Would you believe I'm in the market for a Chippendale desk?"

"No," he said. "I would not."

Gino stood from behind an old, well-polished desk and nodded me toward a chair in front of him. He took a seat back at the desk and spread his hands very wide. "Vinnie, please have Michael bring us some coffee. A little cream and sugar for our guest."

I nodded.

"For an Italian crime boss, you often sound a lot like Alistair Cooke."

"My father made sure his children were given the best educations."

Fish smiled. The smile was uncomfortable but controlled. Gino's newest young man appeared with a small tray filled with a French press, a sugar bowl, and a creamer.

Vinnie took a seat on a brown leather couch. He leaned forward in the dim light and made no attempt to conceal the fact that he was listening to every word. I tossed him the flash drive to see his quick hands in action. Vinnie, being Vinnie, caught it in his left hand like a trapped fly.

"Got this in the mail, Gino," I said. "It's a pretty well-detailed account of payments from your various companies to the esteemed Joseph G. Perotti."

Vinnie leaned back into the couch. Gino placed his hands flat on his knees. His skin had become more paper-thin, and the number of liver spots on his hands had grown. His eyes were hooded, and his lips were thin and purplish. He smelled like a basket of potpourri.

"So?" Gino said.

"Thought you might want it back," I said.

"Very generous of you."

Gino and Vinnie exchanged looks. Gino turned to me and slowly lifted his chin. He swallowed and then turned his attention to the coffee. Michael stepped forward and poured a cup for Gino and then for me. As he left, he pulled the curtain shut as if separating first class from coach.

"And what do you want in return?"

"Your undying gratitude?"

Gino looked to Vinnie. Vinnie shook his head and looked at the floor.

"And what else?"

"I want to know who killed Rick Weinberg and why."

Gino leaned back in his seat. He left the coffee on the table, a wisp of steam curling up in the glow of the Tiffany shade. He pursed his purple lips. "And if I had him killed, I would lie to you."

"Yes."

"But you came anyway."

"As a show of good faith."

Gino nodded. He tented his long fingers before him. I never was sure why people did that when they were thinking. I thought they often did that to telegraph contemplation. I usually just tapped at my temple to fire up my brain.

"I have no idea who killed Rick Weinberg."

"You say that with such conviction."

Gino nodded.

"Obviously, there are some who have benefited by Rick Weinberg's death."

Vinnie and Gino exchanged another look. Gino nodded to Vinnie.

"Mr. Fish and Mr. Weinberg had been business partners."

"Till death do you part?"

"Yep," Vinnie said.

"And now Mr. Fish does not care to work with Jemma Fraser?"

"She did not impress me," Gino said.

"I figured you would be immune to her obvious charms."

Gino took in a long breath. He leaned forward and added a lot of cream but no sugar to his coffee. His eyelids drooped. "I don't owe Rick Weinberg or any of his people a thing. I've found it may be to my advantage to work with another party."

"And that would mean Harvey Rose and his group in Eastie," I said.

Gino sipped his coffee. He artfully crossed his legs, his ankle touching the edge of his knee. He just smiled with the thousand-yard stare.

"May I infer from your silence that I'm correct?"

Gino smiled and sipped again.

"You do know who sent you that fucking thing," Vinnie said.

I shrugged.

"Do you really think we wanted to kill that broad?" Vinnie said. "Jeez. Mr. Fish only wanted to speak to her."

"About taking something that didn't belong to her."

"Now you got it, Spenser," Vinnie said. "Now you got it."

"I will do you another favor," Gino said. "There has been an ill wind blowing in from the west since Mr. Weinberg's death. There are individuals who have arrived in Boston who have not been invited, nor do they have any business being here."

"Jimmy Aspirins and the Angel of Mercy."

"Wouldn't you like some sugar in your coffee?" Gino said.

I added a couple cubes and milk. I sat back and drank coffee. Say what you want about Gino Fish, but he was a solid host. If he had brought out tea biscuits, I might have been convinced to work for the other side.

"And who hired them?" I said.

Gino widened his eyes. "That is the question, isn't it?"

"Did you have them killed?"

"No."

He drank some coffee. He looked to Vinnie, who leaned forward with his elbows on his knees. Vinnie popped a piece of gum into his mouth and waited.

"Anyone else ask you to make inroads on Beacon Hill?"

Gino touched the parchmentlike skin that hung from his neck. He took in a deep breath, eyelids slowly drooping back into place. "Those men you mentioned do not come cheap. They are well connected and well paid. And they got in my way."

I nodded. I was not thrilled with the way this was headed.

"Vinnie knows a man named Zebulon Sixkill who has recently fallen under my tutelage," I said. "If you find him caught in the crossfire, I would appreciate him remaining unharmed."

Gino uncrossed his legs. He stretched his neck and rubbed his fingers across his jawline. "And I would like the same arrangement for Mr. Perotti. Can you see to this?"

"That may be more difficult," I said. "Some other people know."

"But can they prove it?"

I shrugged.

"Let's keep it that way, Mr. Spenser."

Vinnie looked at me, seeming odd in his tailored suit and neatly barbered hair, and blew a huge bubble. The bubble popped in the brick room like a gunshot.

59

"That lying little bitch is making a goddamn mess out of everything," Rachel Weinberg said.

"It certainly appears that way."

We sat together in the back of the black Lincoln, with Lewis Blanchard at the wheel. I had been summoned to accompany Blanchard to Logan to pick up Rachel. I had dressed in jeans, a herringbone jacket, a blue button-down, and no tie. I did not want to appear overly eager. But I did come armed with news of the winds swirling in Boston, ill and otherwise.

"First she hires some local hooligans to scare people from a condo we need," Rachel said. "And now she's breaking into Harvey Rose's offices to blackmail him. This is why she has no business running our company. Rick would have never acted like such an idiot. She has gone batshit crazy."

Rachel smoked down one of her thin

cigarettes. The windows were up because of the rain and fogged the car. The windshield wipers sliced water from the gray landscape of overpasses and on-and off-ramps.

"I don't know if she broke into his office or if she had someone do it," I said. "I am merely speculating."

"Who the hell else would do it?" Blanchard said from the front seat. He did not turn around; the Town Car dipped down into the Sumner Tunnel. The sound of the engine roared, muffled in the enclosure.

"Were you aware that Jemma had studied under Harvey Rose?" I said.

"We knew she worked for him and we knew she went to Harvard Business School," Rachel said. "Hell, she wouldn't let us forget. But when she came over to us it wasn't like Harvey Rose was gonna write a recommendation letter. He was pissed. That was the start of some bad blood between him and Rick."

"She never told you that they had been close," I said. "Or that she had been his intern while in Boston."

"No."

"Why do you think she'd keep that a secret?" I said.

"Because she's a lying piece of trash," Rachel said. "She has blindsided me about every order of business since Rick's death." Rachel pounded the armrest with the bottom side of her fist.

"Did you know she would be his successor?"

"Of course," she said. "I had to vote on it. Rick wanted it so damn badly. But Jesus, I didn't imagine what would happen. Or that she would try to fuck me over with the board. I just got back from a meeting in Vegas where they offered me a buyout. They want me off the board and to take a fucking check. Who do you think broached that simple subject?"

"What did you say?"

"You ever see that scene in *Mommie Dearest* when Faye Dunaway stands up and tells the board at Pepsi-Cola, 'Don't fuck with me, fellas'?"

"Yep."

"That's the G-rated version of my little speech."

"And Jemma was there?"

"Of course."

"Was a young man with her," I said. "A big Native American guy."

"No," she said. "But why the hell not? I bet she's fucked her way around the world. Twice."

We emerged from the tunnel, the river appearing to the right. We passed under the Longfellow Bridge and by the boathouse. I assumed we were headed back to the Four Seasons, though Blanchard had not said. I did not speak until we turned left at Arlington and the Public Garden, nearly at the Four Seasons' front door. "You heard about those two dead sluggers from Vegas," I said. "Ever hear of them?"

"You think they worked for Jemma?"

"Or against her," I said. "They weren't local talent, and therefore not in my personal Rolodex."

"Who were they, then?" Rachel said.

"Jimmy Aspirins and a guy they called the Angel of Mercy."

"Are you shitting me?"

"I would not shit you, Mrs. Weinberg."

"Lew?" Rachel said. "Sound like anyone we know?"

"No, ma'am."

"I would recommend taking extra precautions," I said.

"A turf war between Jemma and Harvey Rose?" Rachel Weinberg said. "Christ. Just what we need. A whore and a dolt."

Blanchard turned onto Boylston and quickly under the porte cochere. The valet, in his crisp green uniform, approached the rear door. Blanchard looked back, right arm

350

resting on the passenger seat. He waited. Rachel looked at me with pursed lips, crushing the cigarette into the tray.

"Rose doesn't have the stomach," Rachel said. Her jaw was clenched very tight, and she repeatedly shook her head in frustration.

"And Jemma?"

Rachel Weinberg nodded in thought. "Goddamn bitch."

Lewis Blanchard half turned, drumming his fingers on the back of the headrest. The windows dripped with rainwater, the windshield wipers still going.

"You have enough people?" I said.

He nodded, lost somewhere in thought. "That's all been covered."

"If you don't," I said. I made an offhand gesture.

Blanchard nodded. The valet opened Rachel Weinberg's door and she stepped outside without a word. If someone was going to harm Rachel, under the porte cochere of the Four Seasons would have been impolite as well as ill conceived. Blanchard drummed his fingers some more, looking off.

"Listen, Spenser," Blanchard said. "We got this thing now. But we appreciate what you've done."

"I haven't done much."

"You'll be paid."

"Never doubted it."

"But for now . . ."

"Kind of hard to leave mid-stride."

"I may have overreacted, hiring you."

"How's that?"

"You got to understand, I report to a whole fucking committee," he said. "If it was just you and me, it would be simpler."

"I don't need money."

"You got to get paid." He paused. "You stay on it, it'll be my ass. Legal issues."

"Wish to elaborate?"

"Nope."

Rachel stood close to the Town Car and lit yet another cigarette by the hotel entrance. Four valets waited nearby for the smallest word from their guest. Blanchard turned off the ignition and stepped outside the car. I followed. He offered his hand, and I shook it.

"Effective immediately?"

"We got this thing," Blanchard said. He grinned. "We got it."

60

Now gainfully unemployed, I returned to the Harbor Health Club to see Henry and perhaps beg for a free protein shake or even a smoothie. Alas, Henry had other things on his mind and took me to the apartment he'd loaned Z. After knocking a few times, he reached into his sweatpants pocket for a key, unlocked the door, and pushed inside. I followed.

The apartment consisted of a wide-open room with an open kitchen, one bedroom and one bath. The walls were bare Sheetrock, the furniture basic and impersonal. The view was nice. Three picture windows looking out onto the harbor. Henry looked into the bedroom and returned, shaking his head.

Z was gone. He had stripped the bed and left drawers empty. A pile of twisted sheets and towels lay in a heap by the bathroom. Z had always traveled light; most everything in the apartment belonged to Henry. It might have taken him five minutes to pack.

"Didn't know he left," Henry said. "Saw him yesterday. He came in to work out and that was that. He was alone. I didn't see the broad."

"The broad had gone back to Las Vegas," I said. "She had important business."

"Hell of a body," Henry said. "Getting pretty good with her hook."

"All in the hips," I said.

"Isn't everything?" Henry said.

Rain came in droves, the clouds black and endless out on the harbor. There seemed to be a battle with the dregs of winter and the arrival of spring. Neither one wanted to cede to the other. I took a seat on a couch facing a big-screen television. On a large wooden coffee table stood the last remnants of Z's tenure at Henry's gym, an empty bottle of Jack Daniel's. Henry and I saw it at the same time.

Henry picked up the bottle, twirled it in his fingers, inspecting the label. He nodded and sat across from me. The rain pinged pleasantly on the glass. I wished Z had left us a couple drops of the whiskey.

"Didn't see this coming," Henry said.

"All may not be what it seems."

"Looks like he's hitting the hooch."

"He's working for me."

"Did he tell you he'd left?"

"Nope."

"What does that say?"

"It says he'll shout when he needs it."

"That's nuts."

"Got to trust him."

"How long since you heard from him?"

"Two days."

"Two days," Henry said. "Christ."

Henry placed the bottle back on the coffee table. Wind kicked up from the harbor, rain hammered the glass, and the masts of boats bobbed up and down and side to side.

"He's in trouble," Henry said.

"He wants to do this alone."

"Now you're talking like a shrink."

"It's how he'll finish the business," I said. "He needs me, he'll let me know."

"I say he needs help," Henry said. "Hadn't been for me, you wouldn't have met the Weinbergs."

"Hadn't been for you, I might be dead."

Henry shrugged. "That's an oversimplification of my role in your life."

"Discipline and self-reliance."

Henry leaned into the chair. We both sat, watching the storm crack to life across the waterfront. Thunder rattled the picture windows. Lightning zipped in crooked patterns. The harbor churned and seemed to turn black. Quite a show.

"How come we never thought about training anyone else?"

"Never saw anyone with as much potential," I said.

"You coulda let him go like Hawk."

"If he were so inclined."

"But he's not."

"Up to him."

"And you like passing on your skills to the next guy who does what you do."

I shrugged. "Something like that."

" 'Cause we can't go on forever," Henry said.

"Speak for yourself, John Alden."

We watched the rain for a long time. He picked up the empty whiskey bottle again and cornered the last drop of booze. "How was it for you that time you were shot?" Henry said.

"Which time?"

"The really bad time."

"They are all bad times when you are shot."

"But the one that nearly killed you."

"The Gray Man."

"You remember?"

"Hard to forget."

"You think about quitting?"

"Nope."

"Why?"

"The alternative was not attractive."

Henry stood up and walked to the door. He shut off the lights, intensifying the effects of the storm outside, making the grays and blacks more stark. "That woman is a pro," Henry said. "I don't think Z is prepared for where she'll take him."

"I think he got busted up," I said. "He learned being cracked doesn't make you broken. He's ready."

"How'd you get so wise?"

"I'm Irish," I said. "I listen to the wisdom of the little people."

"Okay, then," Henry said. "Let's find the kid."

61

Henry and I had spent eight hours looking for Z. And looking for Jemma. I learned she no longer frequented the Four Seasons. Or the Boston Harbor Hotel. Or the Legal at Copley Place. I had tried the storefront in Revere that Rick Weinberg had rented. I had tried some of Z's favorite brewpubs. Nothing. The next morning I went for a run, with Pearl trotting at my side with great enthusiasm. I missed Z. He always pushed me harder than I pushed myself. He was younger, stronger, and faster, and in turn made me better. I kept my mind off dark thoughts.

The rain had been constant, the remnants of a storm off the Atlantic. It fell warm and salty, hitting my face as we ran east along the river. Pearl and I crossed the Weeks Footbridge, heading back toward the business school, while I considered what I knew about Jemma Fraser. Which was not considerable or specific. She was ambitious and ruthless. She had been a protégée of Harvey Rose's but had chosen to keep that relationship private. She had sent some local sluggers to scare some old folks into selling their properties, possibly against her boss's wishes. She had tried to seduce me and had failed. She had told Z that I forced the issue. Now I learned she had probably stolen incriminating evidence from her old mentor and then sent it to me to show that Harvey Rose was in cahoots with Gino Fish and sever their relationship.

But being ruthless and even highly unethical in business does not make you a killer. However, it doesn't make you Rebecca of Sunnybrook Farm, either.

I kept heading east on the Boston side of the river. I followed the path to Soldiers Field Road to where it would become Storrow. Despite the rain, the rowers were out in force. I watched a four-woman crew aimlessly float and then slow in alignment before falling into a steady dip of oars and muscle. I kept jogging, Pearl's collar jingling beside me. Her constant pant a comfort.

As I approached the Harvard Bridge and Mass Ave, a black car slowed to my pace along Storrow before turning onto Mass and illegally parking on the curb at the edge of the bridge. Healy and Lundquist got out. I stopped and caught my breath. Pearl looked back at me with annoyance.

"Admiring my form?" I said.

"Got a minute?" Lundquist said.

"Is there a statie policy against having a hound in your car?"

"Yeah," Lundquist said. "Might make my commander bullshit."

Healy shook his head and climbed back into the passenger side. Lundquist eased his large frame behind the wheel. I opened the back door, let Pearl in, got in behind her, and closed the door. Lundquist drove out onto Mass Ave and crossed back over the river.

"How's it going out there?" Healy said.

"Rain slows me down a bit," I said.

"I meant with the Weinbergs," he said.

"I was told that my services were no longer needed."

"So you got it all figured out?"

"Sure thing," I said.

"Why'd they let you go?" Lundquist said. His red hair was cut razor short above his thick neck.

"It was implied they now have their own people."

"Anything you want to let us know?" Lundquist said.

Pearl sat at attention in the leather seats, head on a swivel as we passed MIT and the many students bustling about in tight jeans, sloppy T's, and backpacks.

"My apprentice is missing."

"You're getting some rotten luck, Spenser," Healy said.

"I suppose you have something to cheer me up."

"In fact, we do," Healy said. "We know who killed Rick Weinberg."

I raised my eyebrows. Even Pearl perked up. "That is swell news," I said. "Made the arrest?"

"Might be tough," Healy said. "It was those two shitbirds we found shot up in Chelsea."

I waited. Pearl waited.

"Weinberg's DNA is in the trunk," Healy said. "We found a receipt to the cash purchase of a Stihl chain saw. Want me to draw you a picture?"

"Lovely," I said. "You tell Mrs. Weinberg?"

"You're the first to know," Lundquist said. "We don't want it getting out until we get further up the food chain."

"Ideas on who hired them?"

"That's why we came to you, ace."

"Gee, thanks."

"We're looking into their phone records,

and people out in Vegas are doing the same," Healy said. "It will take some time. They have connections to what's left of the Genovese and Polizzi families."

I scratched Pearl's head. Her wet-dog smell and dog breath rapidly filled the car. I felt like I should share something with the staties, but wasn't sure what. I could tell them what Gino Fish suspected about Jemma and perhaps mention the reason he sent his nephews to corral her. Instead, I thought for a moment. "Did your people ever find out what happened with Weinberg's cell?"

"Nope."

"But you subpoenaed the provider," I said. "The provider would have to turn over what they had."

"Takes more time than you think."

"Phone is lost at sea," I said. "But any texts or voice mails would still exist."

"Remember the days when we just dealt with Ma Bell," Healy said. "Jesus, it was much easier."

"I used to send a box of chocolates and flowers every Valentine's Day to my favorite operator."

"Let me see where we stand," Healy said. "You know something?"

"Did you guys happen to find Jemma

Fraser?" I said.

"You don't know where she is, either."

"You looking for her?" I said.

"We are."

"May I ask why?"

"Off the record?"

"Yep."

Healy took a deep breath. "She is what we call a 'person of interest.' "

"That would make Rachel Weinberg a very happy woman," I said.

"Yep," Lundquist said. "She is of interest on a great many things. We have her arriving yesterday in Boston, and then she's fucking Houdini."

"Registered at a hotel?"

"Nope," Healy said.

"Talked to any business associates?"

"She's missed two important meetings," Lundquist said. "Nobody in the company can find their new CEO. That's a little strange."

He slowed the car. We had made it to Kendall Square right by the Longfellow Bridge. "You want us to put you out where we found you?" Healy said.

"This works," I said.

"You'll find your way back?" Lundquist said.

"Does it matter?" I reached for Pearl's

363

leash. "I'm still looking for a place to start."

I tried calling Z again. No answer.

62

After a shower and change of clothes, I was still flummoxed. So flummoxed, I drove back to my office and uncorked a bottle of Black Bush.

A blank yellow legal pad sat on my desk. I had yet to hear from Z or hear from Healy or make any sense of what was going on in Wonderland. I thought maybe it had something to do with me not turning on my office lights. So I did. My door was slightly ajar. Rain blew in from the Atlantic. It was nearly night, and for an odd reason, I didn't care about eating. Instead, I checked the time, and realizing it was three hours earlier in Vegas, called up Bernie Fortunato. Bernie, being one of those guys who kept a cell screwed into his ear, answered after one ring.

"It's a comfort knowing you're there for me."

"Where's my fucking check?"

"In the mail."

"I don't usually go about business that way," he said. "That's like a broad telling you that you're her first."

"Jaded."

"What do you need?"

"More snooping services are required."

"You're lucky this is a slow time for me."

"You'd make time," I said.

"You say."

"I need you to get to the Clark County clerk's office before they close."

"Sure."

"And search for anything of note filed on Rick Weinberg, Rachel Weinberg, or Jemma Fraser in the last few months."

"Sure," he said. "You want to tell me what the fuck I'm looking for?"

"Legal issues," I said.

"A hint?"

"Maybe a lawsuit brewing between Rachel Weinberg and Jemma Fraser. Or maybe something within the company."

"Sure, sure."

He hung up. I hung up. I poured a nip of Black Bush into my coffee cup. I leaned back into my chair, propped my feet on the edge of my desk, and listened to the steady rain and the traffic sounds out on Berkeley. The whiskey tasted more warm and welcoming on a wet day. So welcoming, I drank some more.

After a time, I dropped my feet to the floor, picked up the phone, and called Susan, who also answered after one ring.

"You and Bernie."

"Me and Bernie what?"

"Loyal pals."

"So what's the news from Berkeley and Boylston?"

"How'd you know I was in my office?"

"There is a new thing called caller ID," she said.

"Ah."

"Have you spoken to Z?"

"Nope."

"Found out who killed Rick Weinberg?"

"Sort of."

"What's 'sort of'?"

"I know who committed the act but not who made the call."

I explained.

"And how is Z?"

"Z has disappeared, and so has Jemma Fraser."

"Perhaps a romantic getaway?"

I stayed silent. I told her about Healy and the state police looking for her, too. I told her the abbreviated version of Joseph G. Perotti and his magical bank account. She was not shocked.

"And what will Gino Fish do if his dirty laundry makes it into the *Globe*?"

"Be further annoyed."

" 'Annoyed' is an underwhelming word."

After we hung up, I leaned back in the office chair and watched the odd patterns of light along Berkeley and the comings and goings of cars along Boylston.

I looked at my watch. I called Henry. Still no Z.

"Any more ideas?" I said.

"Aren't you the fucking detective?"

"Yeah, but sometimes I need a reminder."

I hung up, grabbed my raincoat and ball cap, and locked the door behind me.

63

I tried all the spots Z was known to frequent, and some that were just wild guesses. I did not have a picture of him to pass around. The description of a big Indian seemed to be enough. After the happy-hour rush, I found myself sitting at J. J. Donovan's at Faneuil Hall. Z and I often came here for a beer after working out. I ate a cheeseburger and fries and drank some Sam Adams on tap. J. J. Donovan's was a solid bar despite being located in the hub of tourist central.

The Sox game was on, and I watched while I waited for Henry to close up. I had already asked the bartender about Z. She said she had never seen a real-life Indian except in movies. I asked which movies, and she said *The Searchers*. We talked about *The Searchers* for a while.

I drank the beer very slowly. A handful of patrons hustled in and out, their jackets and hats soaked from the rain. The Sox were dry in Toronto, down in the bottom of the eighth.

The waitress smiled brightly and removed my empty plate. She brought me a new Sam Adams without being asked.

I had a few sips and my cell buzzed. Unable to hear much in crowded spots, I took the call outside on the pedestrian mall. The rain swept across the old brick street, but it was quiet.

"Okay," Fortunato said. "I made it to the clerk's office and stuck around till they closed. This'll all be on the bill. But it takes time, this stuff."

"Of course."

"And now I'm on the other side of town," Fortunato said. "And I had to grab a sandwich. If I had been by my office, I wouldn't need to go and get a fucking sandwich."

"Naturally."

"Okay," Fortunato said. "You ready, or you want me to call back?"

"I am all ears."

"So I went looking for any civil suits," Fortunato said. "I cross-referenced anything with Rachel and Rick Weinberg or that broad you mentioned."

"Jemma Fraser."

"Right," he said. "Her. I also had a list of

all the known corporations Weinberg operated in Nevada."

"And."

"And I didn't get jack," he said. "There was some bullshit from a knucklehead who'd run up two hundred grand at Weinberg's casino and now claims he was Weinberg's guest. Basically he stiffed the joint and wants Weinberg to pay him or some crap."

"So," I said. "No lawsuits from Rachel Weinberg. No recent suits against the board of directors or against Jemma Fraser. I'm looking for something with these women trying to get more from the will."

"I didn't see nothin' like that. I went back six months before they turned off the lights on me. You want me to head back tomorrow?"

"Why not?"

There was an old-fashioned iron street clock in front of the bar. If the old clock was right, it was nearly nine o'clock. Henry would be back soon.

"The only thing I saw with both the Weinbergs was motions filed in their divorce."

"Excuse me?"

"Rick Weinberg filed two weeks ago."

"Jumpin' Jehoshaphat."

"I thought you were working for her?"

371

"I was."

"And she hadn't told you?"

"Nope. You said Rick filed it?"

"I wouldn't want to cross the daughter of old man Polizzi," Fortunato said. "Do you know who her old man was?"

"A noted Las Vegas philanthropist?"

"Yeah, sure," Fortunato said. "Christ, Spenser. I would have charged you double if I'd known Weinberg's wife was a fucking Polizzi."

"I guess she didn't advertise."

"You want me to fax it to your office?" he said. "I made copies of this and of the other thing with the deadbeat."

I thought about what I'd learned from Healy about the dead men in Chelsea. "Jumpin' Jehoshaphat."

"You said that already, chief."

"I feel like saying it again."

"The sandwich wasn't much," he said. "But don't go nuts when you see it was eighteen bucks."

"Go get yourself a steak dinner and a bottle of red," I said. "On me."

I spotted Henry coming down Clinton Street, flags American and otherwise popping in the wind. He was still dressed in white workout clothes but had on a ball cap. I told Fortunato I'd call him back.

"Anything?" Henry said.

"Nothing on Z," I said. "Go inside and get a beer. I'll be right behind you."

Henry shrugged and walked inside. I called Healy on his cell.

"This better be worth it," Healy said. "I don't just hand out my personal cell for the hell of it."

"Any luck with those phone records?"

"God's smiling on you today. We got them at lunch and finished them up a few hours later. Lundquist and I both read them. Couldn't see jack shit. Bunch of crazy texts. Nothing jumped out."

"Can I see them tonight?"

"Jesus," Healy said. "You do realize I have a life."

"Thirty minutes?"

"Okay, okay," Healy said. "Christ. Meet you at 1010. So where's the fire?"

"Rick Weinberg filed for divorce two weeks ago."

"You sure?"

"I'll bring you the filing," I said.

Healy was quiet for a long while. "Christ."

"Anything coming back to you about those texts now?"

"Rachel Weinberg uses a lot of colorful language."

"Nothing else?"

"Like she threatened to cut off his fucking head?"

"Yeah," I said. "Like that."

"Not that I recall."

"What about between Jemma Fraser and Weinberg?"

"Some dirty shit," Healy said. "But nothing illegal in Massachusetts."

"Ms. Fraser seems to have dropped off the face of the earth with my former apprentice," I said.

"Maybe they took off to Tahiti and he's drinking mai tais and getting laid."

"Susan suggested the very thing."

"He's a big, tough guy, Spenser," Healy said. "I bet he's just trying to lay low with this woman till it's safe. She's got a dead boss, an attempted kidnapping with one of the guys dead. Not to mention the two sluggers who got whacked who may have been coming for her, too. I wouldn't mind being locked up with her for a few days."

"He would call."

"This divorce thing doesn't crystallize it."

"Maybe not."

"Did he say he'd be off the grid?" Healy said.

"Yep."

"I'm sure he's fine."

I tucked the cell back into my pocket. The

pedestrian mall had emptied. I stood alone in the rain. Everything oddly silent and hushed.

64

It was past eleven when I called Lewis Blanchard and asked if he could meet me. He sounded sleepy but agreed. I waited for him on a park bench in the Public Garden, halfway between my apartment and the Four Seasons. The rain had stopped, but I brought an umbrella anyway, along with my .38 and the thick, unmarked envelope Healy had handed me in the parking lot of 1010 Commonwealth.

At night, the Garden was green and vibrant in the glow of the streetlamps. The tulips wavered in the soft wind, dappled with moisture, air smelling of fresh-cut grass and rich wet earth. The swan boats had been docked for the night, and in the near distance, a trickle of people walking home from bars and restaurants crossed over the lagoon bridge. Blanchard appeared, wearing a tan raincoat, unshaven and bleary-eyed.

"Couldn't this wait?" he said.

I asked him to take a seat. Cordial. The bench was wet, but we both wore long coats and were tougher than the rain.

"Would've been nice to know about the divorce," I said.

He rubbed his bristled jaw and leaned back. He actually slumped farther into the bench, letting out air like a deflated balloon. "Why?" he said. "It was nobody's fucking business. And with Rick dead, it never happened."

"It would've come out sooner or later."

"Sure," he said. "But why bring it out in the middle of this circus?"

"Of course," I said.

Blanchard didn't speak. More people passed over the lagoon bridge. Somewhere some ducks quacked. Perhaps making way for ducklings.

"If everything is being kept so private," I said, "why did you hire me?"

"We thought you could help. But Rachel wants it with the cops now."

I offered him Spenser's look of doubt. The look was quite formidable.

"What? You sore about being let go?"

"Confused."

"By legal issues."

"By a lot of stuff," I said. "Mainly why Rachel wanted me to find out who killed her husband if she was the one who called it."

"You're fucking crazy," he said. "What? You want to blackmail her or something, get some cash or you'll spin this shit to the newspapers?"

"Nope."

"What, then?"

"I don't think you knew."

Blanchard looked at me with both disdain and pity, two emotions tough to convey at the same moment. "What?"

"Weinberg got by you that night because he was told to come alone."

"Jesus."

"Rachel was the one who drew him out," I said. "She paid to have him killed."

"You're fucking nuts."

I handed him the thick envelope. He looked at it like I'd presented a professionally wrapped turd. "Text messages between Rachel and Rick," I said. "The instructions were very specific."

I kept the eye contact. When bluffing, eye contact, no flinching, was key.

He opened the envelope and glanced through the first few pages. Blanchard stiffened. He looked straight ahead, watching traffic roll past on the wet asphalt of Boylston. "You making this up?"

"Rachel orchestrated all of this. The slight with Jemma was bad enough, but the divorce would cut her out of the company completely."

"Complete bullshit."

"I guess it doesn't matter what you believe," I said. "I'll hand it over to Captain Healy."

"Why tell me first?" he said.

I shrugged. "Professional courtesy?"

He turned to watch my face, his own jaw hanging open slightly. He glanced down at the envelope. "Where'd you get it?"

"I know some people."

"And Healy doesn't know."

"Not yet," I said. "But he will."

Blanchard studied my face. I waited.

"If we keep staring at each other on this park bench, people may begin to talk."

The automatic was in his hand sooner than I would have guessed. He had it out and pointing into my side. "Get up," he said. "Now."

"Now that the rain has stopped, it's turned into a lovely night."

"Shut up," he said. "Just shut the fuck up."

"Was it really Rachel's family who helped Rick get started?"

"Yes." His voice sounded tired and old.

"Hell of a slight."

Blanchard did not answer. The lamps on the lagoon bridge shone in creamy globes of light, reflecting on the water. "Why protect her?" I said. "She killed your boss."

"If you shut your fucking mouth," he said, "it'll make things easier."

"You gonna just shoot me right here?" I said. "Right in the middle of the Public Garden?"

"Be quiet."

I put my hands up in mock surrender and stood. Blanchard nodded at a footpath heading toward the Common. We walked, with Blanchard following a few paces behind me. I could not feel the gun but knew it was there.

"So who killed the sluggers from Vegas?" I said.

Blanchard didn't answer.

"Oh," I said. "I'm slow, but it's making sense."

"Shut up."

"That's loyal, Lew," I said. "She kills your boss, but you still look out for her."

I was throwing spitballs, but a great many of them were landing. We passed over Charles and into the Common, leaving the path into a sliver of darkness under a large tree. Blanchard told me to lie facedown.

"I'd rather not."

"Shut the fuck up and lie down."

I turned to him, hands still up, and smiled. "Slow and easy, or you'll get a bullet to the spine," I said.

He kind of laughed but half turned. Henry Cimoli stepped from the darkness, looking a little comical holding my .357. The gun nearly outweighed him. "Put down the piece, fucknuts, or I'll blow your goddamn head off."

"Say it like you mean it, Henry."

Blanchard let out another long breath. I'd seen the look before in fighters when they were most certainly beat. Blanchard loosened his fingers and the automatic dropped to the wet ground. I kept my eyes on Blanchard as I knelt, picked up the gun, and tossed it toward the footpath.

"Where is Jemma?" I said.

He shook his head.

"And Sixkill?"

He shook his head. "You'll never know."

I couldn't come up with a clever reply, so I shot an overhand right at his jaw. He stumbled a bit but remained on his feet. He wiped some blood from his mouth and nodded. I looked to Henry and waved him off. Henry remained still. Blanchard came at me in a fighter's stance, sure-footed and dead-eyed. I still had the .38 on my hip but

lifted my hands and stepped forward. Blanchard grunted as he lunged at me in a flurry
of hard but uncalculated punches. One of
them hit me hard in the temple and another
in the kidney. But I had a reach on him,
slightly shifting and knocking him with a
left in the nose and a right uppercut under
his chin that lifted and startled him a bit. I
stepped back and circled. I watched his
eyes. I was pretty sure he wanted to kill me.
He ran for my legs, tackling me down to
the soft earth and decomposing winter
leaves. I rolled away and kicked loose, then
kicked him hard in the stomach and face. A
man who has nothing to lose is a terrible
opponent. Blanchard kept coming. He
lunged for me and I slipped him. He ran at
me again and wrapped me in a bear hug,
squeezing all the breath from me and picking me up. We were face-to-face, and he
head-butted me several times, and I saw
stars and heard Henry yell to me to get my
head out of my ass. For a moment, I thought
he might have been geographically correct.

I head-butted Blanchard back and
knocked out my elbows, breaking free. I hit
him hard, square in the face, and harder in
the solar plexus. He made a sound not un-
like "oof" and stumbled back just one step
and dropped to a knee. He was winded and

bloody. My hands were scraped and throbbing. I caught most of the breath he had squeezed from me.

Henry stepped up, large gun in hand. "That the best you got?" he said.

I shrugged.

"Where's Jemma?" I said.

"Dead."

"And Sixkill?"

"Dead, too."

"Why?"

"You don't understand Rachel," Blanchard said. He wiped the blood from his lip and tried to stand. He fell back down to one knee. "It's fucking over. It's done."

"You killed those men because you didn't know Rachel had hired them. Not until after the fact."

"You should check her family tree sometime, Spenser," he said. "And ask yourself how her family had enough money to bankroll Rick."

"Where did you take Jemma and Z?"

"I didn't take them anywhere," he said. "Those guys from Vegas didn't come alone. There's another guy. They call him the Executioner. He was going to take care of everything. He was going to take them out to the dog track, find out what they knew, and then bury them deep."

I picked up his automatic from where it lay. I jacked the magazine from the butt and thumbed out the bullets into my palm. I placed the bullets in my coat pocket and tossed Blanchard the empty weapon. Then Henry and I jogged back to my car, leaving Blanchard in the dark.

65

"So I guess I'm screwed on the condo deal," Henry said.

"Afraid so."

"I had already made plans to expand the gym," he said. "Another room for Pilates or maybe some spin classes."

"How about a larger boxing room?"

"That would attract more boxers," Henry said. "You guys are gonna give me a fucking heart attack."

"He'll be okay," I said.

"You believe that?" Henry said.

"Got to." I wasn't so sure, but thinking Z was dead didn't help us. We would search until we found him.

"Blanchard said they used a special guy," Henry said. "I know animals like that. In fact, we both know an animal exactly like that. They don't make fucking mistakes."

"Neither do I."

We drove through the Callahan Tunnel

toward 1A. It was past midnight now as we rolled past the cut-rate motels, big rusting oil tanks, and barges running along the Chelsea River. We made it to Revere in fifteen minutes. Across the highway the condos stretched north along Revere Beach like dominos, red lights blinking from rooftops. You could smell the ocean.

The parking lot at Wonderland had been cleared of most of the cars, revealing buckling asphalt and potholes. The broken pieces of the old amusement park stood as still sentries. There was still crime scene tape marking the front entrance to the grandstand and someone had thought to install a new stretch of chain link across the front of the whole racetrack. Off the lot, near a couple of ragged construction trailers, I spotted Z's Mustang. I suddenly felt like I'd swallowed sand.

"Better to know," Henry said.

"I'll call Healy," I said.

"Maybe he's inside."

"I'll call Healy," I said. "You stay here."

"Fuck I will."

"When the cops get here," I said, "send them in."

"I'm coming."

"If someone is with him, I need to handle

it," I said. "If he's dead, you don't want to see it."

"Remember what I taught you about taking a hit?"

"Sure."

"Answer it back," Henry said. "Times two."

"Henry, this isn't your work."

"I started this," he said. "I'll goddamn well finish it."

He opened the car door and started for the chain-link fence. After I left a message for Healy, I opened the hatch of the Explorer and threw a tarp from two pristine Winchester 12-gauges. I pocketed a flashlight and a box of shells. I did not want Henry to come. Nor did I want to wait around all night while we debated the point. Against my better judgment, I handed the old man a shotgun.

"Times two."

"Goddamn right," Henry said.

My heart felt displaced in my chest. I took a deep breath and searched for a way to get through the chain link. I kept a Leatherman in my jacket and used it to pry open the end of a section attached to a metal pole. At the very top of the rounded brick entrance was a big fancy sign for WONDER-LAND, with the image of a muzzled greyhound in full sprint. I handed several shells to Henry.

He loaded the 12-gauge with great dexterity.

I nodded my approval.

"What do you expect after hanging out with you and Hawk all these years?"

"Style and class," I said.

We stepped through the ragged opening and approached the wide red-and-white tiled entrance. I clicked on the flashlight and lifted open the bent and cracked door frame. Broken glass crunched underfoot as we passed abandoned ticket booths and turnstiles and walked up a gentle ramp to the concession stands and the wide, empty space that was once a temple to the glory of off-track betting. Empty wires and cables hung loosely from the walls. I pointed the flashlight toward the south end of the building. The ticket stubs of the losers still littered the floor like ticker tape.

Henry walked beside me. We did not speak. There wasn't much to say.

I held the flashlight tight against the barrel while I walked. There was a smattering of puddles and the long stream of backed-up sewage. The smell was unpleasant as we briskly took stairs up to the Club House and into the booth where Sammy Cain used to announce. There were a lot of overturned chairs and hamburger wrappers and empty Budweiser cups. A large bank of windows looked out onto the dirt track itself, barely visible except for the lights to some warehouses next door. We pushed through one room. And then another. We went through a half-open door; the weak light from outside gave the room a noirish patchwork of shadow and light. That's where we saw the fallen figure of the woman, fallen at an impossible angle on the red-and-black linoleum. I moved closer and edged the flashlight onto her face.

From the bruises and torn clothing and halo of blood around Jemma Fraser's head, it was clear she'd been killed in a very ugly manner. Henry walked away, gagging and coughing, and toward the bank of windows. A warm wind hustled in from the track, whistling through the cracked windows and cavernous space of the Club House.

I took a breath and searched outside for anything.

"What a fucking waste," Henry said.

I nodded.

From beyond the broken windows was a mechanical sound, a low humming, coming from deep in the bowels of Wonderland. The place had been closed up for nearly five years and I seriously doubted the electric bill had been paid. Henry and I followed the sound, out of the Club House, down the stairs, and out into the grandstand. The humming came from somewhere out into the track. Every thought was of Z and how I'd failed him. Henry patted me on the back as we walked. I had not let go of the shotgun. I held it in my hands, wishing for some violence.

"Does he have anyone back in Montana?" Henry said.

"Nope."

"No mother, no father," he said. "Holy Christ."

Some old metal starting boxes lay in a heap at the far side of the track. Beyond the track, just off the dirt now grown up with weeds, was a cinder-block kennel. A bit of light came from the mouth of the kennel, and Henry and I walked toward it. I pocketed the flashlight, holding the Winchester steady in both hands.

There was no door, just a wide passage into the kennel. Dog cages ran down both sides of a straight shot through the center of the building. At the end of the passageway, a mechanic's light had been snaked through some pipes and hooked to a generator. Along those same pipes, someone had hung thick chains where the figure of a man twisted in the dim light. The generator made the walls and metal cages shake.

Henry held the gun in his hand as if the dead man might spring to life. I did the same. The face of the dead man turned away, slowly rotating on the chains. Under the lifted feet lay an old car battery, a bucket of water and sponges, and some kind of metal brushes attached to wires. The setup was crude but probably effective.

I used the shotgun to turn the dead man. His face was black, and his purple tongue hung from his open mouth. He was a large man with large hands that had turned black in death. He was not Z.

I took a breath. Henry called out to me and I ran toward him.

Z was in the back corner of a cage, fallen to the concrete in a crushed pile. There was a lot of blood, one eye swollen shut, and deep searing burns and open wounds across his bare chest. Z had found a way to take out his torturer, but barely.

"He's breathing," Henry said. "Christ, he's breathing. Give me something to stop the bleeding. Give me something. He's bleeding like a fucking stuck pig."

I tossed off my jacket and tore off my shirt. Henry pressed the shirt to the wounds and patted Z's face with soft, tapping slaps. "Come on. Come on."

I knelt down and helped move Z from the wall. I could hear sirens coming from the highway. I reached for the water bucket. Henry dabbed my shirt in the water and ran it over Z's almost unrecognizable face.

Henry held Z in his lap, pressing the shirt against the bleeding and bruises, the broken ribs and bones.

"Breathe," Henry said. "Come on. Come on. Breathe."

"He'll make it."

Henry dabbed more water across his face and busted eye.

"How do you know?" he said.

"Because he finished it," I said. "He won."

There were more sirens, coming closer, echoing from the parking lot. Z opened his good eye and smiled. Henry grinned and shook his head. "Son of a bitch," the old man said.

66

Very early that morning, I stood with Healy on the right side of a two-way mirror, watching Brian Lundquist interview Rachel Weinberg. We'd been there for more than two hours at 1010 Commonwealth and the interview had been ugly to watch. Rachel started off indignant and that soon spooled into rage. Henry stayed with Z at Mass General.

"What do you think?" Healy said.

"I'm glad we're on the right side of the mirror."

"She's nuts," he said.

"Perhaps."

"She blames Jemma Fraser for her husband being a cock hound."

"She blames Jemma Fraser for being the right kind of bait."

Healy shrugged. "Same difference."

"All the other women didn't bother her," I said. "What bothered her is being replaced."

"You know how much money she gave up?" Healy said.

"You know how much power she gave up to Jemma?"

There was no place to sit on the other side of the looking glass. The room was bare and clean. In the old days, places like this were filled with empty coffee cups and cigarette butts. The cleanness of the space made everything seem very clinical.

"But she has not confessed," Healy said.

"Nope."

"And she won't."

"Nope," I said. "Still, she won't have much of a choice but to make a plea."

Healy nodded. When they picked up Rachel Weinberg at the Four Seasons, Lewis Blanchard had followed. Blanchard had spent an hour with Lundquist, Healy, and me before they interviewed Rachel. He had been very forthcoming.

"Can he trade what he knows for a deal?" I said.

"Don't see why not."

"Even though he killed two men?"

"Fucking Jimmy Headaches and the Angel creep?"

"Jimmy Aspirins," I said. "The Angel of Mercy."

"Whatever."

We were both tired of listening to the one-way conversation, most of it through Rachel's harried attorney. He was a young guy in smart black glasses wearing a pajama top under a khaki overcoat.

"Why not," Healy said. "I'm not crying for those guys. You think a jury would?"

I watched Rachel Weinberg lean back in her chair and firmly shake her head. She wore a lavender sweatsuit, her face a dull white without makeup. Gold and diamonds sparkled on her fingers and around her neck.

"Fucking bastard," she said. "Fucking bastard."

"Who's she talking about?" Healy said.

I shrugged. "Maybe all of us."

"How is Z?" Healy said.

"Busted up and broken."

"I've seen you that way a time or two."

"It's character building."

"If you make it through."

We watched while Rachel Weinberg's attorney stood, held up his hand, and stopped the questioning. He looked silly with his overcoat open, revealing his poorly buttoned pajama top. Rachel Weinberg sat looking down at her hands, deep in thought. No more rage but something like resolve.

"Oh, tiger lily," I said to the glass. "If only you could talk."

"What?"

"She was pushed," I said. "And now she's trying to make sense of it."

"By what?"

"By a mathematical system."

I left 1010 and got into my Explorer. I drove to Mass General and stayed there for ten days. Susan flew home. Henry watched Pearl.

67

I met Vinnie Morris nearly a month later at one of the big open pavilions at Revere Beach. The weather was good that day, with a bright, strong sun and heavy waves that broke across the sand. I had brought Pearl with me. I had strategically parked across from Kelly's Roast Beef, promising her a few morsels in exchange for the company.

Vinnie walked up onto the empty pavilion and threw down a copy of the *Globe*. There had been a front-page story that morning by Wayne Cosgrove. Gino Fish had been featured prominently.

"What the hell?" Vinnie said.

The tone of his voice made Pearl scatter back a couple steps and bark. I put my hand to her head.

"Easy."

"Easy?" Vinnie said. "You want me to be fucking easy?"

"I was talking to Pearl."

"We can't have this," he said. "You gave Gino your word."

"I told Gino others were aware of the flow of money."

"You said it couldn't be proven," Vinnie said. "I was right there. I fucking heard you."

"I said I wouldn't help prove it one way or another."

"But you told this reporter about Gino and Perotti."

"Actually, he told me," I said. "I only had the bank information. I'm terrible with math."

"Jesus," Vinnie said. "The FBI raided Gino's office this morning. They pulled Perotti out of the State House. You know what this looks like?"

"Business as usual?"

Pearl still stood at attention. She was still not overly fond of Vinnie's tone. But the sudden whiff of Kelly's on the ocean breezes calmed her. I patted her head again.

"You know what this means?" Vinnie said.

"I'm off Gino's Christmas card list."

"You damn well know."

I nodded.

Vinnie stared at me. I was reminded of long-ago meetings in the company of the late Joe Broz. The newspaper pages fluttered between us. Seagulls glided on light breezes off the breaking waves. "You damn well know."

He left the pavilion. I sat down with Pearl. We both watched Vinnie get into his car and disappear north. Pearl sniffed at the shifting wind.

We walked a bit on the beach and then drove back to Cambridge. Susan was waiting for us, four bags packed and ready for five days on Cape Cod. Half of one of the bags was mine. Z was staying at my apartment while I was gone, closer to physical therapy and a therapist Susan had recommended.

As we hit Route 3, Susan turned to me and said, "How did it go?"

"Vinnie is perturbed."

"Vinnie will get over it."

"Not this time."

"How can you be so sure?"

"I think we all got played a little," I said. "Some more than others."

"Z said you believe Harvey Rose was aware Jemma Fraser would destroy the Weinbergs the whole time."

I nodded.

"That's very confident."

"Not if you know the odds," I said.

"And Rose walks?"

"Yep."

"Hands clean."

"You tell me," I said.

"Do you think Harvey Rose is a sociopath?"

"I think Harvey Rose is an interesting addition to the Boston ecosystem."

"And perhaps a system now minus Gino Fish."

"Charges of bribery won't harm Gino Fish," I said. "It will only enhance his reputation."

Susan nodded. I turned to look at her on a straightaway. Her black hair was down and flowed loose and very thick. She wore a black cotton dress and leather flats, a thin gold chain around her neck.

In the backseat, Pearl's collar jingled as she reached with a hind leg to scratch her ear. Gold afternoon light filled the car as I placed my right hand on Susan's. She leaned in to my shoulder, and I could feel a familiar swelling in my chest. We were quiet all the way to the Sagamore Bridge. Crossing the canal, I had hope for a great many things, and tried not to dwell on things I could not change. I thought about Z and wished the same for him.

"Together again," Susan said.

I nodded and drove, the road open and wide across the bridge.

ABOUT THE AUTHORS

Robert B. Parker was the author of seventy books, including the legendary Spenser detective series, the novels featuring Jesse Stone, and the acclaimed Virgil Cole/Everett Hitch westerns, as well as the Sunny Randall novels. Winner of the Mystery Writers of America Grand Master Award and long considered the undisputed dean of American crime fiction, he died in January 2010.

Ace Atkins is the author of thirteen novels, including the *New York Times* bestseller Robert B. Parker's *Lullaby*. He was nominated for an Edgar Award for Best Novel in 2012 for *The Ranger*, the first book in his Quinn Colson series, which also includes *The Lost Ones* and the forthcoming *The Broken Places*. Atkins, whom the bestselling author Michael Connelly has called "one of the best crime writers working today," lives on a farm outside Oxford, Mississippi.